PRAISE FOR *WHENEVE[R*

'Tender, warm-hearted and wise. B[
Toni Jordan, author of *Prettier If She Smiled More*

'It's so damned refreshing to read a novel in which three dimensional older female characters are at the centre of the action . . . Friendships, betrayals, secrets and lies, romances, revelations— Trish Bolton tackles the gritty stuff that we inevitably confront in the second half of our lives. A page-turner of a novel.'
Sian Prior, author of *Childless*

'What a joy this book is. Deft and effortless storytelling, vivid, poignant characters, and a deep undertow of social commentary shot through with wicked, laugh-out-loud humour. I loved it.'
Lucy Treloar, author of *Days of Innocence and Wonder*

'Engaging, moving and full of heart, *Whenever You're Ready* is a touching story of friendship, forgiveness and second chances.'
Suzanne Leal, author of *The Watchful Wife*

'*Whenever You're Ready* is a rich portrait of inner lives and the stories we tell ourselves and each other as a way of dealing with the world. Each of the women in this compassionately drawn, inherently relatable novel feels like she could be a friend.'
Sophie Green, author of *Weekends with the Sunshine Gardening Society*

'*Whenever You're Ready* is a compelling and astute exploration of friendship, grief and families in the rapidly changing and generally rapid world ruled by real estate and Instagram . . . Big-hearted and entertaining, Bolton is a natural-born storyteller and her debut novel is a gift to us all.' **Lee Kofman, author of *The Writer Laid Bare***

Trish Bolton is a Melbourne writer whose words have appeared in *Overland*, *New Matilda*, *The Big Issue*, *The Age*, *Sunday Age*, *Sydney Morning Herald* and *Canberra Times*. *Whenever You're Ready* is her debut novel.

WHENEVER YOU'RE READY

Trish Bolton

ALLEN&UNWIN
SYDNEY · MELBOURNE · AUCKLAND · LONDON

First published in 2024

Allen & Unwin
Cammeraygal Country
83 Alexander Street
Crows Nest NSW 2065
Australia
Phone: (61 2) 8425 0100
Email: info@allenandunwin.com
Web: www.allenandunwin.com

Allen & Unwin acknowledges the Traditional Owners of the Country on which we live and work. We pay our respects to all Aboriginal and Torres Strait Islander Elders, past and present.

A catalogue record for this book is available from the National Library of Australia

ISBN 978 1 76147 027 1

Set in 12.7/17 pt by Midland Typesetters, Australia
Printed and bound in Australia by the Opus Group

10 9 8 7 6 5 4 3 2 1

The paper in this book is FSC® certified. FSC® promotes environmentally responsible, socially beneficial and economically viable management of the world's forests.

For Frank

PROLOGUE

CLAIRE LOOPS THE TWINE BETWEEN her fingers, secures her life with a neat bow.

Bank statements, tax file numbers, passwords. Wills.

She has thought about this day for months. Planned and prepared.

But still she has not found peace.

She places the letter to her daughter on the mantelpiece where it can't be missed, traces a finger over Jane's name.

These last weeks she has busied herself, going through drawers and cupboards, throwing out spices past their use-by date; starting up a shopping list, then realising there was no need. Organising great bundles of clothing for the Brotherhood.

She stands at the window, taking one last look at her garden. Venturing outside, she braves the icy wind. Somewhere, there is snow. The cold stings and goosebumps rise on her arms. Stepping

1

off the verandah onto the path, she brushes past lavender planted last spring. She closes her eyes and feels the rush of wind across her face, the mess it's making of her hair.

Back inside, she eases herself into a favourite chair, the spike of pain a reminder her painkillers are almost due. Her legs are heavy, her once-slender ankles fat with fluid, and there's a tiredness she's never felt before. She hears Jeremy wandering up and down the hallway—she is sure he senses something—his grunts of frustration as he rattles the back door.

She hated taking away his last little piece of independence, believing him somehow when he promised never to go beyond the front gate. When his wanderings grew more frequent, she had a handyman add a snib, sure it would bamboozle him and be much too high to reach.

One day he wasn't bamboozled and he did reach.

He had been gone twelve hours when police found him beside a busy highway, arms wrapped around his knees, rocking and weeping and calling her name.

Claire doesn't believe in God. Or heaven and hell. But these last weeks, she has found herself praying . . .

She hopes not to be judged too harshly.

Not by her daughter. And not by Lizzie.

Lizzie, her oldest and dearest friend, the only person she might have told. Lizzie, no matter how distraught, would keep her secret. But there was another secret, one Claire had left too late to confess.

When she and Lizzie kissed goodbye after meeting for coffee—how long ago last Tuesday seems—Claire had clung to her, almost giving herself away. She hurried off, waving goodbyes and agreeing to catch up properly in a week or two.

So many times she had tried to write Lizzie a letter asking her forgiveness, but always she returned to the same place: some things were unforgivable.

She glances around the room then closes the door behind her.

With his hand in hers, Claire guides Jeremy to the bathroom, helps him pull down his track pants, removing his pad as she nudges him onto the seat.

She looks down at his still-thick head of hair, feels, as she so often does, a great surge of tenderness. Their life together has not been perfect. But he loved her in spite of her failings, and she, mostly, loved him.

Gripped by a moment of doubt, she trembles, then catches herself.

There can be no going back.

Claire organises wine: a toast to their life together.

She goes through the CDs and chooses Charles Aznavour, one of Jeremy's favourites. Whenever she teased him about his daggy taste in music he would laugh and waltz her around the room.

Jeremy opens his arms wide.

Soon they will go to bed, bodies and lives entwined.

But now, they will dance.

CHAPTER I

THE BAD NEWS CAME UNEXPECTEDLY, as bad news often does.

Lizzie was down on all fours when Jane rang, knees protesting the bare timber floor, playing horsey with Jack. She phoned again when Lizzie was throwing the dice, Molly about to beat her at Snakes and Ladders.

She ignored the calls—she wasn't interrupting her time with her grandchildren, not even for Jane.

When the phone rang a third time, screen lighting up with Jane's name, Lizzie was in bumper-to-bumper traffic. She reached to take the call with a vague feeling of unease, withdrawing her hand when she remembered the fine she'd paid a few months before, the police officer who'd called her *luv*.

It will be nothing, she told herself. Jane, who'd been busy organising a surprise party for her mother's seventy-fifth, would be chasing Lizzie for photos or an amusing anecdote, a question that needed answering.

The traffic had only just started flowing when a man in a high-vis vest, face grimed with dust, held up a STOP sign. Lizzie tapped an impatient beat on the steering wheel. More roadworks. Particularly annoying, she mused, when she might not be around to enjoy the promised benefits.

Dusk was descending, the sky a hazy mauve of traffic fumes and dying light, footpaths rushing with people clutching bags and briefcases, bodies slanted towards home. She turned up the radio and hummed along to a piece by Mozart. Music always gladdened her heart.

It had been a good day, better than most. She and her daughter, Margot, hadn't had words, not even when Margot wagged her finger at Molly and told her not to be bossy—*No one likes a Miss Bossy-Boots.*

Lizzie was of a mind the world could do with a few more Ms Bossy-Boots, but she wasn't one to preach.

A young woman in the car beside her was touching up her lipstick. She pouted into a tiny circle of mirror, head angling this way then that, pleased, so far as Lizzie could tell, with what she saw. At her age, why wouldn't she be?

She envied that generation; not their youth so much as the opportunities laid at their feet. Had she had the same choices, she doubted she would have pledged her life to a man. Or a woman either, for that matter.

The question of motherhood was more vexed: would she have denied her maternal longing—for longing is how she remembered it? Would she have willingly given up her freedom? The answers eluded her. What did it matter, when there'd never been that choice. You married, you had children.

And then, just like that, you were seventy-something.

When Lizzie's grandmother was in her seventies, special privileges applied: she abandoned her bra, ate what she wanted when she wished and rarely-to-never ventured out in the evenings.

Nowadays, ageing was out of the question. You were encouraged to enrol in weight-lifting classes and walking groups. And to socialise, too often meaning afternoons spent listening to detailed updates of the latest medication regimes. On bad days, it was the demise of an acquaintance, most usually relayed in excruciating detail.

Any hope of a quiet moment was taken up volunteering, now referred to as *giving back*. It was expected you make an annual trek overseas—never mind the toll the ascent to the Airbnb had on your knees—your derring-do provoking affectionate aren't-old-people-marvellous smiles.

High-vis-vest man tapped the bonnet and waved her on.

'Hold your horses,' she said, hitting the accelerator a little too hard and stalling the car.

Lizzie could hear the phone ringing before she was through the front door. There was something about a landline she couldn't ignore. Racing down the hallway, she remembered to take a leap over the corner of the rug where the fringe was detaching.

It was Jane again, but the frantic voice on the other end sounded nothing like the laidback young woman who organised surprise parties.

'Lizzie, dreadful news.'

Lizzie remembered another call, the radio on in the background, the whirr of a printer nearby, the sickly sweet smell of banana. 'Jane . . .' was all she could say.

'Mum and Dad,' Jane sobbed. 'They're dead. Both of them . . . gone.'

Claire? Dead? Lizzie reached blindly for the arm of the sofa, elbow knocking a vase of nasturtiums to the floor, their velvety faces drowning in a puddle of water. She sank down, still holding the phone to her ear.

'A car accident?' What else could it be?

Silence.

'Jane?'

'They took sleeping pills.'

The room shifted in and out of focus.

'Mum had been planning it for months.'

A sob rose in Lizzie's throat.

'Did Mum tell you . . . ?'

'No . . . no. I had no idea.'

'. . . that she had ovarian cancer?'

'Oh, Jane.'

'It was in her letter.'

Lizzie closed her eyes, everything making terrible sense.

'No, I . . . she didn't tell me.'

She felt almost betrayed.

She could hear Jane gulping back tears. 'Could you tell Margot . . . I just can't . . .'

'I'll tell Margot.'

'And Alice . . .'

'Alice, too. Is Sam with you?'

The phone went crash; muffled voices in the background.

'Lizzie, it's Sam. Jane had to go.'

'Look after her.'

'Look after yourself, too.'

She hung up, head falling to her knees, body swaying side-to-side, something terrible and familiar filling her chest.

Lizzie had seen Claire only days before. She pictured them kissing goodbye, Claire pulling her so close Lizzie stepped back and held her at arm's length. 'Is everything okay? Jeremy?'

Claire answered with a bright smile that of course it was. Jeremy was fine. *Stop worrying.*

Claire must have known then, known they wouldn't see each other again. *Why hadn't she realised? Why hadn't Claire told her?* She sat a long while, unable to raise her head. She could not think of Claire dead, Claire who brimmed with life, who filled rooms and lives and hearts. She could not believe it. She would not.

Tom snuggled up beside her. He came to her when she needed him most. She had once told Claire about his visits. Claire didn't mock or make her feel foolish. *When you're ready, you'll let him go.*

'It's all right, Mummy,' he was saying. 'It's all right.'

She hugged him to her chest, kissing his dear little head, telling him over and over how much she loved him. And then her arms were empty and the room was cold.

She could hear Fred whimpering and pawing the back door. Willing herself up, she stumbled through the kitchen, door creaking as she held it against the wind, icy air and moonlit sky. Fred rushed inside, circling her legs and snorting with relief. She tipped leftovers into his bowl, Jane's words on repeat in her head.

To call Margot now . . . dinnertime, bathtime, storytime. She wanted for as long as possible to protect her daughter from the terrible news. Tomorrow. She would phone first thing tomorrow.

Lizzie rang Alice: a gasp of disbelief, a stifled sob. Silence.

'Alice?'

'I'm coming over.'

Lizzie fell into the chair. Protesting would be useless. Alice would already be on her way.

They always came together when crisis struck, at Alice's side when she was going through chemo, with Claire when Jeremy was diagnosed with dementia. They came to Lizzie when she lost Tom.

In that first terrible week Claire never left Lizzie's side, listening as Lizzie raged and wept, wrapping herself around her and Ed—they'd been together then—mothering Margot, who couldn't understand why she would never see her little brother again.

Lizzie splashed her eyes with cold water. She patted her face dry and tidied her hair, managed a swipe of lipstick. How she wished Alice wasn't coming. Not tonight, not yet.

Outside, the wind whipped at the trees and rattled the windows. Wind always unsettled her. There was a loneliness to it, a lament, as it searched for a place to rest. She turned on lamps, lit the fire and stared into the flames.

She'd first met Claire at boarding school. They were in the same class during the day; their beds, in a dormitory of ten, were next to each other at night.

Lizzie had known immediately that she and the long-limbed, golden-haired Claire came from different worlds. The girls Lizzie grew up with left school at fifteen to work in a shop or help out around the farm. Married by twenty, usually to a local farmer, a baby along every year or two, they were old at thirty.

Determined to escape a lifetime of milking and shearing and varicose veins, Lizzie had put her mind to winning one of the scholarships offered by a Melbourne boarding school, a school her parents could never have afforded.

In her home-sewn uniform, she had been lonely and friend-less, out of place from the day she dragged her fraying suitcase up the stairs to the dormitory that would be her home for the next six years.

The bed beside Lizzie's remained empty until Claire had come along mid-term after travelling abroad with her family. One night when Lizzie was crying into her pillow, a hand reached out in the darkness. 'Lizzie,' Claire whispered, 'I'm here.'

They became unlikely friends—Lizzie earnest and naive, Claire worldly and carefree. They were rarely apart, on the phone when they were, sharing secrets, whispering dreams. Never imag-ining a life without the other.

And now Claire was gone.

Fred galloped down the hallway before the bell chimed, slipping on the floorboards, his excited yelps signalling that he was friends with whoever was on the other side of the door.

'Lizzie.' Alice's face was haggard and ghostly, eyes wide with shock. Specks of wattle caught in her hair. Their arms went around each other.

Recovering herself, Lizzie ushered Alice down the narrow hallway, reminding her, as she always did, to watch the corner of the rug, while shooing Fred, who was getting under their feet, to his bed.

'We knew that sooner or later . . . but not like this. Never like this,' said Alice, unwinding her scarf and removing her gloves.

'I spoke to Jane. Claire had ovarian cancer.'

They clutched each other's hands.

'She didn't tell you?'

'No one knew,' said Lizzie. 'It was in her letter to Jane.'

Alice slipped out of her coat. 'Why didn't she tell us? She should have told us.'

Lizzie placed a hand on the back of the sofa to steady herself. 'I met her for coffee last week. She hugged me goodbye as if she wasn't going to let go . . . I should have known.'

Alice sat Lizzie down, put an arm around her friend. 'How could you have known? How could anyone?'

It seemed impossible that Claire was gone. All beauty and grace; people went out of their way to please her, darling Jeremy among them.

Lizzie rested her head on Alice's shoulder. She would never hear Claire's laugh again, never again see her lovely face, a face she knew as well as her own.

'I can't stop thinking about Jane,' said Alice. 'Losing both parents like that.'

Lizzie could not even contemplate. 'Sam will look after her.'

'How could Claire put her daughter, everyone, through this?'

'Think what it must have been like for Claire,' said Lizzie, 'planning those final moments, sparing Jane, us. How alone she must have been.'

'I know, I know,' said Alice, tears welling. 'If only she hadn't always refused our help.'

There was much about Alice that Lizzie loved, but if Alice had even once offered Claire support, Lizzie would be surprised. Alice had often stayed with Lizzie after one of her breakups, a day or two becoming days on end, helping herself to everything from jewellery to food to alcohol. Then she would disappear, leaving piles of dishes in the sink, the bathroom a mess of wet towels, wine bottles empty. She was too bohemian and creative, Alice said, to manage the more mundane aspects of life.

'I just can't imagine how anyone could end someone else's life. I just can't.'

How could Alice, who'd never had a relationship that lasted, know what it was to love someone for a lifetime?

And how Claire had loved Jeremy. Lizzie remembered Claire telling her that she and Jeremy still enjoyed a little sip of wine in the evenings. She'd put on music, and they'd dance and laugh, in love all over again.

'Just you and me now,' said Alice.

Who would they be without Claire? thought Lizzie. How would they be?

'Have you told Margot?'

Lizzie shook her head. Margot was as close to Claire as she was to Jane. 'I will. First thing tomorrow.'

Jane would endure—she was resilient, like her mother. But Margot . . .

Alice stood with her back to the fire. 'Will you tell Ed?'

Lizzie looked up, surprised. 'I hadn't thought about it.' She tried never to think about Ed.

Alice dropped to her knees and stabbed at the logs with the poker. 'He'll know soon enough.'

Those days long ago, thought Lizzie, when she couldn't imagine a life without Ed, when the five friends had been inseparable: lunches that went on way past midnight; weekends at Jeremy and Claire's holiday house, rooms with views of the ocean. And then, after Tom, they had all unravelled.

'Do you remember us? I mean, when we were young?' asked Alice, climbing awkwardly to her feet. 'How beautiful we were, how free. We were amazing.'

Lizzie laughed. 'We're still amazing.'

'I've got this photo of us hanging out at Jo's, smoking rollies and drinking that terrible coffee.'

'Oh God,' Lizzie laughed again. 'We thought we were so avant-garde.'

'You and Claire talking politics and philosophy and boring the crap out of me.'

'That novel you were writing that was going to change the world.'

'I still have that chapter somewhere.'

They laughed and cried.

'She can't be gone,' said Alice. 'She can't.'

Lizzie put her arms around her friend, never wanting to let her go.

'We should toast Claire,' said Alice. 'With a whisky. Claire liked a whisky.'

Alice was back in front of the fire when Lizzie returned with glasses and a bottle of whisky, flames dancing across the floor-boards, everything off-kilter.

They raised glasses to Claire, the crackling of the fire the only sound in the room.

After a tearful farewell, consolatory words hanging useless in the air, Lizzie poured another whisky and added logs to the fire. She wandered the room gazing at photos of Claire and Alice that went back decades.

She reached for the photo taken with Claire on graduation day, law degrees unrolled for the camera, two young women with their lives ahead of them. Beside it, a framed newspaper clipping of Alice, the weather girl who'd won a best-new-talent award.

She flicked on the television, company that expected nothing in return. Ed's face filled the screen. A few years younger than

Lizzie, her ex was tanned and slim, his head of silver curls a shiny halo under the studio lights. He flashed his pearly smile, a slight crinkle around the eyes, a few scribbly lines to the possibly-botoxed forehead.

She changed the channel. Ed again, denying rumours he was plotting to oust his leader, his focus, he said, on putting Australia and the Australian people first. His sincerity, as always, making a downright lie seem an absolute truth.

It came naturally to him. To lie. And to justify. When that didn't play out: contrition. Short-lived.

Had Ed heard about Claire? she wondered. They hadn't seen each other in years. Still, it would be sad news. He would be remembering.

She brewed a pot of tea, found some comfort imagining Claire and Jeremy sinking into a peaceful sleep, arms around each other.

Ed was still droning on. She hit mute.

She and Ed had once been quite the team: Lizzie's law background put to use as a political adviser, Ed a political new blood who had everyone sitting up and taking notice. Young idealists, they both worked for the same party. It was a couple of years before Lizzie succumbed and said yes to a date. He'd loved her well enough; she'd loved him too much.

Lizzie had moved on from Ed long ago. He'd been single for years when, quite unexpectedly, he married Charlotte, the granddaughter of a venerated ex-prime minister.

Charlotte was Margot's age, and only weeks separated their daughters. They babysat for each other, they were friends on Facebook—Lizzie's Facebook invitation to Margot still unanswered—and shared photos of their children on Instagram. She should have been happy for them. She wasn't.

'Mummy.' Tom cuddled up close, pressing a book into her hand. 'Story.'

She held up the cover. *'There's a Hippopotamus on our Roof Eating Cake,'* she recited, her eyes opening wide. 'No, that can't be true?' He gurgled with anticipation, little fingers prising open the first page. He vanished before they reached the end.

Fred put one huge paw on the sofa, eyes hopeful. Lizzie spread his blanket and asked him up, staring at the soundless images on the screen until the fire sputtered and went out completely.

CHAPTER 2

'CAN YOU PULL IN THAT tummy, darling girl? Oh dear, we'll have to do something about that wobble. Smile big, but not too big—don't want you looking long in the tooth, my love. Now give us your best zany—oh come, come, anyone would think the whole ship was throwing up behind you.'

Alice's tummy was pulled in, so pulled in she hadn't taken a proper breath all afternoon. Starving yourself to death when you were twenty was one thing, quite another fifty years later. 'But aren't we on one of those all-you-can-eat cruises?'

The in-his-twenties *creative*—that's how he referred to himself on his groovy business card—sighed. 'We're not in the business of realism.'

In the past, Alice would have stormed off if anyone dared criticise her, everyone rushing after her, wondering what whim they could meet, what could be done to assuage her ego. But that was then and this was now.

'Give me a minute,' said Alice.

She headed to her dressing-room, a curtain screening an area no bigger than a cupboard, and wriggled into the supplied Spanx. The problem was those ghastly old-lady slacks Wardrobe expected her to wear.

She assessed her reflection in the mirror, turning to one side then the other. She had to agree that the girdle or whatever it was had done the trick. If only she'd worn it when she'd been cavorting, in white, with supplied husband on a windswept beach.

'There, that's better,' the creative said. 'Now, if you can gaze into your handsome husband's eyes . . .'

Handsome Husband was also wearing some sort of corset beneath his smart open-necked shirt. He had on the thickest layer of pancake, and his porcelain teeth grinned grotesquely. He creaked when he walked.

'Imagine you're on deck, surrounded by a glittering Mediterranean ocean, sun sinking, sky golden, drinking French champagne, a hint in your eyes of what happens after glass number three . . .'

Alice sipped the lukewarm soda water.

Five takes and the sun had set, the adoring look in Alice's eyes replaced by relief that the foreplay was over.

'That's it, we're done—big tick, you two.'

'Don't I know you from somewhere?' Handsome Husband asked as Alice was saying her goodbyes.

Alice feigned disinterest.

'Oh my God, yes, of course! Didn't you used to be that weather girl?'

Alice turned on her heel, ignoring his invitation to adjourn somewhere more intimate for real champers.

Weren't you once . . . Didn't you used to be . . . ?

Yes, she'd been a weather girl, like forty years ago. She'd been a journalist, too, and a model—a real model. She'd been a lot of things.

Alice had been working for a local newspaper covering the usual human interest stories—cats rescued from drains, couples celebrating fifty years of marriage without a cross word spoken, the sprained groin of the local cricket hero—when she was spotted by a scout from a top modelling agency.

She didn't hesitate. Modelling was so much more lucrative and glamorous than journalism. She'd swayed down catwalks all over the world, glared from the covers of fashion magazines, her tempestuous love-life filling gossip columns. Ten years later, it was all over.

She had hoped to get back into journalism, applying for one job after another—who's going to take an ex-model seriously, the predictable response—when the producer of a top-rating news program thought she'd make a hot weather girl.

And for a few years she did. Until they dumped her—*too weathered, ha-ha,* they said. *Need a bloke,* they said. *Lacking gravitas,* they said.

Fuck off, she said.

If she hadn't needed the money, she'd have cancelled the shoot but this had been her first job in weeks. Her agent had assured her that signing with a modelling agency that specialised in mature women would bring her more work than she could manage. It was the older woman's moment, apparently.

Mature, she soon discovered, was somewhere between thirty and forty. At sixty—she'd fudged her age—she was positively antediluvian.

The interview with the twenty-something from the agency was not so much an interview as a forensic examination—legs, arms and everything in between—with a focus on décolletage and dentistry. It had been as humiliating as any audition.

Alice had endured the piling-on of indignities, certain she would again be pursued by Australia's top designers—gowns, streetwear, indie—as well as Tiffany and Maybelline. *Vogue* would want her on their cover. Instead, she was expected to swoon over incontinence pads and make out with a geriatric who, after fifty years of marriage, probably didn't know where his socks were kept.

Baby boomers, she thought with contempt. They were so . . . well, old. Present company excepted. She was much more millennial in her outlook. And she could pass for a Gen Xer. Everyone said so.

Dodging a tram and keeping an eye out for cyclists flying past in skinny bike lanes, and lithe locals in t-shirts asserting holier-than-thou diets and minimal ecological footprints, she wondered, not for the first time, why Lizzie loved this side of town. Give her the other side of the river any day.

Shit. A parking fine. Alice would have kicked the tyre if it hadn't been so bald.

Oh God, she was crying. Not crying, weeping. She'd hardly stopped since hearing of Claire's death the day before. Mortified someone would see her, she hurriedly unlocked the car and searched for a tissue.

She was crying, not just for herself, but for Lizzie, too. Lizzie forever fragile, the loss of Tom still there in her eyes. She gave her nose a good blow and checked her face in the mirror, surprised she was feeling Claire's loss so keenly. Although friends, they hadn't been close; tensions going back to their university days.

Alice, like Lizzie, had won a scholarship, not to boarding school, but to one of Melbourne's best universities. Until then, she'd never met anyone who'd been to university. The girls she went to school with found work in typing pools and factories, jobs they'd leave as soon as they married. Clever girls went off to be nurses and schoolteachers. Alice wanted to be a journalist. You don't need a degree to become a journalist, she told her mother. In those days, you ran messages and made coffee and learned on the job. They called it a cadetship. But her mother insisted. 'Education never goes to waste,' she'd said.

Alice did not have the rounded vowels of her classmates, she didn't wear the brands they wore, she didn't have their affectations or perfect teeth. She wasn't part of their circle. They'd all gone to the same half-dozen schools, lived in the same suburbs, learned the same musical instruments, went to the same orthodontists, travelled abroad to the same handful of destinations during semester breaks. When they asked her where in Melbourne she was from, the inner circle exchanged amused glances. *Where's that?*

So, Alice listened and observed. She dressed as they did, but at half the price and with way more panache; she read the books they claimed to read and listened to the bands they listened to. She brought the rising inflection under control, expunged all but the occasional adjective and adverb from her vocabulary, and worked on sounding less earnest. By second year, she was fully assimilated. Except for her teeth. They would have to wait.

Claire and Lizzie, who had known each other since boarding school, were more like sisters than friends. They'd met Alice, who was working at the student magazine as part of her Arts degree, when they answered a call for volunteers. It didn't take five minutes for Claire to take over—out with the light and breezy, she'd said, and in with serious journalism. She was quickly appointed assistant editor, the position Alice had been sure was hers.

Alice had never considered that Claire might die before her—or before Lizzie, for that matter. Everything Claire was, and had done, and known, just vanished. There was a conversation they should have had: if Claire were to die first, what would that mean for the story she had shared with her, that now only she knew.

She pulled out from the kerb and, for some silly reason, turned on the windscreen wipers to brush away her tears.

CHAPTER 3

IT WAS PAST MIDDAY AND Lizzie was still in bed. She had been awake for hours, unable to rouse herself except to open the door for Fred who had curled up on the rug beside her. She hadn't wanted to sleep, knowing that waking would deliver the shock of Claire's death anew.

She lay there, eyes closed against the cold brittle light, an ache filling her chest. The hands on the clock felt meaningless. Everything at a standstill.

Flinging off the doona, she sat on the side of the bed, head in her hands, crying again. It wouldn't do. She gave herself a shake. It simply wouldn't. There was Margot to ring, Fred to walk. Breakfast.

Instead of breakfast, she stood under the shower, hot water coaxing the stiffness from her neck. She knew this feeling, knew she could wait it out, that eventually a whole day would pass without tears. She knew also that nothing would be the same again.

She and Claire had every now and then considered the manner of their passing. They'd joked about booking flights to Switzerland or locating a drug dealer in a dimly lit alley and buying a big hit of heroin. Anything to avoid the death throes of a nursing home. But even in their seventies, death had somehow seemed far away.

She reached into the wardrobe and went with the first item her hand fell on. She didn't care what she wore, if the top didn't match the skirt, if the hem was coming adrift, if the elasticised waist had given up the ghost.

After treating Fred to yoghurt and blueberries, coffee all she could manage, Lizzie went searching for her phone in the sitting room. She had put off the moment, throwing out the drowned nasturtiums and blotting the still-wet rug with paper-towels.

She eventually gathered herself, as mothers always gather themselves, and called her daughter.

Margot adored Claire; she was everything Lizzie was not. She'd wished many times there had been more of that love to go around, but she'd never been jealous of the affection between them. How could she be?

'Darling, I was wondering if I could come over.'

'Today?' Margot sounded surprised. 'Did you forget something?'

'No, I . . . I wanted to talk.'

'We're talking now.'

'I could be there in forty minutes.'

A moment's hesitation. 'Is it Grandma?'

At ninety-five, Lizzie's mother's passing could only be a matter of time. 'Grandma's fine.'

A sigh of relief, Margot's voice fading in and out as she took the stairs. 'It's just that I've got so much on . . .'

To pass on news of Claire's death over the phone felt careless and cruel. 'It's important.'

A cupboard door banged open and closed. 'If it's so important, tell me now.'

Lizzie paused, wanting to somehow prepare her daughter for that one thing no one can ever be prepared for: someone you cared about who cared about you, someone you were sure you could never live without, gone.

'Mum?'

'It's Claire.'

'The surprise party?'

'Claire passed away yesterday.'

Margot was silent.

'Darling . . .'

Lizzie could hear Jack's voice in the background. 'Don't cry, Mummy.'

'I'm leaving now.'

Margot opened the door, lips pale, eyes disbelieving.

How Lizzie loved her.

'You didn't have to come.'

Lizzie put her arms around her. 'I wanted to.'

Margot disentangled herself, Lizzie following her through the elegant marble-floored entrance into the lounge room, deep-cushioned sofas, a palette of clotted creams.

'Is Jack asleep?'

Margot nodded and burst into tears.

Lizzie pressed a crumpled tissue from her bag into Margot's hand and guided her to a sofa.

'Was it a heart attack?'

Lizzie placed a hand over Margot's. How was she going to do this?

Margot bowed her head. 'Poor Jane.'

Jane wasn't just Claire's daughter, but Margot's closest friend. Jane had been only a few months old when Claire and Jeremy returned from the UK. Margot had been ecstatic: someone to love almost as much as she had loved Tom. Jane had loved her back, trailing after Margot; wherever Margot was, Jane was only a few steps away.

'And Jeremy. My God, what will happen to Jeremy now Claire's gone?'

Lizzie brushed away tears.

'There's something I haven't told you.'

No matter how carefully Lizzie chose her words, they were shocking to hear.

Margot put her head in her hands, elbows sliding to her knees. 'Claire did a dreadful thing.'

Lizzie was struggling, too. 'It was a decision she would never have wanted to make.'

Margot's hands fell from her face. 'I'm trying to understand.'

'That's all Claire would ask.' All any of us would ask, she thought.

Margot was crying again.

'I can stay if you like, pick up Molly from school, make dinner.'

Her daughter shook her head, as Lizzie knew she would.

'Would you like me to ring Julian?'

'He's in Sydney.' Margot reached for her phone. 'He was fond of Claire. He'd want to know.'

'You ring Julian, I'll make coffee.'

Margot nodded, phone already to her ear, voice breaking as she struggled to find words.

Margot was scrolling through her phone when Lizzie returned, a flash of images beneath her daughter's thumb. How, in this moment . . . it was as if no one wanted to be in the moment anymore, distracted by another moment, then another.

'Did you speak to Julian?'

Margot didn't look up. 'He can't believe it, either.'

Lizzie closed her eyes, the finality waylaying her yet again.

'He's right, though,' Margot put down her phone. 'How many people die at home with the person they love beside them?'

Lizzie's cup trembled in the saucer.

Their eyes met.

Lizzie knew they were both thinking of Tom.

Lizzie had been in Canberra the morning the call came.

She'd hardly been home for weeks. It was the beginning of an election year: frenetic, relentless, with twelve-hour days extending into sixteen. The air buzzed with anticipation—everyone thriving on adrenaline, frozen dinners and booze, pumping out policy and press releases, schmoozing and back-scratching anyone who might turn a vote the party's way, on the scent for anything that could put their opponents in a bad light. She loved every crazy Shakespearean moment of it.

Margot and Tom missed her. Lizzie, promising that after the election . . .

Ed was often away from home, too, on the road with his minister or in Canberra putting out spot fires, both of them pretty much on the job twenty-four hours a day. He was in Canberra that week, but when she asked if there was any way he could get home a day or two early to look after Tom, he'd said it was impossible, in fact, it was looking more and more likely that he wouldn't make it home for the weekend.

Lizzie had phoned home, as she usually did, just before the children's bedtime.

Tom was still grizzly. 'Come home, Mummy, come home.'

He'd cried that morning when she left, dragging at her skirt as she climbed into the taxi that would take her to the airport. Tired and guilty, she'd snapped at him. He'd clung to Mandy, the children's nanny, looking accusingly at Lizzie. Lizzie noticed the bright spots in his cheeks and the runny nose, but he'd had a runny nose ever since he started kinder.

As the taxi drew away, Tom started crying. *Mummy, Mummy* . . . Lizzie was about to tell the driver to turn around when her to-do list flashed through her head.

Just a few more weeks, she told herself, blowing kisses, Tom inconsolable. She tried not to feel too guilty—they'd have lots of time together once the election was over.

She was alone in the office early the next morning, her break-fast, a half-eaten banana on the desk while she hammered out a media release, when the phone rang. She picked up, thinking it would be a journalist wanting a response to the latest polling.

'Lizzie, it's Mandy.'

There was something odd in Mandy's voice but Lizzie was too distracted to give it attention. 'Let me guess, Margot's refusing to go to sch—'

'Is anyone with you?'

'No. Why? Is something wrong?'

'It's Tom.'

A cold feeling in the pit of her stomach. 'Is he unwell?' The runny nose had turned into a cold, the flushed cheeks, signs of a temperature. She shouldn't have left him.

'I couldn't wake him this morning.' Mandy's voice was high and thin. 'I gave him a little shake,' she gasped, 'but he wouldn't wake up.'

Lizzie was falling through space, hand still clutching the phone, screaming to Mandy to call an ambulance.

Mandy was sobbing. 'It must have happened while he was asleep.'

'No, no . . .' Lizzie doubled over, all the breath gone from her.

'Mummy . . .' Margot's voice. 'Tom-Tom won't wake up. Why won't he wake up?'

Lizzie was vaguely aware of Ed rushing through the door. 'Mandy left a message—something about Tom—' He looked at Lizzie on her knees, the phone clutched in her hand. 'Oh God, what's happened? What's happened to Tom?'

Lizzie hung her head. No force on earth could make her say those terrible words. Saying them would make the unthinkable true.

Ed wrenched the phone from Lizzie's hand and spoke to Mandy. 'I see,' he said. 'Yes, I understand. Please ask them to ring me as soon as they arrive.' He hung up.

Lizzie was never to forget his anguished cries echoing through the empty corridors.

It wasn't until months later, that Lizzie realised they hadn't put their arms around each other.

Lizzie didn't remember the flight home, only that she was sure there had been a ridiculous mistake. Mandy was overreacting; the paramedics who'd spoken to Ed were good, but they weren't doctors. Tom had caught something from kindy and needed to sleep.

Ed was beside her, staring, unblinking, fists clenching, unclenching; every now and then dropping his head to his chest, saying, *Oh no, God no.*

They arrived home to an ambulance outside their house, Claire rushing through the front door, her arms around them, whisking them inside.

Tom was so peaceful, her little boy on his bed, football on the floor, colouring pencils and book spread over his bedside table. He was such a good sleeper, always, from the beginning. No trouble. Ever.

Ed scooped him up and held him to his chest, head buried in him. Lizzie kissed and rubbed his little hands between hers, trying to warm them. Claire still had one arm around Lizzie, one around Ed, all of them weeping.

Lizzie turned to Mandy who was kneeling on the floor beside Margot, cruel in her grief. 'Couldn't you see he wasn't well? Why didn't you phone earlier? We could have called the doctor, done something.'

'We watched TV and read a story. He was fine when I said goodnight.' She dropped her head, shoulders shaking. 'And then this morning, when I went to wake him . . .'

'Lizzie, it's no one's fault,' said Claire.

Lizzie took Tom from Ed and cradled him in her arms.

'He kicks his football very high now,' said Margot.

Lizzie knew she should go to Margot, gather her close and tell her what a lovely big sister she was, how much Tom loved her, how much they would always love each other. But her arms and heart were too full of Tom.

A paramedic stood quietly in the doorway. 'Have as long as you need. Just let us know when you're ready.'

Lizzie held Tom closer. 'Where will you take him?'

He shuffled his feet. 'There'll have to be a post-mortem.'

'No!' she cried. She wouldn't allow them anywhere near his precious little body. 'No post-mortem.'

Claire squeezed her hand. 'Lizzie, it's the law.'

Ed laid Tom on his big-boy bed, Lizzie and Ed beside him, each of them holding a hand. There was a scrape of dirt beneath his thumbnail and a scratch on his arm. His lovely brown eyes were closed and his little mouth was soft.

They talked to him and held him and kissed his forehead, his eyelids, the scab on his nose, Lizzie running her fingers through his thick springy hair, loosening a knot between her thumb and forefinger.

Claire brought cups of tea and made Margot a cup of Milo. She took the little girl to her room and read her favourite stories, bringing her down when it was time for Tom to go.

Margot kissed her brother goodbye, crying because he was so cold. She told him she would look after his room until he was home again and promised not to pinch his colouring pencils. But would it be all right if she borrowed his Lego.

Lizzie and Ed went with Tom in the ambulance.

And then they took their little boy away.

CHAPTER 4

THE WAITING ROOM WAS PACKED, almost every seat taken. Alice had been waiting two hours, and the woman next to her complained she'd been waiting longer. Bored children fidgeted and whined, ignoring the crate of broken-down toys supposed to keep them entertained. Doctors emerged every now and then from surrounding rooms, struggling with the pronunciation of their next patient's name.

'Alice Miller,' a weary-voiced doctor called, with a surprised expression he quickly masked when she approached him. His surprise, she was sure, was that she looked so young.

He guided her into a shabby colourless room, indicating the chair into which she should sit, not bothering to introduce himself. She'd contacted the hospital a few weeks earlier, concerned when she read that breast implants might be putting women at risk of cancer.

She'd been incredulous. Surely the media reports were exaggerated. How was it possible that she had survived breast cancer, only to again be put in jeopardy by the breasts that replaced those she had had removed?

'Let's not get ahead of ourselves,' the doctor said, when Alice explained the reason for her visit.

Did he use that patronising tone for all his patients, she wondered, or reserve it for women in general, post-menopausal women, in particular?

'The advice at the moment is to wait and see,' he said, still not making eye contact.

Claire's ovaries, her breasts. When it came to women's bodies, the carelessness and contempt of the medical profession astounded her.

'The chances of the implants causing cancer is tiny,' he said, demonstrating the infinitesimal probability between his thumb and forefinger. 'One in ten thousand, they're saying.'

Alice nodded, convinced he would not be quite so blasé if his penis, which he no doubt held in huge regard, was in similar statistical jeopardy.

'There's only been a couple of dozen or so cases worldwide,' he said, raising his voice so he could be heard over the trucks emptying the bins lined up outside his window.

It was as if the thirty years that had elapsed since she'd been told her breasts might be the death of her were but a brief intermission. The news, then, had come on a Saturday evening, her surgeon not abandoning her to an anxious weekend, phoning to tell her, that very unfortunately, the lump in her breast was cancer.

Her most pressing concern at the time was Christopher. They'd been living together almost a year. She'd been sure he was 'the one'. But things weren't going well. He disliked her friends, constantly belittling them, creating a fuss when she met them for dinner or drinks, complaining if they visited. He seemed to be chronically short of money, and he'd had another of his outbursts.

The doctor continued to peer at his computer screen. 'I see your implants are about due for replacement.'

Ten years had gone very quickly.

Alice waited while he scrolled through her history, wishing that Lizzie was with her. She would ask all the right questions, put this doctor back in his box. She thought of Claire, who would have attended her medical appointments alone. No one to take her hand or reassure her, no one to share her frightening news.

He swivelled his chair to face Alice. 'Given your age, there doesn't seem much point in replacing them.'

Was he implying she'd be dead before another ten years were up or that no one would be interested in her, or her breasts, false or otherwise?

The doctor glanced at his watch. 'If you'd still prefer to go ahead, I could put you on a waiting list.'

'I'll need to give it some thought.'

'Of course.' He swivelled back to his screen. 'Any questions?'

Shaking her head, Alice reached for her bag. She didn't want to spend another minute with annotated diagrams of breasts, and doctors who made assumptions about women and age and what was best for them.

He stood and opened the door, a faint smile farewelling her.

A gentle whirr as the lift carried her downwards, the hiss of doors opening, outside, the sky high and wide, buildings sunlit and shadowed, cigarettes held between trembling fingers, wisps of smoke carried on a gentle breeze. The clang of a tram.

*

Alice stood naked in front of the mirror. She had not forgotten the discoloured, puckered skin; the scar that ran across the flat terrain of her chest. She cupped her breasts, the weight of them reassuring. Her only disappointment had been the nipples. Made of silicone, they looked real enough. Their one drawback? No feeling whatsoever.

Her surgery and treatment had been gruelling, her recovery long. If not for Claire . . .

She'd quite forgotten that Claire had visited almost every day bearing gifts, those silky pyjamas the nurses went mad over, the girliest dress to wear home after discharge.

Alice shook her head. It was easy to be generous when you were wealthy and successful. When you had the perfect life. Lizzie had made an effort, but she hadn't long lost Tom, his death becoming a lifelong excuse for self-pity.

If the worst happened, Alice's thoughts returned to her own mortality, and the implants did cause cancer, her personality couldn't be blamed. Champagne wouldn't be a suspect, divine retribution for a teenage abortion neither the cause of her cancer, nor what she deserved. No, if she were the one in ten thousand to get cancer, it would be a cancer entirely man-made.

Should she decide to go ahead and have her implants replaced, it would be replacement number four. She supposed she could try those ghastly moulds in her bra instead. But no matter how they may have improved, they wouldn't give her cleavage, a wonderful distraction from the neck. And she had her career to think of: if she couldn't get modelling work with breasts, how much harder would it be without them?

She hadn't wanted to live without breasts then, and she didn't want to now.

It was better in the end that Lizzie hadn't accompanied her to the appointment. She would be insisting before they were out the door that Alice take the sensible course and have her implants removed immediately, for good.

Reaching for her prettiest bra, the lime green with watermelon-coloured straps, she realised with some shame she was more fearful of losing her breasts than she was of cancer.

She logged in to her bank account. Puny savings, fast diminishing. She knew she was being irresponsible, knew that later she would be filled with guilty regret, but it had been weeks and weeks . . . It wasn't the sex, okay the sex was nice, it was the company, the affection; feeling, if only for a few hours, interesting and desirable again.

Yes, she had sworn she'd stick to her budget. But not today.

Today she would ring Emilio.

Alice leaned forward and spoke into the intercom, another of the intrusive devices that cluttered modern life. 'It's me, Alice.'

'Alice, you are here,' said Emilio.

Emilio lived in a high-rise apartment in Southbank. He was tall and dark and toned. She was smitten. She thought he might be a tiny bit, too.

He was often fully booked. But he always made time for Alice. She had in the past tried Tinder and other dating apps, but they were terribly hit and miss. Mostly miss. And no matter how she embellished her bio and filtered her photo, no one other than sixty-somethings were interested in sixty-somethings. She lied about her age, and by the look of them, they did, too.

She had been on some truly awful dates. Oh glory, the man with the wheeler complete with built-in seat, which he shuffled around to her side of the table to sit closer, saliva bubbling in the corners of his mouth. Men, no longer with a woman in their life to moderate bad habits, turned up to potentially romantic evenings squeezed into too-tight pants, specs swinging from chains, last meals embedded in dentures.

Emilio greeted her with a wide smile. 'Alice,' he kissed her on each of her cheeks, 'you look always amazing.'

And always, when in Emilio's company, Alice felt she really did look amazing. She was twenty again, waist slight, hair luxurious, skin velvety. She laughed like a girl, the croak of the past smoker, vanquished, as he showed her into his apartment.

Alice was one of the few clients who came to him, Emilio mostly visiting them. But he was sympathetic to her concerns that her neighbours might cotton on that the beautiful boy who occasionally visited might not be a relative or even a boyfriend, and neither was keen on a hotel room.

His apartment, windows soaring to the ceiling, walls unadorned but for one huge poster—something abstract and challenging— was nothing like the stuffy over-decorated houses people her age lived in.

They sat by the window, sipping cocktails, the sky a washed blue. An aspiring actor, he told her about the auditions he'd been to, his small role in an up-and-coming musical, the call-back for a major television production. 'Any day now, the big break.'

Alice doubted Emilio would get his big break. The problem would not be his talent or craft but the colour of his skin. In an industry uncomfortable with difference, his roles, if he was lucky, would be limited to criminals, drug-dealers, gang members or token minorities.

They toasted to big breaks.

Between auditions and the occasional role, Emilio visited women and, sometimes, couples. Not so unusual. But among his clients were people with a disability. At university he studied sociology and psychology. In his first years as a psychologist, specialising in sexual dysfunction, he saw a great unmet demand for the services he now provided.

He understood women, their needs and vulnerabilities. Like every job, it had its moments, he said, an emotional burden that he managed through regular debriefs with his own psychologist. Although Alice knew theirs was a business transaction, his attentiveness reminded her of how invisible she had become.

Not even Lizzie and, when she was alive, Claire, took her seriously, laughing dismissively and shaking their heads if she ventured an opinion on matters important. *Silly Alice.* She had for a long time comforted herself that they were jealous of her youthfulness, that she, unlike them, had cheated time rather than let it have its way with her. And she had *joie de vivre*, something Lizzie, who was so often a mope, did not have. Not in abundance, anyway. But after a time, she realised it wasn't jealousy. It was pity.

It had hurt, that realisation, it still did; but they were her friends, lifelong friends.

What would Lizzie say, she wondered, if she were to tell her about Emilio? Lizzie, who had grown to appreciate the monastic life, would think Alice foolish and narcissistic, and find the whole thing distasteful and post-feminist.

She told Emilio about Claire.

He put a hand on her knee. 'You must promise . . .'

She shook her head. 'Are you afraid of getting old?'

'My father died when I was very young,' he said. 'I am more afraid of not getting old.'

'I grew up without a father, too.'

'It is hard. My mother is both my mother and father. She is why I love women. And my grandmother, who looked after me while my mother worked, is why I love older women. Women, they have the life force.'

'Your mother, your grandmother. Are they . . . ?'

'They are both gone.'

Later, when Alice cried, he held her.

'Life,' he said, 'it is sad and beautiful.'

CHAPTER 5

SHE SHOULD RING HER MOTHER, she really should.

Margot was staring into the mirror, brushing her teeth. It wasn't her face she saw but her mother's, pale and stricken with tears. She closed her eyes. When she opened them, her mother had gone.

Margot had had a sudden urge to call her, to say that they would be there for each other, that together they would remember Claire and all she had meant to them. It was what she should have said when her mother put her arms around her. It was what Claire would have wanted, what she really wanted, too. It was the threat of her mother's tears that stopped her; tears, that when she was younger, she thought would never end. Year upon year, flowing silently.

She rinsed: one, two, three times. Gargled: ten, twenty, thirty seconds.

Perhaps she'd call tomorrow. Thank her for knowing that Margot needed her. She tried to imagine what it would be like to lose Jane—she couldn't. She would have to keep the conversation with her mother short, though, school pick-up always a good excuse. Her mother was someone to be carefully managed or before you knew it, she'd be taking over your life with her opinions and advice on child-rearing—as if—and what to do and where to go and anything and everything else.

Restless, Margot paced the room. If not for the children asleep in their beds, she would have left the house, a drive somewhere noisy, a walk somewhere quiet.

She turned down the bed, smoothing the sheet—there—tugging the corners so they sat evenly either side of the mattress.

Symmetry was so reassuring.

Julian would have flown home if she'd asked. He was a good man. A loving father. Her husband. *Stay, I'll be fine*, she'd told him.

A spin doctor—he hated it when she called him that—he had more work than he could handle, putting in long hours and often being called away any time, day or night. She had grown to quite like his absences, with the bed to herself, her iPad and phone beside her.

Tip-toeing downstairs, she made herself a cup of tea, tempted to add milk. And something sweet; how she longed for something sweet.

Back in her room, cup of weak black tea on the bedside table, Margot flicked through the leaflet she'd picked up at the library, thinking a course of some sort might pass the hours between school and kindy drop-offs and pick-ups. She ran her eye down the page: she had no inclination to study beekeeping, she couldn't see the point in learning Spanish, and why would she bother with karate when she lived in a safe neighbourhood?

She allowed herself to wonder what it would be like to be someone other than Julian's wife, to have an identity of her own. Someone other than mother. A person people wanted to talk to at parties, not someone they hurried from at the earliest opportunity.

Margot imagined a job, a career. Adults to converse with, a project, a deadline. A purpose? When occasionally she was tempted to look for something part-time, she immediately quashed the idea. Her mother had rarely been home, distracted when she was; away or too busy to be in the audience when she was in the school musical, or to wave her off when she headed to camp.

It was Claire's arms that had held her when she cried for Tom, Claire who stood close at Tom's funeral, Claire who was beside her in those first weeks. Her mother, grief-stricken, threw herself into her work. Soon Margot was living most of the time with Claire: Claire, Jeremy and later, Jane, her de facto family. She still saw her parents, alternating between them, when they could spare the time.

At Claire's she didn't have to sleep next to Tom's room and wake thinking she could hear him rustling around. She didn't have to listen to her mother's crying or her parents arguing whenever they were home together. Mealtimes she had hated most—her parents silent and glaring, no Tom being silly and funny and annoying. At Claire's, she could almost forget about Tom.

When Margot was in her teens, her mother, quite unexpectedly, resigned from her job, a career that until then had been her whole life. Margot remembered her bundling up jackets and suits along with anything navy or tailored and delivering them to the op shop. Any shoe with a heel she threw in the bin. She stopped colouring her hair, going grey and leaving it to its own devices, the occasional trim with whatever pair of scissors she could find, her only concession.

Lizzie had insisted Margot move back home; Margot furious her mother had enrolled her, without consultation, into a new school, public of course, that her mother had said, with misplaced reverence, encouraged artistic and creative pursuits. Students—Skyes and Ferns and Indigos—probably birthed in murky water, with a chorus of women singing them into the world, sounded like youthful versions of her mother as they raged against the patriarchy and whinged about capitalism in their three-hundred-dollar vegan shoes.

Her mother took up chanting and yoga. She became vegetarian. Margot could eat meat, if she must, but wasn't to bring it into the house, everything always more important than her. Her father eventually rescued her from the cliché, happy, he said, for Margot to live with him. But only on weekends. The rest of the week she spent at boarding school.

One of her therapists had once asked if she was still angry with her mother. She'd said no, but that sometimes she hated herself. She'd had no idea where that came from, but then, didn't everyone hate themselves some of the time? She found another therapist.

That same therapist had suggested that perhaps Molly and Jack could see more of Lizzie. She said it was important for children to have a close relationship with their grandparents, and that it might be good for mother and daughter, too. Margot followed her advice, arranging for her mother to come over one afternoon a week to spend time with the children.

Molly and Jack adored their grandmother. She threw herself into every game, every activity. She read to them, took them on nature walks around the garden (then lectured Margot about the use of insecticide), helped them whip up cupcakes and scones—her mother who had never baked—and laughed more than Margot had ever heard her laugh. She was patient and loving and funny.

That wasn't to say Margot didn't keep a careful eye, ready to step in if her mother were to start filling their heads with tales of rising sea levels or melting ice-caps. Not that she'd ever said anything untoward, but who knew what her mother, who got herself arrested at global warming protests, might come out with.

Margot scrolled through Instagram. No *likes*. She'd thought that her very professional photos, her photogenic children and her beautiful house would translate into lots of followers, but nope, the *mummies* and *mommies* mostly ignored her. She swung her legs from under the doona and took the cup and saucer to the kitchen, rinsing before placing them in the dishwasher, giving the bench a final soapy wipe.

It was Margot's habit to pop in on the children before she turned out the light. She picked up the book lying open on Molly's bed, brushed the curls from her face and kissed her goodnight.

Jack was fast asleep, too, a foot poking from the bed, his head nestled into the crook of his arm. She bent to kiss him, the warmth of his breath reassuring.

Margot's watch buzzed a reminder: ten pm. Bedtime.

Margot liked to be up early. A dream, a lovely dream, had woken her. She was having lunch with her mother and Claire in one of those cafés typical of Melbourne's inner north, with scarred wooden tables and an assortment of wonky chairs, that her mother thought was authentic or something.

They were sharing Molly-and-Jack anecdotes: so creative, so intelligent, so good-looking, all outrageously biased, of course.

During the meal, her mother and Claire glanced across the table at each other, smiling. In their eyes, Margot saw how much they loved her. She saw, too, that she loved them back.

When she woke, that brief joyous moment was quickly replaced by a thudding emptiness. Claire was gone. But it was more, even, than that. The three women hadn't had lunch together, not for years. Claire, tiring of Margot's excuses, had given up trying to bring them together. Margot had always thought there'd be a next time, but next times came and went. They'd never had that lunch, and now they never would.

In the kitchen, Margot began packing Molly's lunchbox: a Mediterranean salad, wholegrain bread cut into triangles (Molly refused to eat squares), a small tub of Greek yoghurt, fresh fruit, a handful of nuts. She did wonder for a moment if all the trouble she was going to was for Molly or for the admiration it might unleash on Instagram. She shook her head, of course, she was doing it for Molly. She set the lunchbox against the splashback, hot pink plastic reflected in the satiny stainless steel, positioned the fruit bowl so it was just in frame, and arranged the children's paintings on the fridge, a happy arty blur in the background. Perfect.

She opened the camera on her phone, then stopped. What the actual fuck was she doing? Claire had barely been dead twenty-four hours and here she was messing around with Instagram. In the same moment, early-morning sunshine streamed through the window, bathing the kitchen in a pink glow. She snapped. And posted.

Claire wouldn't want her to feel guilty. She'd throw back her head and laugh and say *go for it*. An amateur photographer herself, she admired Margot's eye for detail and the cinematic quality of her images. And besides, it was a distraction, a positive one that got her thinking about something other than Claire and mothers and mothering and regret.

She slipped the lunchbox into Molly's school bag. Her mother hadn't bothered with school lunches. She had instead pressed coins into Margot's hand and told her to go to the tuckshop and buy whatever she wanted. She was not like her mother. She would never be like her mother.

The phone buzzed: a message from Charlotte: *thinking of u – a walk later in week if ur up to it xxxxxxx*

Margot messaged back: *yep lets xx*

Margot drank a glass of water, her thoughts again with Claire. How she wished she'd phoned Claire more often, asked, even occasionally, if she needed help with Jeremy. They had been supposed to meet for coffee a fortnight ago, but Margot had cancelled. She remembered being surprised that Claire had sounded so disappointed.

She tried to recall the reason she'd cancelled but couldn't. One of those days, probably, when leaving the house, anything, seemed such an effort.

If only she hadn't stretched the time between their catch-ups. It wasn't that she didn't enjoy Claire's company. But the last few times they'd met, Claire had seemed to always bring the conversation back to her mother. Couldn't Margot see just a little more of her? It would mean so much. Yes, Lizzie had her ways. Don't we all? Yes, she could be judgemental—who of us wasn't?—and perhaps she was a little bossy. But Margot must know how fiercely her mother loved her and Molly and Jack. Claire, in her last weeks, had been trying to mend things between them.

Her phoned pinged: three *likes*.

She was scrolling distractedly when she heard the key in the door. Julian.

She shoved the phone in a drawer. He was always going on about the time Margot wasted on Instagram. He thought she might be bored—she heard *boring*—concerned she was lonely—she heard *friendless*. He'd warned her that social media could become a habit—she heard *addictive personality*. And so, she learned to cover her tracks lest he jump to any more conclusions.

He came hurrying into the kitchen, suitcase rattling behind him, face full of concern. And love. She never quite understood what she had done to deserve being so loved.

'You should have stayed in Sydney.'

'I would've been back last night, but the meeting went on and on.'

Julian tilted her chin and stared into her eyes as if to determine the depth of her sorrow.

She dropped her head onto his chest and had a cry. 'I don't want to believe it.'

He wrapped his arms around her. 'Cry as much as you want.'

She tried never to cry. She hated crying. You didn't know what it would raise, where it would end.

'Lizzie must be struggling.'

He had always called her mother, Lizzie, which, of course, Lizzie liked very much. Had Lizzie had her way, Margot, even the grandchildren, would call her Lizzie. Labels linked to mothering were a patriarchal conspiracy, she said, a way of keeping women in their place.

Julian liked her mum even though she'd opposed their marriage—*not your marriage specifically, just marriage in general*—and made a fuss about her taking Julian's name—*you have a very good one of your own.*

Her mother didn't discuss politics with Julian, but they often talked shop: communications and crisis management and stuff

Margot had no interest in. They did occasionally clash, her mother wondering how he could represent those *capitalist over-lords* or protect some depraved person, most usually a man, and sleep straight in bed at night. Julian could always talk his way out of trouble, make her mother laugh so that she eventually forgot what she was bothered about.

Julian said he understood, given their past, why Margot might want to keep Lizzie at arm's length. But she always felt his sympathies were not entirely with her. On the few occasions she'd raised it with him, he said it wasn't for him to take sides. He liked Lizzie, he loved her. They must sort it out. He hoped they would. Counselling might help.

He thought it was that simple.

'I don't think it's quite sunk in,' said Margot, seeking an explanation for her mother's composure when she'd told her about Claire.

'And Jane, how's Jane? I wanted to call her but thought it might be too soon.'

'Numb, I think. The unexpectedness of it, the shock. I'm spending tomorrow with her.' She shook her head. 'We're choosing photos for the farewell.'

He stroked her hair. 'You love someone your whole life and then they're gone,' he said. 'Just like that.'

Just like that, thought Margot.

'Gets you thinking, doesn't it? A death.'

Margot's plan was not to think about it. Not now. Not ever. Another ping. Four *likes*. Finally, her posts were getting some love.

Julian looked vaguely irritated. He pulled open the drawer, raised an eyebrow.

Margot removed the phone and without a word placed it on the bench. They'd argued a few nights before. She was almost permanently distracted, he said. She'd rather be on her phone than with him. Even when they were making love, he felt she was elsewhere. *Well, yes, maybe . . .*

'Posting? Today?'

He was laying another guilt trip on her. 'Could you not?'

Julian stared at her as if he was about to say something but then changed his mind. 'Kids still in bed?'

'I was about to wake them.'

'After the photoshoot?'

'Not funny, Julian.'

He laughed and pulled her close. 'Come here, you.'

He was never mad at her for long.

Kissing her forehead, he said, 'I'll take Molly to school, get Jack to kindy.'

Julian disappeared through the door, the enthusiastic stamp of his feet on the stairs.

Jane was sitting in the corner of an old sofa in the lounge room of her share-house avoiding the dip in the middle where the springs had given way, photo albums in a pile beside her. Margot was on the floor rummaging through yet more photos, sepia-toned and black and white.

The unbearable news of Claire's and Jeremy's deaths, the shock of their sudden loss, was inscribed in the pallor of their faces, the protective hunch of their bodies. It was a very different mood from the hilarity a couple of weeks earlier, when they'd been sorting through the same photos for Claire's surprise seventy-fifth.

The house, normally full of activity and chatter, was unusually quiet, a respectful silence; Jane's loss only three days long. Jane's housemates came and went, offering coffee, leaning over the back of the couch to kiss the top of Jane's head or give her a quick neck massage before disappearing to allow them privacy.

'Look at this,' said Jane, passing a photo of a young Claire and Lizzie.

Two girls, very proper in school uniforms, stared at the camera. Already, there was a sadness in her mother's eyes, Margot noticed, a faraway look, her half-smile lost beside Claire's big grin. She could see Claire's fingertips brushing her mother's hand.

Margot had often thought you couldn't tell where Claire ended and her mother began. She would be kinder, she would follow her back on Facebook. She might even ask her out to lunch.

Jane blew her nose.

Margot reached up and squeezed her hand, eyes red-rimmed and salty, too. 'We can take a break if you want.'

Jane shook her head, wept tiny breathy sobs into her tissue.

Margot moved the albums to one side and sat with Jane on the couch, arm around her friend, slowly sliding into the dip.

'You're sinking,' said Jane. They burst out laughing, arms around each other.

Back on the floor, Margot opened another of the albums, its pages filled with Claire and Jeremy's time in the UK. She passed the album to Jane. A letter, old-style airmail, fell into Jane's lap. She opened it. 'It's from your mum to my mum. Wow, like decades ago.' Jane slid to the floor so they could read the letter together.

30 January 1984

Darling Claire,
You have been gone only a few weeks but already it feels like years.

Did you get my last letter? Perhaps it's been held up.
International mail can be so slow. I hope you are settling in
and enjoying London—still wonderful, no doubt.

I have been worrying terribly—you know I love to
worry terribly—that something is wrong between us. You
did not seem yourself before you left. I fear I have worn
you out, I wear myself out.

I know I have said it before, but I can never thank you
enough for all you have done for me, Ed too, and for the
way you have looked after Margot. You have been much
more of a mother to her than I could be. She is still having
those night terrors and I've lost count of her tantrums . . .
I try to comfort her but I know it's you she needs.

I have seen Alice only twice since you left. She seems
always to be busy. When we do get together, it feels strained
between us. Things are not the same without you. So, you
see, we are both bereft.

Silly, I know, but I miss Ed. He was so rarely home and
when he was, we argued or ignored each other.

Jane glanced at Margot. 'You okay?'

Margot nodded, she remembered the night terrors . . . and
the tantrums. The arguments and the silences.

They resumed reading.

I don't know if it's our separation or the end of this latest
affair, but whatever it is, he is at a very low ebb. I think
perhaps this last one was more serious. It seems you guessed
correctly when you said it might be more than a fling.

It's almost fourteen months since we lost Tom, but it
still feels so awfully raw. I sometimes think I will never

*experience joy again, to know it, even for a moment, can
only mean I have forgotten Tom. And that I cannot do.*

*Oh, my goodness. All about me, as usual. Do tell me
how you are enjoying your time in England. How lovely it is
to be away. This country sometimes so insular . . .*

*A lovely summer so far, warm days and long evenings.
I do love this time of year. I know you do, too.*

Your friendship is everything to me.

Please write and tell me how you are.

My love always,

Lizzie

'That can't have been easy to read,' said Jane.

Although her mother never spoke of her father's affairs,
Margot knew he saw other women. The rows at home, the innu-
endos in the media, her father's absences. When she was younger,
she'd made excuses for him, telling herself *no wonder*. But now she
did wonder about a man who was so often unfaithful and
the hurt he must have caused her mother.

'He's not like that anymore, he's changed.'

Jane picked up the wedding album, a picture of Claire
and Jeremy sealing their vows with a kiss.

'Look at them,' said Margot. 'Perfect.'

'Perfect,' said Jane.

CHAPTER 6

LIZZIE WALKED INTO THE DAY room of her mother's nursing home, the room to which residents who could still maintain a sitting position were dispatched each morning. She picked up the remote and flicked it from the kiddie cartoon channel to ABC24—just because they were old didn't mean they weren't interested in the world. It was the world that wasn't interested in them.

It was the loneliness that struck Lizzie, the waiting and hoping someone might find an hour in their day to sit with them, to hold their hand, to read from a favourite book. To reminisce. She had seen the joy when they did.

Lizzie had visited every nursing home within a ten-kilometre radius of her home, hoping to find at least one like those advertised on television. Some looked pretty swish on the website but when she did the turning-up-unexpectedly test, it was always the same: residents crying out for want of attention, a couple of fish fingers for dinner, one nurse on duty if you could only find them.

She had put her mother's name on the waiting list of one of the better nursing homes, but even if a bed became available, it would be heartless to move her when she was so frail and had only just settled in.

Bypassing overfilled skips and a trolley loaded with an open dressing pack, Lizzie wound her way through the warren of corridors to her mother's room. She paused a moment when she saw the blue plastic bag tucked into a corner, AGGIE NEWSTEAD written in Texta on a carelessly applied sticker.

Lizzie knew immediately what the blue bag signified. Since her mother's admission a few months before, Aggie was the second person in the three-bed ward to have died. Lizzie took a breath, relaxed her face into a smile and stepped into the room.

'If it isn't my darling girl.'

Lizzie kissed her mother hello, her cheek a bony ridge against Lizzie's lips. 'So sorry about Aggie.'

Her mother crossed herself. 'With the angels now.'

Aggie's bed had been stripped of its sheets and pillows. The photo of her cat, Hugo, who'd been put to sleep because there was no one to care for him after a broken hip stole Aggie's independence, and another of her husband, who'd died years before, already whisked away.

Lizzie flung open the curtains. Her mother, and Grace in the next bed, shrunken faces mired in pillows, blinked as they turned towards the trickle of sunshine. She switched off the lights and wound open the window, curtains fluttering in a drift of cool air.

Lizzie pulled a chair close to her mother's bed. 'Did she go during the night?' They so often did.

'Here when I went to sleep, gone when I opened my eyes.'

'Has anyone spoken to you?' Reassurance that Aggie didn't suffer, that someone was with her in her final moments, that Aggie's life meant something.

She shook her head.

When the residents of Hilltop Manor took the only exit available to them, they were rarely mentioned again. A kerfuffle in the night, a vacated bed in the morning. Little thought for those who'd roomed with them or sat next to each other in the dayroom, sharing a joke or exchanging a profound glance about the situation in which they found themselves. Nothing to remember them, nothing to mark their passing.

'If only I could go back to my dear little house and sleep in my bed. I had it worked out to die in that bed with people all around praying me into the next world.'

'Oh, Mammy, I wish it, too.'

Joyce had lived in a small country town until her stroke the year before. It affected her swallow—pureed meals and thickened drinks all she was allowed—and withered her right side, arm and leg heavy flaccid things, balance teetering.

'I'd be having a proper cup of tea now and a crumpet and the fire would be on and I'd be watching the telly. All nice and cosy.'

Whoever had thought that herding older people together—as if they were all of the same ilk, their basic needs tended to but little else—was a good idea? To take from them, in their last little while, all that was comforting and nurturing and familiar. Why would you not do everything to keep them in their homes and their communities?

Lizzie had been determined that she would never put her mother in a nursing home. She had resolved to find a carer but soon discovered that the cost—even with a few subsidised hours—of the round-the-clock care her mother required, was out of reach. She'd considered selling Joyce's home, not that it was worth much, and moving her into a little flat. But how cruel, in her mother's last days, to condemn her to little more than a box with a rotating roster of carers, anything affordable so far from Melbourne, so Lizzie's visits would be limited to once or twice a week.

Her parents had lived modest lives, her father had worked hard and long, her mother, too, when she was well enough. They had given much and asked for very little, and yet . . . Dignity at the end of life shouldn't come with a price tag attached.

'You sold your house to that nice young couple. You liked them. Remember? They promised to look after your garden and make sure there was water in the birdbath.'

'Aye, I remember.'

Lizzie scraped up the medication, a pink and blue dribble down the front of her mother's nightie, feeding what she could into her mouth, her mother screwing up her face.

'If only your father were here.'

Poor Dad. A lifetime of trying to meet her mother's demands— her mother impossible to please, her father feeling he always disappointed—and there she was calling him back from the afterlife.

Lizzie attacked the over-bed table with paper towelling, wiping away anything sticky or crusty. She replaced the flowers bought on her last visit with a bunch of bluebells from her garden, arranging them in a vase and placing them where her mother could enjoy them.

'Has the doctor been in to see you?'

'If you can call him walking past my bed and saying, *How are you today, Mrs Kavanagh*, then I suppose he has.'

Lizzie cleaned and tidied, searching for the right words. Her mother had always liked Claire: she was pretty and clever and well-to-do.

Lizzie's family had not been well-to-do, but not quite so poor as her mother made out. Accusations of poverty a weapon used against Lizzie's father, who wasn't the provider her mother said a wife had a right to.

Lizzie chatted on about the garden, rueing that the wind had made short work of the magnolia, huge cream and magenta blooms fluttering like broken wings over the path.

'Mum,' Lizzie sat on the bed and took her mother's hand, 'there's something I have to tell you.'

Joyce's eyes narrowed. 'Who is it that's passed now?'

Almost everyone Joyce had known—family, friends, neighbours—was long gone. Occasionally, she'd pick out a name from the obituaries, an acquaintance long forgotten, unashamedly delighted she'd outlived them.

Lizzie stroked her mother's hand, bruises blooming through paper-thin skin, finding the wherewithal to say once more that Claire was dead.

Her mother blessed herself, lips moving in silent prayer. 'She took her own life and Jeremy with her?'

'Claire didn't have much longer. Nor did Jeremy.'

Joyce held tight to Lizzie's hand. 'I wish it were me instead of Claire.'

'Oh, Mammy.'

'It's not natural, young woman like that.'

At ninety-five, Joyce thought anyone under the age of eighty was young.

'Something to have a friend like that. Something to have someone who's known you your whole life long.'

'It was, it really was.' Lizzie closed her eyes. Unthinkable to be speaking of Claire in the past tense.

'Will there be a Mass?'

Lizzie shook her head. 'Claire wanted a farewell instead.'

Her mother raised an eyebrow. 'Not sure how she'd have gone finding a priest, not with two mortal sins on her soul.'

'I don't think it's like that anymore.'

'I'm sure the Lord will take into account the good Claire did and save her from damnation.'

Lizzie was annoyed to feel reassured. 'Of course He will.'

'I've been thinking about my funeral, matter of fact.'

Joyce was often thinking about her funeral.

'I'll be wanting a coffin, solid wood, and a Mass and prayers. And "Ave Maria" and "Danny Boy" playing, the sweetest versions you can find. And I'll be wearing the blue dress, the one that sets off my eyes, not that my eyes will be open. It might be a bit loose but who's going to notice. And shoes, the ones with the little heels. I don't want to be meeting my Maker barefoot.'

'Shoes, definitely shoes.'

'Make sure my wedding ring's on and my dentures are in. And I want flowers, lots and lots.'

'There'll be lots of flowers.'

'And someone to say something nice about me. Someone who knows I did the best I could.'

There was a time when Lizzie had little nice to say about her mother, a mother often too ill to care for her, long lonely months passing before she was recovered enough to leave her room. And then, without warning—she came to know the pattern—Lizzie would wake to her mother bustling around the house doing great loads of washing, humming as she began a spring clean that lasted weeks.

It had been baffling, her mother's sickness. It wasn't until Lizzie was older that she realised her mother's illness was not of the body but of the mind. Her mother hadn't been selfish, she wasn't a bad mother. She needed help, help she didn't get.

It was hard on her father, a simple man, good-hearted and uncomplaining. He did his best to care for Lizzie. He loved her mother but was without a clue as to why his wife, for half the year, would lock herself away from her family. Looking back, Lizzie realised that not only was he proud of her when she won a scholarship to boarding school, but relieved as well.

Her mother eventually sought treatment, if a doctor writing out a script for Valium was treatment. In older age, her mood swings had become less dramatic; after her stroke, disappearing altogether. Lizzie sought an explanation from her mother's geriatrician. It was common, he said, for emotions to be affected after a stroke.

'There are lots of nice things to say.'

Linda, a smiley face on her badge, walked hurriedly into the room, balancing two trays in her hands. 'Hey, Joyce. Hey, Gracie.' She dropped one tray in front of Lizzie's mother, another in front of Grace.

'Busy time of day,' said Lizzie.

Linda rolled her eyes and nodded. 'Come on now, Gracie.' She loaded a spoon with more food than Grace could possibly manage, Grace wide-eyed as she tried to keep up.

Her mother refused to go to the dining room. The few well enough to sit out of bed were either wheeled in or made their own way. Hair uncombed, clothes caked with food, unshaven and often bewildered, they were the saddest company.

One or two staff would do their best, racing between residents arranging bibs and non-slip mats, cutting up meals, placing a fork or spoon into a trembling hand, encouraging those with no appetite—almost all of them—to eat and take a few sips of their drink, a spoonful here, a spoonful there, for those who couldn't manage themselves.

Some cried into their food, others flung it about, most just pushed it around the plate or sat and stared. For if the point was that food sustained life, then what was the point?

Lizzie helped her mother sit higher in the bed and tied a bib around her neck. She lowered the over-bed table and placed her meal within easy reach.

Linda wiped away the food dribbling down Grace's chin. 'Sorry, darl.' Grace clamped her mouth shut. 'No more? You sure?' She dropped the serviette on the tray. 'That's me then. See you tomorrow, same time, same place, hey, Joyce.' She hurried away, more feeds waiting for her in the next room.

When her mother had finished her meal, Lizzie went to check on Grace. She motioned at the tray still sitting on Grace's table. 'You must be hungry—you've hardly eaten a thing.'

Grace's eyes met Lizzie's, all the will and light gone from them. She shook her head and turned away.

You could live too long, thought Lizzie, screening her mother's bed and filling a bowl with warm soapy water.

'She's never had a visitor,' said her mother. 'Not a one.'

Lizzie removed her mother's gown and unfastened the nappy, covering her nakedness with a towel. She moistened the face washer and patted it over her mother's face and neck, then gently beneath the loose flesh that once formed her breasts. She wet the washer again and sponged her tummy, stretch marks telling the story of a baby carried. Carefully, she released the fingers of the hand, balled into a fist after the stroke, removing a square of gauze there to prevent the skin breaking down and fingernails biting into the palm. She guided her mother's hands into the water, giving them time to wallow in the warmth.

They had been a family private about their bodies, Lizzie with no memory of seeing her parents undressed. In adolescence the swelling of Lizzie's breasts went without comment, the first threads of pubic hair unexplained; the desire at night, in bed alone, the heat and moisture between her legs, as mysterious as the bright blood that spotted her undies.

When Lizzie first saw her mother naked, she averted her eyes: a few brusque strokes, a quick wave of the towel, a nightie jerked over her head and the job was done.

Lizzie rolled her mother onto her side, embarrassment long gone. Tending to her had become a meditation, soaping and rinsing, massaging cream into heels and elbows and bottom.

'It used to be lovely.'

Lizzie slipped her mother's affected arm into the sleeve, then the other. 'What used to be lovely?'

'My bottom.'

'Your bottom?'

'Glory days long gone.'

'Mine's nothing to write home about either.'

They burst into laughter.

Lizzie's eyes flicked to the photo of her parents taken when they'd been courting. Her father, hands deep in his pockets, looked shy and handsome. Beside him, smiling mischievously into the camera, her mother, hand resting on his arm. Lizzie had the photo laminated and taped it to the bedhead to remind anyone who might come to her mother's bedside that Joyce, too, had once been young and in love with life.

'You haven't forgotten that Margot will be in to see you tomorrow.' Margot visited every week, sometimes bringing the children with her. Occasionally, Lizzie and Margot visited together, three generations of women bound by love, duty and blood.

'I like it when she visits, it's the goodbyes I don't like. I find them hard, the goodbyes.'

Lizzie combed the thin strands of her mother's hair and pushed it into a wave the way her mother had always done. 'There now.'

Her mother fell against the pillows. Her eyes flickered then closed. Lizzie lay her on her side and tucked a pillow into her back, placing another under her arm to support her hand. 'Comfy?'

'It goes so quick.'

Lizzie kissed her goodbye. 'I'll see you the day after tomorrow.'

She hurried away, the salty dampness of her mother's cheek on her lips.

CHAPTER 7

IT WAS A STILL DAY, chilly, but with winter sunshine warm enough to coax off coats and scarves. Mourners were gathering in the garden of Claire and Jeremy's beach house, lawyers, community leaders, celebrities and politicians, people Claire had put to work in support of her various causes. Even those who hadn't always agreed with her had made the journey to pay their respects.

Claire had always insisted she wanted a party, not a funeral, champagne and music and laughter—speeches if you absolutely must. She wanted a good death and a good send-off. Jane had honoured her mother's wish.

Claire's human rights advocacy had put her in the spotlight, something she courted and enjoyed. Jeremy, a radiologist, forever in his wife's shadow, tagged along as he had always done.

Opinion pages and blogs filled with commentary, people who had never met Claire, passing judgement. Social media had been full of the murder–suicide, Claire's and Jeremy's deaths trending on Twitter.

It had been hard on Jane, the press stalking her for days. But Jane, who was a producer at an independent radio station, understood how the media worked. In an interview with a journalist she knew and trusted, she said her mother would take great comfort knowing she had encouraged discussions about death and dying and the right of people to by-pass doctors and hospitals and drawn-out treatments. Jane wanted it known that her parents had talked about the manner and timing of their passing long before her father became ill. They had both agreed they did not want to languish in their old age or end their days in a nursing home.

Her mother, Jane said, had realised that time had come.

Everywhere Lizzie looked, she saw Claire. The days since her death a blur; grief descending without warning, once in the cereal aisle of the supermarket of all places, casting her adrift.

Lizzie, who had for so long lived with grief, was still surprised by the ache of it, the world faded and unendurable.

But her heart lifted when she saw Margot, with Jack tucked into one arm, Molly trailing alongside. Wearing a black dress, silk scarf artfully draped, long black hair a soft fall of curls, there was something wonderfully elegant about her beautiful daughter that had always reminded her of Ed. Not only did Margot have her father's good looks, she had his carriage, his taste for the expensive, the exquisite. And something of his disposition, too.

Molly was the first to see her. 'Grandma! Grandma!' she called, pulling free of Margot and bounding towards Lizzie.

Lizzie scooped her up, smelling her lovely Molly smell. 'How did you grow so tall in one week?'

Molly kissed a big wet kiss on her lips. 'Mummy wouldn't let me wear my fairy dress,' she said, her voice full of six-year-old indignation.

'Your fairy dress doesn't have pretty pink polka dots like this one.'

'Mummy says you don't like pink, not even on girls,' Molly said, wriggling out of the cuddle.

Oh dear. 'I love polka dots.'

'Mum,' said Margot, leaning forward to kiss her; a graze of shoulders, an ocean between them.

Jack stretched chubby little arms towards Lizzie. 'Ganma.'

'Dear little Jack,' Lizzie said, kissing his head.

Margot lowered him until his feet touched the ground. He was off immediately, chasing Molly in and around their legs, laughing hysterically.

'Is Julian with you?'

'He's back in Sydney—something he couldn't get out of.'

Margot snapped some photos of the children playing, Lizzie laughing at Jack, stout little legs doing their best to keep up with the other children who had joined them, the air ringing with their squeals.

Margot looked up from her phone. 'Have you seen Dad?'

Happily, Lizzie had not. 'Not so far. Is he coming?'

'He said he was.'

Molly and Jack hurtled into them, pink-cheeked and out of breath. Molly was holding Jack's hand just as Margot used to hold Tom's. 'We're hungry.'

'Why don't you go find your father and I'll get these two something to eat?' said Lizzie, plucking a twig from Molly's hair. She knelt beside Molly and Jack. 'And then, if Mummy says yes, we can go and see the fish in the fishpond.'

Molly jumped up and down. 'Can we, Mummy? Can we?'

'Afterwards,' said Margot.

'But Mummy—'

'We have to find Grandpa and Charlotte.'

Molly huffed.

'You go with Mummy and we'll visit the fish later,' said Lizzie.

Margot took hold of her children's hands, Lizzie staring after them.

Lizzie found Jane in a quiet corner of the garden, her face grey and pinched. Grief was such a lonely place.

'Lizzie!' Jane's eyes lit up. 'You don't know how good it is to see a familiar face.'

'So many people,' said Lizzie. It was hard saying goodbye, harder when you were surrounded by strangers.

'I was expecting a crowd.' Jane shook her head. 'But nothing like this.'

They hugged, Lizzie wanting to be strong for her, for Margot.

'I was thinking of you yesterday, collecting their ashes . . .'

'Sam came with me.' Jane guided Lizzie to a nearby seat. 'You can't ever imagine that could be all that's left of two lives.'

Lizzie put a protective arm around her.

'The urns are on a shelf in my bedroom. I can't bear to think of them alone.'

Lizzie could see tears threatening. 'Can I get you anything? A cup of tea, a glass of wine?'

Jane shook her head. 'If only I'd known . . .'

'Oh, Jane.'

'I could have stayed with them until the end.'

Lizzie drew Jane closer. 'Claire would never have wanted to put you through that or let you take that risk.'

'It shouldn't be this way,' said Jane.

'No, it shouldn't.'

'People should be able to decide.'

'They should, of course they should.'

The sun reappeared from behind a drift of cloud, warming and reassuring.

Jane pulled the sunglasses perched on her head over her eyes. 'We're lucky with the weather.'

One of those perfect winter days, thought Lizzie, feeling a great rush of sadness.

'Is Sam with you?'

Jane nodded. 'I just needed a few minutes.'

'These things can be so overwhelming, but when they're over you hardly remember a thing.'

'Jesus, the things people say when they don't know what to say.'

They both laughed.

'I miss them,' said Jane.

'I miss them, too,' said Lizzie.

They were silent for a moment.

'I still haven't seen Margot.'

'She's here with Molly and Jack—we were chatting a minute ago.'

Even though they'd led very different lives, Jane and Margot had remained close. Jane had idolised the older Margot, waiting at the window for her to come home from school, wanting only Margot to read her stories. They were often found sleeping together—Jane, when she was only a few years old, coming to Margot when Margot had one of her night terrors. And yet, Claire had often commented, that when Margot was away on a weekend with Lizzie or Ed, Jane, from the beginning, was entirely self-sufficient. It wasn't until Margot graduated from university that it was she who needed Jane. Though, perhaps, thought Lizzie, that was how it had always been.

Lizzie was grateful for Jane's steadying influence on her daughter. Jane had always been reserved and bookish, preferring to work behind the scenes to occupying the spotlight. She'd once joked that only one person per family could be the centre of attention.

'I hope you've got someone looking after you?' Lizzie was thinking about Jane's partner, Sam, but didn't like to ask specifically. Claire had often complained that there was nothing easier than saying the wrong thing when it came to Jane's love life. *Heaven forbid you ask a question.* Although they'd been together for . . . Lizzie couldn't remember how long, they'd never shared a home. Jane and Sam saw each other spontaneously, apparently, nothing planned, just when they felt like it. In between, they went about their own lives. *Whatever that's supposed to mean.*

'Sam's been great, so have my housemates.'

Claire had been incredulous that Jane, in her early thirties, was still in a share-house. *Is she ever going to grow up?* Jane didn't care what people thought. She did, as Claire liked to say with a sigh, her own thing. Claire would often joke that somehow they'd ended up with each other's daughters.

Jane looked at her phone. 'The speeches will be starting soon.'

'You're okay?'

Jane took a breath. 'I am.'

They walked arm in arm, stopping to give directions to someone who was looking lost.

'Ah, almost forgot.' Jane reached into her bag and pulled out an envelope. 'This is for you. From Mum. The police found it under the bed.'

Under the bed?

'They returned it a few days ago. I haven't opened it, obviously.'

Lizzie had hoped there might be a letter. In it, Claire would explain everything, she would remember their friendship, ask Lizzie to understand. They had exchanged dozens of letters over the years, writing to each other when they were travelling or away, letters sometimes arriving unexpectedly: an anecdote Claire wanted to share, something that was making her sad or mad. She said that when anything important happened, she sat down and wrote Lizzie a letter. She took the envelope from Jane, Claire's last words to her folded in her hand.

Row upon row of chairs had been set up at the rear of the garden, a hedge providing protection from the winds that sometimes blew icy and ferocious off the ocean. Most of the seating had already been taken; a few people sat on the grass, others milled around the edges. It was a mixed crowd, some in jeans, others beautifully turned out, dresses swishing, jewels gleaming. Sam, a classical guitarist, played the 'Cavatina', haunting and poignant, it was one of Claire's favourite pieces.

Jane spotted Margot. They held each other for a long moment.

Alice, who had just arrived, hurried towards them. 'Jane, oh, Jane . . .' She pulled Jane and Lizzie and Margot into an embrace. 'Oh my God, you poor dear girl.'

'It's lovely to see you, Alice. I'm so glad you could be here.'

'I can feel your mother among us,' said Alice.

Jane smiled. 'I can, too.' She glanced at her phone. 'Better go.'

'Yes, yes, off you go,' said Alice.

Lizzie kissed Alice hello. 'Two now instead of three.'

'Oh, Lizzie,' said Alice, weeping extravagantly.

Molly passed Alice a tissue. 'You can sit beside me,' she said.

They took their seats, Molly sitting between her mother and Alice, compelling Margot and Lizzie to sit together. Molly, who was talking quietly to Alice, little hands clasped in her lap, seemed to have absorbed the gravity of the occasion. Claire was nice, Lizzie overheard her say. She was always kind. Alice agreed that she was and put an arm around her. Jack played with a truck at Margot's feet.

Lizzie remembered very little of Tom's funeral: Ed and Claire on each side supporting her; Margot clutching Claire's hand; the tiny white coffin holding Tom; one last kiss before he was gone forever, his little mouth so blue and cold, his busy hands so still. Hair much too neat.

Jane adjusted the microphone. Lizzie wondered if the assembled were a little taken aback that Claire's daughter was tattooed and pierced. She had Claire's good heart and gentle manner, but where Jane was diminutive, Claire was tall, Jane's wild curls the antithesis of Claire's smooth blonde do. Jane thanked everyone for coming, a wonderful turnout. Her mother, who did like an audience, would be delighted. Laughter rippled through the crowd.

Jane's eulogy was not concerned with her parents' achievements; it was her Mum and Dad she wanted to talk about. Lizzie did not have to turn her head to know Jane's words had moved many to tears. She put her hand over Margot's, and Margot didn't pull away. Photos of Claire, Claire and Jeremy, Claire and Lizzie and Alice, Jane, Margot, Ed, a life, a lifetime, flashing across a screen. Jane invited Lizzie to join her at the microphone to remember her friendship with Claire, a friendship more than sixty years long.

And just like that, it was over. Claire and Jeremy had been farewelled.

Mourners stood, many wanting to pass on their condolences to Jane, Margot among them, managing a watery smile when Lizzie extracted a promise that she wouldn't leave without spending some time with her and Alice. 'We'll be in the usual place.'

Feeling light-headed, Lizzie returned to her chair. She felt again the warmth of Margot's hand beneath hers, the slight tremor in the long, beautiful fingers, the gently beating pulse. The hand she should have held at a funeral long years ago.

The photos were still sliding across the screen. What hopes those three young women had had of living extraordinary lives. Instead, they'd stumbled along as most people stumble, trying to make the best of things.

How strange to be taken back fifty years. How discombobulating. It was as if no time had passed and yet it felt a lifetime ago. Had that young woman made different choices . . . but she had not. She had married, she chose not to marry again. She had given birth to two children, one taken from her. She had grown old.

The future, whatever it was to bring, would be short; the past, a little faded, stretched long.

Alice asked Lizzie to keep an eye on Jack as Molly led her away in search of butterflies. Out of nowhere, came a foolish urge to go to Mass, to kneel in prayer—Claire would be rolling her eyes—the comfort of ritual, she decided.

Lizzie glanced over at Alice, who was flattered by Molly's attention. The inevitable thought at her age, of who would be next. For a moment, she hoped she would go first. And then she looked at Molly and Jack and wanted to live forever.

*

'Your words were beautiful. They made me cry,' said Margot.

Jane wrapped her arms around her. 'I can't remember a thing I said.'

Margot had often thought that had they met in their teens or twenties, so different were they, they would never have become friends. But friends they were. Jane had been there when Margot's life unravelled, and was the only person, she felt, who hadn't judged her.

Margot, aware of a growing cluster of people hovering around them, all hoping to speak to Jane, stepped aside. Jane, always gracious, smiled and nodded, giving each person her full attention. 'Make sure you grab a drink,' she said, as they departed.

Back with Margot, Jane asked how she thought Lizzie was doing.

'She's sad, we're all sad,' said Margot, feeling anew the empty weight of loss.

Jane looked over at Lizzie. 'She looks like she could do with a hug.'

Her mother, sitting alone with Jack playing at her feet, looked tiny and vulnerable.

When Lizzie had put her hand on hers during Jane's eulogy, Margot had wanted to grasp it and not let go. But she remembered that other time, so many other times, when she had reached up searching for that hand, and it hadn't been there.

A young man excused himself for interrupting. He wanted Jane to know how grateful he was to Claire for her support of his small dance company. Jane said her mother loved the arts and thanked him for coming.

Another queue had formed, more people waiting to speak to Jane.

'Catch up later?' Margot said.

Yes,' Jane was saying. 'Lots of happy memories.'

CHAPTER 8

ALICE GLARED AT THE YOUNG couple who looked settled in for the afternoon until they were so uncomfortable—less than five minutes later—they left.

'Honestly, Alice,' said Lizzie, laughing.

They arranged themselves around the table, Alice half-expecting that at any moment Claire would sweep by in one of her floaty pastel dresses, kiss them hello and chide them for thinking she would leave without saying goodbye.

'Jane spoke beautifully,' said Lizzie.

As goodbyes went, Claire's was one of the better Alice had attended. And she'd attended quite a number. She loathed funerals and wakes, particularly dry wakes, with only a cup of tea to sustain you. At her age, something stronger was required, to cast reality in a softer light.

It was also the not knowing what to say, and when eventually whatever it was had been said, hearing immediately how meaningless the words you'd searched for sounded.

Lizzie filled their glasses.

They toasted. 'To Claire and Jeremy.'

How strange it was to see Lizzie, no Claire beside her. Thank goodness for the grandchildren, thought Alice. And Margot.

Margot hadn't been an easy child, headstrong and defiant; the loss of Tom, and absent parents, had surely contributed to Margot going off the rails. Alice might have had her suspicions about what *going off the rails* had meant, but it was one of the many things Claire and Lizzie hadn't shared with her.

Still, Alice had been terribly afraid when Margot disappeared that Lizzie might lose her daughter, too. She'd rallied around, but it was Claire to whom Lizzie turned; Claire always with the right word, unfailingly optimistic that Margot would return. And one day she had.

A young man, shy and slender, hair upswept, offered canapés and replenished the dwindling champagne.

'Those deep-fried thingies,' said Alice, pointing to the tray, 'are they vegan?'

'Ham and cheese, madam . . . perhaps you would prefer a falafel?'

'Oh, yes, please,' she said, smiling up at him. 'You are such a life saver.'

Alice looked longingly at the young man as he disappeared into the garden in search of falafels.

Lizzie shook her head. 'Flirting at your age.'

Alice smoothed her black velvet pants. 'So what?'

'A five-decade age difference is what.'

'You don't get a pang every now and then?'

'Not that I'm telling you about,' said Lizzie. She did occasionally have those dreams: quite confounding. She wished they'd come along more often.

The young man returned bearing a tray of falafels. He placed the tray on the table and offered serviettes, Alice cooing her thanks. Blushing, he made a quick exit.

'Anyway, even if we did,' said Lizzie, 'what are we going to do about it?'

Alice tossed her disconcertingly red curls. 'Do I really have to tell you?'

'Men don't want to have sex with any woman over fifty,' said Lizzie. 'Even men our own age won't come near us.'

'They don't know what they're missing,' said Alice.

'Is there something you haven't told me?'

Alice kept Emilio to herself.

Lizzie dropped her voice. 'I've heard that death can make you . . . is there a polite way to put it?'

'Horny,' said Alice. 'Makes perfect sense if you think about it. When someone dies, you're reminded that time's running out. It's like, how many more Christmases? How many more trips to Bali? How many more times will I have sex?'

Lizzie covered her mouth to muffle her laughter.

Alice topped up their glasses. 'It used to be birthdays and weddings, then you turn sixty and suddenly you're in permanent mourning.'

The sun had disappeared, the wind picking up, people buttoning their coats and pulling their scarves close as the chill settled in.

Lizzie skewered a falafel. 'No one tells you.'

'I couldn't do what Claire did,' said Alice.

'We put animals out of their suffering, don't we?'

Alice bit into her falafel. Lizzie could never hear a word against Claire. Lizzie's devotion to Claire had rankled, many times, rankling more so as the years passed. But that was life: it rankled even when there wasn't much of it left. 'That's different.'

'How is it different?'

Alice hesitated. 'You can't compare putting an animal out of its misery to topping your husband.'

'A husband who had dementia.'

At their age dementia was the blackest spot on the horizon, constantly on their minds and on the minds of watchful relatives, so much so that misplacing the keys could be interpreted as befuddlement, a story told twice to the same person seen as a sign; forgetting a word, telling. Any lapse of memory interrogated as an indication that the brain was in terminal decline.

'Must we talk about death?'

Lizzie raised an eyebrow. 'We are at a wake.'

'All the more reason . . .'

'I can't help thinking the stress of caring for Jeremy caused Claire's cancer,' said Lizzie.

Alice's hand went protectively to her breast. 'I'm convinced stress caused mine.'

'I should have done more,' said Lizzie.

'You had enough going on,' said Alice. 'Your mother's stroke, finding a nursing home.'

'You can't help wondering if you'd just done this, just done that . . .'

'Claire wouldn't want you to feel guilty.'

The crowd was already thinning, people finishing their glass of champagne before hurrying back to their lives.

'Do you think Claire worried about going to hell?' asked Alice.

'What a question.'

'Catholics believe if you die with a mortal sin on your soul, you go straight to hell.'

'Claire left the church decades ago.'

'Once a Catholic, always a Catholic.'

Lizzie shrugged and brushed falafel crumbs from her dress. 'We should mingle.'

Alice paused mid-sip. 'I didn't know Ed was coming.'

Ed was moving through the crowd, shaking hands, charming men and women alike; Lizzie, too, if she wasn't careful. He spotted her, turned his smile on high-beam and made his way towards her.

Lizzie could always convince herself she was no longer attracted to Ed. Until she saw him again. And then those old feelings . . .

He was more beautiful than handsome. The pale blue eyes—she didn't notice until too late, how cold the blue—the dark curls, the effortlessness of him. She had been determined not to be one of the women who fell all over him. Marriage and children had been off the agenda. It was the only way women could get ahead.

She had resisted him for two whole years.

Alice put down her glass. 'Why is he here?'

'Why shouldn't he be here?' asked Lizzie. 'He and Claire were close once.'

Ed might have stratospheric approval ratings in the polls, but Alice was no longer persuaded.

Alice and Ed had been close, too. But once he and Claire fell out, Alice had kept her distance. On the few occasions they ran into each other, Alice had bordered on rude. Alice being loyal, Lizzie had supposed.

'Ladies,' Ed said, with a slight bow.

Alice stayed only long enough to exchange niceties before withdrawing.

Ed's eyes, blue pools of concern, fixed on Lizzie. Those eyes that made everyone he met feel they were somehow special.

As usual he was beautifully dressed; he had always had style. Lizzie took in the tailored grey blazer, virgin wool no doubt; the polo shirt, which, once the blazer was off, he'd wear with sleeves gently rolled; the linen trousers.

'Lizzie.' His arms were around her and it felt warm and safe and familiar. A split second of insanity, when she wished they were still together,

From their union had come Margot and Tom, so they made a play of being friendly and civilised, even though within ten minutes, they couldn't stand being in the same room.

'You look wonderful,' he said. 'You always look wonderful.'

Lizzie came to her senses and twisted out of his embrace.

'I haven't stopped thinking about you since I heard the news.'

She almost believed him. 'Have you seen Margot? She's been looking for you.'

He shook his head. 'I'll text her.'

Ed looped his arm through hers and they walked to a quiet spot in the garden.

'Did you get a chance to speak to Jane?' Lizzie asked.

He nodded. 'I passed on my condolences.'

'It's a shame you never got to know her—you'd like her.'

'How could Claire do that to her daughter?' He shook his head. 'What on earth possessed her?'

Lizzie was immediately defensive. 'Claire had it all planned, probably for months. It wasn't something impulsive. She knew exactly what she was doing.'

He took a mouthful of beer, wedding ring glinting. 'That's not what I heard.'

Ed, always in the know.

'There's all sorts of gossip flying around.'

'Got a mate who works at the Coroner's Court.'

Ed had lots of mates, mates who owed him. She bet he owed them, too. 'What did your mate say?'

He spoke quietly. 'That it all went terribly wrong.'

Lizzie's heart raced. 'What do you mean *wrong*?'

'Are you sure you want to hear this?'

She wasn't at all sure. 'Claire was my friend.'

He inclined his head so his mouth sat close to her ear, slid his arm around her waist. 'It looks like Jeremy fell out of bed— broken arm, head injury.'

Lizzie closed her eyes and leaned on him for support.

'From what they can piece together, Claire was trying to get help but was so affected—the place was bedlam, apparently— they found her in the hallway.'

Lizzie felt as if she'd been struck. 'Does Jane know?'

'Patched him up, said you'd never know.'

People were glancing their way, ready to pounce on Ed as soon as their conversation finished.

'Incredibly selfish of Claire.'

Lizzie removed his hand from her waist. 'Perhaps you could save your judgement for another time.'

He looked around. 'Who here is not thinking the same thing?'

'If they are, they have the decency to keep it to themselves.'

'Come on, Lizzie. You've got to admit it was a helluva thing to do.'

'You were friends for a long time, good friends. I thought this might be a sad day for you.'

Some show of emotion. Something. Anything.

'I am sad, very sad.' Ed cleared his throat and for a moment Lizzie saw something she couldn't identify in his eyes. 'I was very fond of Claire.'

'Please don't tell anyone . . . especially not Margot.'

'Of course not . . . how could you even . . . ?'

She didn't trust him. Who knew who he'd tell? And if the media were to discover it had all gone wrong, Claire would be further damned.

She made one last effort to defend her friend. 'Claire would have thought she was doing the right thing.'

'Herself, okay, but poor defenceless Jeremy?'

'They'd made a pact long ago not to prolong things.'

He turned on her. 'You of all people should know how precious life is.'

'Shut up,' she said, and walked away.

CHAPTER 9

MARGOT VEERED FROM THE PATH and cut through the garden, Molly stopping to pick flowers, Jack adventuring ahead. Her father had texted to say they were on the back lawn. Molly and Jack saw them before she did, running to join Hamish and Amelia.

They'd spread a blanket on the grass, her father leaning back on his elbows watching the children play, Charlotte sitting next to him, knees drawn to her chest. He jumped to his feet, gave Margot a big hug and hurried off to get them each a drink.

'It was a very moving farewell,' said Charlotte. 'One of the nicest I've been to.'

Margot dropped down beside her. 'Thanks for being here.'

'I wanted to be here, for you, for your dad. He's been so quiet since he heard the news. Not himself at all.' She squeezed Margot's hand. 'How are you? I know how much Claire meant to you.'

Margot rested her head on Charlotte's shoulder. 'You know Dad and Claire had a falling-out? Something to do with politics.'

'He told me, but not the details.'

Margot didn't know the details either, but she had memories of her father and Claire in, as they said, happier times. 'I wonder if he's regretting not sorting things out.'

'I was thinking the same thing.'

'How's your mum doing?'

'A bit dazed, still in shock, I think.'

'Awful for both of you.'

Margot thought about the letter her mother had written to Claire. Reading it had revived memories she'd have rather stayed buried. Like those times her father hadn't turned up for birthdays, the year he missed Christmas. She'd be broken-hearted, but not for long. He would bring gifts, something unexpected and beautiful. He'd kiss her *cross tears* away and lift her high in the air and tell her that Daddy was held up and he was sorry, he loved her. He was funny and silly, and for a little while, she'd feel at the centre of his world.

'My two favourite ladies,' her father said, passing them each a mineral water.

Charlotte took a few sips before disappearing—*leave you two alone for a bit*—to play ring-a-rosy with the children, giggling as they all fell down. Her father laughed, too. He was happier than he had ever been with her mother.

Margot couldn't remember her parents ever getting along after Tom died; the house was always either loud with argument or strained with silence. Even after years apart they still grated on each other, polite but wary when family commitments forced them together.

It was weird the way things had turned out. When her father told her he was re-marrying, Margot had been determined to hate his new wife. Her resolve escalated when she discovered Charlotte was her age. Instead, they had become friends.

There were things they didn't discuss—sex, her mother, who Charlotte seemed oddly fond of, The Past—a mutual but unspoken understanding. Otherwise, they shared everything.

Margot glanced at her father. He really was awfully quiet. 'You caught up with Mum?'

His jaw tensed. 'I did.'

'I know you and Claire . . .' Margot hesitated. 'I just wanted you to know Claire often asked after you. And Charlotte and the children.' *Often* was a bit of an exaggeration but Claire did inquire occasionally.

'Did she?' He smiled as if he saw through her.

He was good at seeing through people. She supposed it went with the job.

Charlotte flopped down next to her father, out of breath. He brushed a strand of hair from her face. Margot wondered if he'd ever been that in love with her mother—she was sure he hadn't.

The children were getting over-excited. Soon there'd be tears over something or other. Her father was much more laidback than when she'd been growing up: no set bedtime, picky eating indulged, Amelia and Hamish allowed to run wild. A complete lack of discipline, really.

Margot drank the last of the water. 'I promised Mum I'd say hello to Alice.' She'd never hear the end of it if she didn't.

'Pick you up for yoga Friday? Understand if you want to give it a miss, though . . .'

Margot smiled. 'Friday's good.'

The children were circling, her father sweeping Jack onto his shoulders.

'You go,' said Charlotte. 'We'll look after the kids.'

Winding her way to the main gates, Margot stopped to speak to one or two people whose names she couldn't remember. They patted her arm, murmuring predictable platitudes.

She found her mother sitting with Alice, holding court in one of Claire's favourite corners of the garden, sad eyes magnified behind her glasses.

Her mother looked up as she approached, her face breaking into a smile. 'Margot.'

Alice leapt from her chair and clasped Margot to her breast as if she were a long-lost lover. 'Darling Margot, look at you—gorgeous.'

Margot couldn't remember when she had last seen Alice: a year, maybe two.

'Such a sad day,' said Alice, hand on brow in dramatic pose.

Everything was still about Alice. 'We're all going to miss her terribly,' said Margot.

They looked at each other, not quite knowing what to say next.

'I follow you on Instagram,' said Alice, breaking the silence. 'Your photos . . . like, stunning.'

'Margot's a very talented photographer,' said Lizzie.

'Where are those beautiful children of yours?' asked Alice.

'With their grandfather.'

Alice didn't ask after her father. She didn't like him; he didn't like her much either.

'Your mother never stops talking about them—Molly so clever and pretty, Jack her darling little man.'

Lizzie nodded. 'They take after their mother.'

'And their grandmother,' said Alice.

'How old are they now?'

'Molly's almost seven and Jack's four.'

'I bet you're itching to get back to work?'

Her mother's generation of feminists clung to the idea that work gave women freedom when all it did was burden them with two jobs and turn their children into orphans. 'No plans.'

'You don't mind being a housewife?'

Who even said *housewife* anymore?

'I enjoy being a mother.' *You know, like the most important job of all*, was what she wanted to say.

'Of course you do,' said Alice.

Margot had recently seen Alice on television advertising hearing aids. She'd thought then Alice had had some work done. And she'd been right. She was still pretty, if you could be pretty in your seventies.

'Let me get you a glass of champagne,' said Alice.

Margot shook her head. 'I'm driving.' It was an easy excuse, one people didn't question.

'We're all so sensible these days,' said Alice.

'Not everyone,' said Lizzie, eyeing Alice's rapidly emptying glass.

Margot had known both these women all her life. Rather than age changing them, they seemed more themselves than they had ever been.

'It all went well, don't you think?' said Alice.

'Claire would have been chuffed,' said Margot. 'Jeremy, too.'

'Poor Jeremy,' they murmured.

Alice finished her drink. 'Can you believe how old we are?'

Margot wasn't sure what to say. 'You both look so . . . so well.'

Alice laughed.

'You do,' said Margot, looking from Alice to her mother.

'An in-joke,' said her mother. 'At some point in life people start telling you that you look well when once it was beautiful—'

'Glorious, divine, spectacular,' said Alice.

'Brilliant, intellectual, formidable,' said Lizzie.

'Some hoon called me an old bat the other day,' said Alice.

'I hope you told him where to go,' said Margot.

'I called him a cunt.'

Her mother snorted.

Margot stood to go. 'Well, it's been lovely . . .'

'I demand to see you more often,' said Alice. 'And the children.'

'We'll organise something,' said Margot, bending to kiss each of the women, powdered faces cracking like putty.

Her mother looked at her watch. 'Meet you in half an hour?'

Margot had completely forgotten. 'Oh, yes, the goldfish.'

Extracting herself again from Alice's arms, Margot retreated from their collective gaze. Making the most of her freedom, she wandered the paths, stopping to enjoy the herb garden.

She noticed a man seated near the sundial, an arrogance about him making her hurry by. He was staring, his eyes narrow, their glint predatory. And knowing.

Did she know him? She didn't think so. But it was hard to remember, harder as years went by. Did he know her?

It had happened before. Someone recognising her. Usually, they turned away as quickly as she did, neither wanting to identify or be identified.

All in your head, she told herself. Men did check her out, they always had. Oh God, was he walking towards her? She turned, quickened her step.

A man's voice called, 'Excuse me? Excuse me!'

She was walking so fast she was almost running.

A tap on her shoulder, her heart cold in her chest.

'Your scarf, it got caught on one of the bushes.'

He passed it to her, the beautiful silk scarf, a gift to her from Claire, bought on her last trip to Rome.

She drooped with relief. 'Thank you.'

He smiled and walked away.

She hugged the scarf to her face.

It smelled of rosemary, rosemary for remembrance.

CHAPTER 10

LIZZIE STARED INTO THE POND. Claire's and Jeremy's last moments were all she could think of. Jeremy's injuries, the terror Claire must have felt, the guilt, her careful planning gone awry. Claire's voice in her head, calling for help. Claire's letter in her bag.

In the background, she heard the clink of glasses, toasts being raised to the dearly departed, the hum of conversation. Neil was singing, Joni and Nina—the usual suspects.

A waiter offered Lizzie a glass of champagne. She gratefully accepted.

Where on earth was Margot?

'Lizzie.'

She turned, Charlotte, smiling hesitantly, blonde hair beautifully arranged in a topknot, diamonds glittering in her ears. 'Charlotte, hello.'

'I was squeezing in a walk around the garden before we head home.'

'It's a lovely garden to wander in,' said Lizzie, feeling for Charlotte. What misfortune—the new wife stumbling over the ex-wife. She looked over Charlotte's shoulder hoping to see Margot, Molly and Jack straggling behind. 'Have you seen Margot?'

'She left a few minutes ago.'

Lizzie felt her carefully curated face collapse, words spilling out before she had a chance to swallow them. 'But we'd arranged to meet . . .'

Charlotte flushed a flattering shade of pink. 'I'm sorry, I didn't realise.'

Lizzie tried to manage the quaver in her voice. 'Such a long day for Molly and Jack.'

'Jack totally wore himself out.'

'I'm not surprised,' Lizzie said, regaining control. 'He was running his little legs off before.'

Charlotte toyed with the charms on her bracelet, manicured nails settling on the heart. 'Jack was having a tantrum . . . Margot thought it best to get him home.'

'When they get like that, sleep's the only thing.'

Charlotte nodded. 'And such an emotional day.'

Ed's wife was so much nicer than he was, another woman in his life he didn't deserve. For some unfathomable reason, she felt a slight sting of jealousy.

'I didn't meet Claire, but she sounded like a wonderful person.'

'Yes, she was.'

What did Charlotte see when she looked at her? Lizzie wondered. An old lady who, unbelievably, used to be married to her impossibly attractive and youthful husband.

'I can't imagine how sad it must be to lose someone you've been friends with your whole life.'

'Very sad.'

What had Ed said about their marriage, thought Lizzie. What had he said about her? Unlikely to be flattering. And what had Margot confided? Still, Charlotte had always gone out of her way to be friendly. It was even possible that Charlotte liked her.

'But such a lovely way to say goodbye.'

Poor Charlotte, having to make conversation with the ex. 'It really was.'

'Oh, well . . .'

Lizzie could see her eyes seeking escape.

Charlotte took a tentative step back. 'Ed will be wondering where I've got to.'

'It really was very nice of you to come, Charlotte.'

Charlotte hurried away, turning to give Lizzie a last wave.

Lizzie had the awful thought that perhaps Charlotte didn't so much like her as pity her, the reviled ex-wife whose daughter didn't love her all that much.

Tom was beside her, little hand in hers. 'Breadcrumbs, Mummy.'

Lizzie knelt to tie his shoelace, Tom laughing when the big orange fish gobbled up the crumbs. 'The daddy fish is greedy,' he said. The little fish he named Tom and Margot. His friend at kindy had a goldfish, he told her. 'He swims round and round all by himself.'

When the breadcrumbs had all been eaten, Tom slipped away. The fish swam round and round.

'Dear friend,' said Alice, as Lizzie made her goodbyes, 'I'm here if you need me.'

They were as there for each other as they had always been, thought Lizzie.

She went looking for Jane, hoping for a few moments alone with her before she left, but Jane was still caught up.

'Call me,' Jane waved. 'We'll talk properly in a few days.'

Lizzie knew this would only be the beginning of Jane's grieving, that over the next months it would ebb and flow, that just when she thought she'd found some equilibrium it would swoop, surprising her with its ferocity.

'I'll look after her,' promised Sam, who was putting the guitar in its case.

'You played so beautifully.'

'Claire liked those pieces,' said Sam.

They shook hands and said goodbye.

Lizzie had hoped she wouldn't see Ed again, but moments later, she bumped into him, Amelia clinging to one hand, Hamish the other. The perfect husband, the perfect father.

'Hello,' she said, smiling at the children and ignoring him.

'Feeling better?' asked Ed, that patronising smile she knew so well.

'Until now,' said Lizzie.

And for the second time that day, only this time with head held high, she swept away.

As soon as she was home Lizzie checked her phone, a foolish hope that Margot had thought to ring. If she hadn't run into Charlotte, Lizzie might still be waiting by the fishpond. No message.

If Claire were here, she'd tell her how busy young mothers were, how exhausted. Margot wouldn't remember they were supposed to meet until her head hit the pillow. Way too late to call. She'd reason that anyone who was a mother would understand.

Claire would be right as usual, Lizzie reassured by Claire's certainty that Margot would come round. *Give her space*, she'd say. *You'll see*, she'd say.

Whenever anyone asked after Margot, Lizzie had the narrative down so pat, she almost believed it herself. Margot was always dropping by, shopping trips, lunch, babysitting, excursions here and there. The lie once begun, took on a life of its own, a life yearned for, easy to invent. Only Claire had known the truth.

Claire. How lonely life felt without her. She poured herself a whisky, a molten shimmer in the firelight, and took the envelope from her bag. She speculated again, why the letter was under Claire's bed and not with the letter she left for Jane? She peeled open the flap. Her hand shook, her breath caught in her throat. The letter was little more than a few scribbled mostly indecipherable words on a torn scrap of paper. She gulped a mouthful of whisky and held Claire's last words to the light:

Dearst lizzie
for give . . . all those years so . . . afraid
Ed alice
Jane, dear jan
father forgive . . . all my sin

Lizzie was falling, her heart and head trying to catch up.

Lizzie's eyes sprang open—she didn't have to look at the clock to know it was 3.08 in the morning. Shivering, she disentangled herself from the sheet and rescued her pillow from the floor. For the first time in a very long time, Lizzie wished for someone beside her, someone she could wake, or who would wake knowing she needed an arm around her, a whispered *it's okay, you're fine, just a nightmare* . . .

She wanted her mother. But her mother had never been there, not even when Tom died. She had planned to come and stay with Lizzie after Tom's death, to look after Margot, she'd said. But her mother, already struggling, was so overwhelmed, she couldn't stay longer than a day.

It struck her that with Claire gone, her mother was the only person who had known the young Lizzie: the tomboy who climbed trees and never wore a dress; the teenager who fell too easily in love; the uni student who waitressed and studied all night; the ambitious career woman; the head-over-heels-in-love bride who refused to wear a wedding dress or give up her surname. And yet all people saw now, if they saw her at all, was a grey-haired old woman, a burden on the system, with little to offer.

Lizzie stared into the darkness. Claire hadn't intended to write her a letter. She had had months to pen her last words, words she knew Claire would have written with the greatest thought and care. She would never have left something so momentous to the last minute. So why, in those last moments, had Claire changed her mind?

Why had Claire asked for forgiveness: for taking her life? For taking Jeremy's—was that what she meant? Was that the sin she had committed? What had she been afraid of? For years? And Ed? Was she sorry they hadn't made up? Did Claire even know what she was saying? Her mention of Jane, her dear daughter, was the only thing that made any sense.

Claire's reference to Alice was the most bewildering. She and Claire were the least close, Alice often blowing up at Claire. Lizzie had spoken about it with Claire, with Claire saying airily that she never took Alice's petulance too seriously.

Alice and Ed had once been good mates. Ed loved pretty frothy girls, and Alice loved good-looking in-charge men. Lizzie had never taken much notice of their flirting. She certainly hadn't been jealous. Alice was her friend . . . She trusted Alice then. She did now.

She thought about that time she'd stayed at Claire's during school holidays, Claire waving a newspaper clipping above her head. 'Lizzie Kavanagh, you are going to die when you read this.'

'Race you,' laughed Lizzie. Breathless, they chased each other, clambering over bales of hay to the very top of the hayshed, their secret place, somewhere to swoon over their most recent crush and read favourite passages from their latest favourite book.

Dearest. Claire paused dramatically, then read on.

Lizzie clutched her heart: Virginia's letter to Leonard, before she took her life.

Poor Leonard, they said, and wept at the sheer romance of it.

But suicide wasn't romantic: for those left behind, there was only guilt and grief and what-ifs.

Lizzie lay awake until first light pushed through the blinds. She would have stayed in bed, but there was Fred to feed and her mother to visit.

Claire's note was sitting on the coffee table where she'd left it. She held it in her hand, somehow finding the wherewithal to read it once more.

Sad and confused, she slipped the note into the envelope and went back to bed, staring at the ceiling until she fell into a troubled sleep.

That evening, unable to settle, Lizzie walked Fred by the creek. They wandered the path that took them beneath great old bridges, the wattle a golden tapestry against a moonlit sky. Sitting on a worn timber seat, she looked out over the creek, leaves whispering, everything in shadow.

She had once dreaded the sun going down: no Tom splashing in the bath, eyelashes dark with water; the desolate space next to Margot at the table; bedtime story unread.

Life went on. That's what people said. That was the cliché. And it was true. More or less. If nothing else, you went through the motions. You put yourself to bed at night. You woke in the morning. You dressed, brushed your teeth, went shopping if you had to. Walked the dog. You might even, when the occasion demanded, summon a smile. Your blood still pulsed, your heart still beat. Yes, you went through the motions. Because what else could you do.

Darkness enveloped the creek, a mist lacing the water, fog descending. How many times she had sat on that old seat: the scent of eucalypt; the ribbon of muddy brown water; tonight, a spangle of stars. She often wondered how it must once have been, the creek unpolluted, the fishing and hunting, the sharing of food, the holding of ceremonies. And then, the land taken, the people slaughtered. *Dispossessed.* She always felt she was a trespasser, treading on land that didn't belong to her.

Lizzie climbed the steps to the main road, two men with large plastic bags brushing past, a strong smell of alcohol. She felt guilty for her thick coat, scarf warm around her neck, hands nestled into fleece-lined gloves. 'Missus,' they said, politely. Headlights caught their faces, sad-eyed and damaged.

Back home, Lizzie fed Fred leftovers. He was putting on weight while she was losing kilos she couldn't afford to lose. She should have something. An egg, perhaps. On toast. Her stomach lurched at the thought. She'd have more of an appetite tomorrow.

She'd organise something tempting, something that took her mind off things.

Lizzie had never been much for cooking when her children were young. She didn't have the inclination or the time. But these days she made an effort, often trying out new recipes that sent her off in search of ingredients.

Cooking for one seemed such a lonely pursuit so she cooked for two, always a set table and a proper serviette. The care you'd take if you were having company. On weekends, she made dessert.

The television stayed off during meals, chair placed so she could look into the garden, watch the birds argue over the figs or squabble about whose turn it was in the birdbath.

She would sometimes hear Tom and Margot at the front door waiting for Ed, fluting voices calling *Mummy, Mummy, Daddy's home*. There'd be a rush of little feet, Ed laughing and gathering them in his arms or chasing them into the kitchen. Those fleeting, precious moments she'd been too busy to notice.

If she were granted one wish it would be to prepare a meal for her children. Lizzie wanted it so much, she sometimes talked herself into believing Tom and Margot were coming to dinner; her son and daughter all grown up, the three of them the greatest of friends. They would bang through the front door, throw their arms around her and sit themselves down, Lizzie eager to hear all their news.

More than thirty years had passed since Lizzie lost Tom. She still wondered, all these years later, if his cold had warned of something more sinister, that had she heeded that warning . . . There was nothing she could have done, the doctors said.

Sudden Unexplained Death in Childhood, they called it now, but back then no one could tell her why he'd died, the post-mortem inconclusive. Very like Sudden Infant Death Syndrome, they told her, shaking their heads. *Rare, but it happens.*

It happened to Tom.

For a long time, Lizzie didn't close the door to Tom's room, leaving it ajar, afraid that if he found his way back and the door was closed, he would be forever lost. Years passed, but always there was something to remind her of her loss. When Tom's little friends walked past Lizzie's house on their first day of school, shiny in their new uniforms, the ache was so fierce she thought she would have to move far away. But she stayed, eventually taking pleasure in watching those same boys grow. All too quickly they disappeared, work and university their next big adventure.

She had occasionally run into one or other of them in cafés, the barista who made her coffee or the waiter who took her order. Standing embarrassed at her table, they would say a polite hello and scurry off. She wanted to ask if they ever thought of Tom. Perhaps they did, for a moment. Perhaps, later in life when they had children of their own, they would recall the little boy who died in his sleep.

Neighbours and acquaintances, even close friends, were sad for her—*I can't imagine . . . how awful to lose a child*—but as time went on, she saw judgement in their eyes: *so long ago, surely time to put the past behind you.* Lizzie wished it behind her, too, but forgetting would be a worse grief. She had heard it said you die twice; the second death when your name is never spoken again.

Everyday Lizzie spoke Tom's name. While she lived, he would, too.

CHAPTER 11

SHOPPING WASN'T WHAT IT USED to be, Alice grumbled as she went in search of a shop assistant. A twice-yearly trip into the city with her mother to wander the department stores and make a purchase or two at the sales had been quite the event. And always, Alice could choose a modest, but special little something, just for her. But that was long ago. The once-indispensable coiffured matrons in twinsets and pearls, smiling patiently at customers clearly in great need of their wisdom, had since disappeared as had the requisite gloves and hats ladies donned whenever they visited Melbourne.

Alice had been shopping for shapewear, but after sorting through the jumble of intimate apparel hanging haphazardly from hangers and racks, she was exhausted. Oh, the irony of standing in a snaking queue waiting to be served while sublime beings smiled down upon you promising an unforgettable shopping experience. When finally, she flung her shapewear onto the counter, the assistant ran off in a fruitless search for someone experienced enough to manage a complication with the transaction before, hoped Alice, closing time.

Purchase finalised, Alice took refuge on the fourth floor and treated herself to a glass of bubbly, her days of ending her expedition into Melbourne with a cream bun and can of Fanta, a dim memory.

Exiting through the Galerie de Parfum, Alice sprayed a little of Catherine Deneuve's signature fragrance—how wonderful that the French so worshipped older women—on the inside of her wrists. She imagined a perfume named for her. She must raise it with her agent. *Perfectly Alice* would be palest pink, the bottle vintage crystal. Touching her wrists behind her ears, she pictured herself draped in glorious green, hair a fiery tumble. Emerging from her reverie, she ignored the impossibly beautiful sales assistants tucked behind their cosmetic counters, regarding her with a mixture of horror and pity.

She reclaimed the jumble of bags fallen at her feet. Was it any wonder people shopped online?

Alice sat one last time on her sofa and waited for the knock on the door.

She had to admit, it wasn't the most comfortable of sofas—a little firm if you sat too long, its curves hard and unwelcoming. Not a place to nestle or bed down with a book. But discomfort and impracticality were minor inconveniences when, every day, she could gaze upon something so beautiful.

But now it had to go.

She glanced at the bags holding the must-have items from yesterday's shopping spree, boastful department store logos gleaming. On the table, still to be unpacked, they gave rise to a feeling of panic. How could she have been so reckless? It wasn't the shapewear, Alice could justify that as a work-related expense should she earn enough to pay tax. It was the ankle boots, their splendid buckles apparently the latest thing—Alice did so love the latest thing—and the flared turmeric-coloured pants that made her stomach somersault.

Almost homeless, and she'd gone shopping.

A few weeks ago, she decided that if she had to sell every stick of furniture to stay in her dear little home, she would do just that. Her art deco apartment with its lusciously iced ceilings and spacious sun-warmed rooms, in a suburb where streets were named after poets, had been Alice's refuge for nearly thirty years.

Alice had moved in soon after Christopher had fled, an unexpected breakup that set her free. For the first time in a long time, she'd had a space she could call her own. She could invite friends over, wear whatever she wished, go out whenever she chose and spend what she pleased. No more that sense of dread when she woke in the mornings.

She could still remember the young woman showing her through all those years before. One in a block of four, the apart-ment—flats, they used to call them—was weary and wan as if it had seen a little too much of life. Windows had been flung open in a failed effort to eliminate the smell of damp, and there'd been a half-hearted attempt to paint over the faded graffiti that frescoed the walls. Alice wasn't deterred.

Claire had loved the apartment, the only one of her friends to see beyond the peeling wallpaper and disintegrating linoleum to the charming home Alice would create. While Lizzie stood on the balcony sipping champagne saying *how tiny* and *fancy living in a flat*, and *my God, that wallpaper, the filth*, Claire wandered the rooms admiring this, commenting on that. *Perfectly Alice*, she said.

Uni students, attracted by cheap rent and seedy glam, came and went. Alice stayed. Somewhere along the way, her suburb transformed. Suddenly, or so it seemed, real estate billboards were shouting *location, location, location*.

The landlord had, many years before, given Alice the chance to buy her apartment at half its present value. She'd been between jobs and had spent extravagantly on a trip to northern Italy, leaving little in the way of a deposit. The bank manager, when she approached him, had asked about hubby's annual income, escorting her swiftly through the door when she informed him that she, as an independent woman, had no need of a husband.

Late in life, a little too late, had come a longing for a place to call home. Her mother's modest brick veneer with a square of lawn and borders of colourful begonias had been home. Her apartment was home.

Alice opened the doors wide and stepped onto the balcony, a solitary wine glass from the night before smudged with finger-prints and lipstick. The wind had picked up, clouds floated in a pale sky, laughter drifted from the street below.

When finally, she accepted that she could no longer afford to keep her apartment, Alice begrudgingly looked for something more in her price range, only to find that even a one-bedroom unit a million miles from anywhere was out of reach. Terrified she was weeks from homelessness, she put herself on the list for public housing. Alice was told that as she wasn't a high priority, she could be waiting years for a place to become available. She'd grown up in public housing; there'd always been public housing for those who needed it. When had everything changed?

A room in a boarding house was, after much looking, the only thing she could afford. Checking she had the right address, she parked her car and waited for the manager who was to take her through, to arrive. The house, a fifties triple-fronted suburban palace with a springy green lawn and fruit trees looked respectable enough from the outside. When the manager didn't show, she tapped on the front door hoping to convince whoever answered, to let her in.

The door swung open. She paused a moment before poking her head inside.

'Helloooo?' she called.

No response.

She stepped into a long dark hallway, carpet spongey beneath her feet. A few more tentative steps and she was standing in the doorway of a large room, stained mattresses laid so close there was hardly a foot-width between them. A couple of men sitting cross-legged stared at her with lost eyes. One of them muttered to himself, his mate took a long swig from the bottle he was nursing.

Fleeing, Alice thought again about asking Lizzie to take her in. She would welcome her, of course she would, insist she make herself at home for as long as needed.

Alice had occasionally stayed with Lizzie, sleeping in Margot's old bedroom. She'd never told Lizzie that Tom had once come to her during the night, his presence so strong beside her that she had woken and spoken his name. She sensed his restlessness, his confusion when he couldn't find Margot. His big sister was all grown up, Alice told him, with a little boy who looked just like him. It made her sad, that house.

She had resolved to hang on to her apartment for as long as possible, find a second job . . . she'd do anything, anything at all.

An advertisement in her local café for life models, mature-aged, no experience necessary, had caught her attention. Held in a lovely light-filled studio close to her apartment, the work was casual. When she inquired, she was told she could expect at least one sitting of two hours per week.

Why had she not thought of life modelling before? Posing naked in a room full of strangers, who were, after all, artists, did not bother her a jot. And her yoga and meditation practice had taught her stillness and poise.

In the meantime, she was selling off some of her vintage pieces. Her antique glassware, collected over a lifetime, was first to go. The satinwood table shipped in from overseas was next. Today it was the sofa.

Alice hadn't quite found the courage to tell Lizzie, who had scolded her many times, cross she had no eye to the future, about her straitened circumstances. She would go all sad-eyed and shake her head as if Alice was a problem that couldn't be solved. Claire, had she known, would have offered to help, an offer Alice would have immediately refused. And so now here she was. Exactly as Lizzie predicted.

A young couple was at her door, eyes shining with anticipation. A lovely sofa for their lovely home. They adored it, of course.

With the help of an eager friend, they manoeuvred the sofa through the doorway and down the steps into the waiting van. They thanked her and asked if she was moving into a retirement home.

'No,' said Alice. 'I'm not going anywhere.'

CHAPTER 12

'DO I HAVE TO, MUMMY?'

'It will only take a few minutes,' Margot said, winding Molly's curls through her fingers.

Molly made a face. 'You always say that.'

'You don't want your face all screwed up in the photo,' said Margot. 'Now, up on the bed. I'll sit here.' Margot arranged the pillows. 'You kneel behind me, arms around my neck. You're laughing because we've been playing—'

'You never play.' Molly stuck out her lip.

'Now, Molly, that just isn't true.'

'Grandma plays with us.'

'Grandma has lots of time.'

'Ganma, Ganma, Ganma,' said Jack running around the bed.

Margot grabbed Jack and sat him on her lap. 'Molly, I want

you to do your big smile.' She rumpled the doona, a casual laidback vibe.

Molly clambered onto the bed. 'What if he cries like last time?'

Margot tickled Jack's tummy. 'You're not going to cry, are you, Jack?'

Jack squirmed, smiling up at his mother.

Margot ran her eyes over the room: lighting up a notch, the curtains—oh, lovely, a soft breeze making them billow—the blue of the grape hyacinths, Molly adorable in her onesie against the big mess of pillows and cushions.

She gave herself a final critique in the mirror: linen pants, loose tee, hair in a relaxed bun, a touch of makeup.

Despite Molly's complaints, she followed Margot's directions, smiles for as many times as it took to get the perfect photo.

'That's the one,' said Margot, holding up the phone to show Molly. Five minutes and she'd cropped, filtered and posted *#lazyfridayafternoon*.

'I'm starrrrrving.'

Margot slid Jack to the floor. 'I think there might be something nice for afternoon tea.'

Molly clapped her hands and hurtled down the stairs to the kitchen.

Margot's phone pinged approval.

'How many *likes*, Mummy?' Molly asked, as Margot sneaked a look at her phone.

'Two,' Margot said, each blood-red heart making her own beat fast. Margot's posts were beautiful, uplifting, positive. But rarely were any of her one hundred and seventy-nine followers uplifted enough to *heart* her. She persevered, searching for tips on how to get noticed, how to make heart-catching content, how to connect and, most importantly, how to attract followers. It was a full-time job.

Every now and then she'd have a moment—Julian's voice in her head—thinking perhaps she really was spending too much time online. She'd plan a week's break. A day or two later, she'd be back: her children were beautiful, her home was beautiful—why wouldn't she want to share all that beauty with as many people as possible?

'Yummy,' said Molly, 'banana bread.' Its warm sticky fragrance filling the kitchen.

Margot cut the loaf into slices, arranging them on a blue plate, crumbs sprinkled for effect, a posy of johnny-jump-ups in the sweetest vase nearby.

Bananas had been banned from the house when she was growing up. Even the smell of them made her mother ill. An allergy, she'd said, the way some people were allergic to nuts.

The allergy hadn't been passed on: bananas were always in the fruit bowl, and banana bread was a favourite. But not today—that morning, sitting on the loo, Margot had noticed the beginnings of a tummy roll.

Margot poured them each a glass of milk. 'Stop wriggling, Jack, and lean over the plate.'

Another ping: that made three *likes*. She had a talent for photography, and for years had photographed friends' weddings and babies and celebrations, when she much preferred shadow and angles and lived-in faces, black and white her favoured medium. Then someone had suggested Instagram. She put down her camera and picked up her phone, photography swept aside for *hashtags* and *likes*.

Oh my, if Molly didn't look gorgeous with her little moustache of milk.

'Mummy, no more photos.'

Margot laughed and put down the phone.

The phone was always with her, walks becoming less about leisure and exercise than finding that perfect Instagrammable something. Moments were everywhere if only you looked.

All that was missing was a pet. Pets were so Insta—they tugged at the heartstrings and provided endless photo opportunities. But the mess. Even short-haired dogs moulted, clouds of dog-hair levitating across the floor at the slightest provocation.

A poor sleeper, she'd slept even less since Claire's death. A dream from her childhood had returned to haunt her. In it, she wakes to Tom crying. She rushes to his room. He isn't there, but she still hears his cries. She searches the house. When she bursts into the lounge room, his crying stops. But something frightens her. She runs and runs, her father calling after her, a voice whispering words she couldn't remember in her ear.

Margot's memories of Tom came to her in flashes, moments she'd entirely forgotten: together on the floor building a Lego train; tea parties under the jacaranda; being his bossy big sister. Mostly, she remembered loving him to pieces.

He was still with her, in her eyes when she looked in a mirror, in Molly's big smile and Jack's funny knees.

A bird nesting in the vine outside the window screeched, a great commotion of feathers. Protect your babies, she thought. Keep them close.

A final exhalation and it was over.

Julian pulled out, rolled onto his side. In minutes, he was snoring contentedly.

When they'd first started seeing each other, Margot had wondered if her past might come between them. But it had never been an issue for him. So what? he said. What an amazing, fabulous woman she was, he said. He loved her.

She mopped at the damp between her legs with tissues folded and ready beneath her pillow. She hadn't really been in the mood, sadness dulling her libido.

This was what she had wanted, wasn't it? Marriage, security, everything the ring on her left finger promised, her happily-ever-after ending?

It wasn't just her mood, she'd been distracted by tomorrow's Instagram post, too—the picture she'd take, the words she would write. She so wished she could post a family photo, but Julian refused to participate. Enough narcissists in the world, he'd say, without adding to their number. Not, he'd quickly backtrack, that he thought Margot was a narcissist. But darling, she'd give him a look, your clients live on Instagram. He'd laugh, that's strictly business, he'd say, then thank God he had a social media team to handle that side of things. Did he also thank God that he had a wife at home to handle the domestic side of things?

Margot watched him sleeping. While she was growing visibly older, he was becoming more attractive with age. Which, of course, had much to do with the wardrobe she chose for him, the trendy haircut she'd advised. The easy confidence success developed.

She sighed. She would never be accepted into the *mommy/mummy* tribe without Julian being part of her story: the drop-dead gorgeous crazy-in-love-with-her hubby, the fun sporty dad, the high-achiever who cooked and cleaned and hung out the washing, the perfect family man.

She loved him. But Margot sometimes wondered if love was enough.

They'd met at uni. He'd been in one of her tutes, a core subject she couldn't get out of. She remembered him gazing at her, looking away quickly when their eyes met. He didn't stare in a creepy way, more a look of longing.

He wasn't unattractive, slightly pudgy with a severe side part—he just wasn't her type. These were things she thought about later, not then. Then she hardly noticed him.

Julian turned onto his side, his foot seeking hers, sighing contentedly when their toes touched. But that was Julian, he was content. No lows, no highs either. She missed the highs.

She remembered that she hadn't always been so desirable herself: tall and too thin, prone to blushing, a girl who didn't meet your eye. Margot also made the mistake of being clever. She sat alone at recess, watching, from a distance as girls played skipping games and boys fought over balls.

A book was always in her lap, at first to give the impression she had something more interesting to do than play childish games. Lonely months later, books had become her refuge.

Socially, it wasn't quite so painful once she was at high school, though she still found it hard to make friends, difficulty navigating friendships when she did.

That all changed when, in her mid-teens she moved in with her father and started at a new school. In the few months it took her to work out who was who in the pecking order, she transformed into a beautiful version of her awkward self.

Beauty gave her a different frame, with shyness interpreted as cool, aloofness seen as sophisticated. Being clever and bookish added to her allure. Girls fluttered around her wanting her to notice them.

Those same friends introduced Margot to drugs. Not that she hadn't come across drugs before, the odd joint passed around, older kids boasting about smuggling ecstasy into music festivals. But they were novices by comparison.

A weekday boarder at a girls-only school, boys were a weekend novelty. They were crazy for her, she didn't have much time for them. Most of her crushes were on girls. Passive in love as well as friendship, she didn't pursue them.

Margot easily managed the marks needed to get into advertising. But deferred, trekking round Asia, hanging out for months in Nepal, her gap year rolling into two, then three years.

When finally, she started uni, advertising wasn't what she'd hoped, more about manipulation than imagination. She persisted, filling her electives with English and literature subjects. Soon, she was hanging out with wannabe poets and stoned young men who talked about Kerouac and Bukowski. But mostly about themselves.

What might her life have been, Margot wondered, had she not run into Julian in that café across the road from uni? He remembered her, even her name, she struggled to recall his. He said hi and asked if he could join her. She said, sure. He asked how it was going and she told him it was going shit because she had to give a presentation and she was lousy at presentations. Julian, who was in his last year of marketing and PR, said if there was one thing his degree had taught him, it was how to give a presentation.

He came over to hers that night, her audience of one, encouraging her through stumbles and hand trembles and flat delivery. She followed his tips—keep water handy, find a place to focus on at the back of the class, slow down—and gave an A+ presentation.

They hung out a bit after that. He was nice, Margot was fond of him, that's what she told him when a few weeks later he got all intense and said he wanted more than friendship. Couldn't they just stay friends, she said. Margot didn't tell him she was having sex, stoned sex, with beautiful arty boys who kissed lingering kisses all over her body.

Her offer of friendship refused, she hardly saw him after that.

The following year, Margot had had to drop her electives, exchanging pretty boys for boys as straight as their straight As.

Halfway through semester, she accepted an invite to a party from Nick, the self-assured boy who seemed always to sit next to her in lectures. She drove to his side of town wondering what the night might hold, parking the little sedan her father had bought her beside shiny cars that looked as if they'd just been driven out of the showroom. She knew this world, moved through it with ease, enjoying its privileges, perhaps a little too much.

But that was before everything changed.

Nick was waiting for her at the end of a long driveway. He took her by the arm and introduced her around. He pointed to where a crowd was milling and said if she wanted a snort . . .

'Speed?' she asked.

He laughed and looked at her as if she was from another planet. 'Cocaine,' he said.

They started dating after that. Margot liked Nick, she liked the cocaine he provided more. She didn't use drugs at home and did what she had to do to pass her subjects. But her marks were slipping.

She reached for her glasses and the book she'd been reading. Julian's eyes flickered open. 'Still awake?' he asked, thickly.

'Go back to sleep,' she shushed, feeling again that old regret of not making the most of her studies, the most of her youth, that precious, golden once-in-a-lifetime time.

It was through Nick, she met a whole new group of people, all with ready access to drugs and the money needed to buy them. She eventually discovered her relationship with Nick wasn't quite as exclusive as he'd led her to believe. She broke up with him, moving into a share-house with Elle, an architecture student she'd met at one of Nick's parties.

A few weeks later, Patrick moved in. He was in his last year of Arts Law, smooth and sure of himself. It was Margot's turn to be besotted.

He came to her bed that first night, hands silky over her body. It was a weekend, and on weekends he used heroin to chill out.

Heroin had frightened her, made her think of ravaged faces and ruined lives. And injecting was a long way from smoking or snorting or taking pills. But Patrick assured her that most people who used didn't get addicted. Him, for instance.

Alone together one evening, she took the tourniquet from his hands and strapped it tight around her arm, his eyes meeting hers as he injected oblivion into her veins.

CHAPTER 13

LIZZIE KNEW SHE WOULDN'T REST until she talked to Alice about Claire's letter. She'd phoned a few days after they'd farewelled their friend. Could they get together, there was something she wanted to ask. Alice, always keen for an excuse to wear something glamorous, insisted they dress up, celebrate Claire in style. That bar Claire loved with the city views. They'd promised to meet there the next time they had something to celebrate. A next time that had been taken from them.

Lizzie hadn't been keen. Party dresses and celebrations felt a little too soon.

Scouring her wardrobe, she found something that might do the trick, if a ruffle at the neckline and a swirl to the skirt counted. She matched the red of the dress with a lipstick and swept her hair to one side. She could have almost passed for sixty.

*

In the back of a taxi, Lizzie wrapped her thickest coat around her, the smell of cigarettes and leather familiar and comforting. A cheerless winter had given way to spring, the light spilling brighter, summer drawing closer.

She stared out the window, moon low and luminous in a starless sky. People crowded the footpaths, calling and laughing and staggering. Taking a little break from themselves.

Lizzie struck up a conversation with the taxi driver, a habit she'd developed in Canberra, where taxi drivers were more knowledgeable and a deal more trustworthy than the press gallery.

Melbourne taxi drivers came from all over the world, from backgrounds most Australians couldn't imagine. Her driver was from Syria. His curls, cut short, were thick and dark, his eyes, when he looked up, a little wary. He was shy, many of the drivers were, but once they were over their shock an Australian would take an interest in them, they almost always opened up.

He talked about the war that had destroyed his home and forced him to flee. His parents and brother had been killed during the bombing. He'd waited long months for the world to come to their rescue, praying it would not turn its back on them. When his prayers went unanswered, he made a choice no one should have to make. In the night, he escaped with his wife and three daughters to Turkey, where they boarded a dinghy for Greece. For the first time in years, they had much hope. His daughters were excited about going to school and making new friends.

Two died when their dinghy sank. Only in dreams can they be together again.

Lizzie murmured meaningless platitudes, words all she had.

'Thank you,' he said.

She asked his name.

'Essam.'

'Such a beautiful name.'

'This name I do not deserve.'

Lizzie didn't understand.

'In my language, Essam means to protect. I did not protect my family.'

'The failure is not yours,' said Lizzie.

He asked her name, rolling the z's around his mouth. 'Like the Queen of England,' he said. And they laughed.

Essam had been an engineer, graduating from a most respected university, but after applying for more than one hundred jobs in his adopted home, his heart no longer lifted with hope when he sent off an application.

'I weep sometimes when my wife cannot see. But I have good fortune also,' he smiled. 'In this country I have peace.' The persimmon he planted in memory of Najam and Jemila was, last summer, heavy with fruit. His daughter, Amira, growing up in a country free of war, a baby soon to be born.

Lizzie saw the same loss in his eyes she imagined he saw in hers, an old woman and a young man from a country she had only seen on the news, finding connection as they travelled through the night in a bright yellow car.

Essam couldn't know he was one of the reasons Lizzie resigned from a job she once loved.

Over the years, years in which she buried herself in her work, Lizzie had risen to become her party's chief of staff. Both respected and feared, she was frequently in disagreement with her party's changed direction, reluctantly advising ministers how to paper over mean-hearted policy that left people without hope. When she could no longer look away, she resigned.

Claire had counselled her to stay, to work from within the party to make change. 'Don't be a Pollyanna,' she'd said.

Her resignation went almost unnoticed, the job Lizzie had sacrificed everything for—or so it felt—had come to an abrupt end, a younger, more innovative, more flexible, more outcome-driven person taking her place.

After she resigned, Lizzie expected Margot, then in her early teens, to move back home. Lizzie was, after all, her mother. She had hoped Margot might want it, too. Other than weekends here and there, and the odd holiday, which Margot never seemed to enjoy, they hadn't had much of a chance to do mother and daughter things.

Instead of getting to know each other, Margot hardly left her room, her favourite CDs on rotation. She hated her new school, hated her mother for enrolling her, eventually refusing to come down for meals.

Lizzie was patient at first, deciding to wait it out, sure Margot would relent. Margot was hormonal, and she'd had trouble making friends at school, one of the reasons Lizzie thought a new school might be just the thing. But as days dragged into weeks, she became increasingly sad and frustrated.

She eventually snapped, going uninvited into Margot's room, and, in a rage of grief, threw the CD player against the wall when Margot wouldn't turn down the volume. Margot lunged at her.

'Why can't you be like other mothers? Why can't you be normal?' she screamed. 'I hate you! I've always hated you. I wish you were dead.'

Lizzie wished herself dead, too.

Falling to the floor, Lizzie picked up the shattered pieces of plastic. 'Sorry, I'm sorry. I'll buy you a new one, the latest one.' She could hear herself, this woman on her knees begging forgiveness, pathetic in her desperation to mend something between them that had been years in the making.

A few days later, Margot packed her things, and without a word, went to live with Ed.

Another absence filled the house.

Lizzie launched into a new career. Yet again, she had Claire to thank—Claire convincing her university friends that Lizzie would make a fine teacher.

She found, to her surprise, that she loved teaching, perhaps even excelled at it. But the free market she had helped usher in later rallied against her, closing down the only campus for kids living at the furthest reaches of suburbia so that the university might address funding shortfalls.

Her age, she was told, after consulting a recruiting firm, would make it difficult for her to find similar work. Not only could she not find a similar position, she couldn't find work at all.

Lizzie took an early retirement.

Alice was waiting for Lizzie at the bar, liqueurs in pretty bottles a kaleidoscope of umber and topaz and rose, music in the background. Nearby, a cluster of variously tattooed, sleek-haired young women talked in that conspiratorial way women do when the subject of their conversation is another woman, one running a contemptuous eye-linered eye over Alice. Perhaps, thought Alice, she was an unwelcome reminder of their future selves.

Lizzie arrived, surprisingly stylish in a red dress. She could look quite civilised when she made an effort, which mostly she didn't. After hugs and kisses and compliments, they went in search of their table, the throng parting as they made their way to the back of the room.

A handsome young man with a nifty ordering device approached their table. 'A night out on the town, ladies?' He handed Lizzie a menu. 'If you're after something to snack on—'

'We'll let you know,' said Lizzie.

He nodded, looking at them with fond amusement, much like a parent regarding their child on their first day of kinder.

Lizzie fixed him with a cold eye. He retreated.

'He thinks we're on the loose from the nursing home,' laughed Alice, silver dress a shimmer of soft rain. Always a good organiser when it came to alcohol, she took Lizzie's order, and disappeared into the cram of people waiting at the bar.

Lizzie was looking at her phone when Alice returned.

Alice wondered what it was she wanted to talk about. She handed Lizzie her drink, something blush-coloured and icy.

'That was quick.'

'God didn't give the elderly sharp elbows for nothing.'

Lizzie's laughter quickly faded. 'So strange that Claire isn't with us.'

'She's here.' Alice closed her eyes and spread her arms. 'Concentrate and you'll feel her presence.'

Lizzie rolled her eyes. 'We're not here for a séance.'

They raised their glasses. 'To Claire.'

Lizzie manoeuvred the mint floating in her glass to one side. 'There's something I have to ask you.'

CHAPTER 14

IN A GLITZY BAR SURROUNDED by beautiful people, Lizzie told Alice how in her last moments, Claire's careful planning had come undone.

Alice bowed her head. 'Oh, Lizzie.'

Hoots of laughter from the next table.

'There's something else,' said Lizzie. 'Claire left a letter.' She corrected herself. 'More of a note than a letter.' She paused for a moment. It felt hard telling her. 'The police found it under the bed.'

'Claire and Jeremy's bed?'

'I think she'd already . . .'

Alice froze. 'You're not saying . . . ?'

Lizzie nodded.

'Oh no,' said Alice.

They reached for each other's hands across the table.

'It didn't look anything like Claire's handwriting.'

Alice took a long swallow of her drink. 'Could you make any sense of it?'

'Only a few words.'

'Was she saying goodbye?'

'She asked me to forgive her.'

Alice was suddenly still, startled eyes on Lizzie.

'Forgive her for what she was about to do or had already done?'

Lizzie shook her head. 'It was something in the past. She said that for years she'd been too afraid . . . it was as if she wanted to confess.'

Alice, stabbed at the ice in her glass with the straw.

'I know this is distressing.'

'Claire would have been so affected—she wouldn't have been thinking straight.'

Lizzie had expected Alice to be equally mystified but instead she saw something like panic in her eyes.

'Best we put the whole thing out of our minds,' said Alice.

'She mentioned Ed.'

Alice's elbow caught her drink, almost knocking it over.

'She also mentioned your name. And Jane's.'

Outside, the lights of the city glittered against a dark sky. The streets were hectic with people, everyone with a secret they'd kept, a lie they'd told, a heartache they'd caused, a promise they'd broken.

Alice shifted in her chair, fingers sliding up and down the stem of her glass.

Lizzie wanted the feeling that Alice was keeping something from her to go away. 'Is there something I should know?'

Alice looked stricken.

'Well, is there?'

'You're ruining what should be a lovely evening.'

Lizzie fixed her eyes on Alice. 'You haven't answered my question.'

Alice slumped forward. 'It's not what you're thinking.'

It felt to Lizzie as if her heart stopped beating.

'I've hated not telling you.' Alice was on the verge of tears.

The waiter came to the table, took one look at their faces and backed away.

'Ed was having an affair.'

Lizzie's laugh was brittle. 'Ed was always having affairs.'

'You never suspected?'

Surely not her friend. Not Alice.

Alice sat pale and motionless.

A cold hand clutched Lizzie's heart. She had trusted Alice. 'You? You and Ed?'

'No, Lizzie, not me.'

Lizzie stared at Alice, at first uncomprehending. Surely Alice wasn't saying . . . no, impossible. She closed her eyes. Unthinkable. She wouldn't believe it. She couldn't.

'I wanted to tell you . . .'

The music was louder, the revellers rowdier. Lizzie realised she didn't like the bar; she'd never liked it. She preferred somewhere quiet with jazz playing softly in the background, where people could have proper conversations and drinks didn't have sexed-up names and prices, and waiters didn't patronise and make you feel old and ugly and stupid.

'It was all a very long time ago,' said Alice.

'How long?'

Alice stared, white-faced, as if a grenade was rolling towards her.

'Before or after Tom died?'

'After.'

Lizzie looked at the crowd of people, now all a little drunk. She heard their laughter, their light-hearted banter.

'How long after?'

Alice tore at her serviette. 'There's something else.'

Lizzie held her breath. What else could there be?

'There was a baby.'

A baby? What did she mean, a baby?

'Claire was pregnant. To Ed.'

Lizzie looked at Alice, her words, that she could make no sense of, swirling in her head. Had someone spiked her drink? Was she having a stroke?

'Jane is Ed's daughter.'

The baby so unexpected, Jane, a miracle, the joy she had felt for Claire . . .

'Ed . . . does he know?'

Alice shook her head.

A cold fury filled Lizzie's heart.

Alice leaned forward, her face suddenly old. 'I know how upset you must be.'

Lizzie wanted to laugh: *upset* that Ed and Claire had an affair, that Jane was Ed and Claire's child, that the people she trusted most in the world had lied to her for decades?

Alice sagged into her chair. 'I hoped this day would never come.'

Lizzie regarded her friend for a long moment. They had known each other a lifetime; she had thought that nothing could ever come between them. But between them there had always been a lie; a lie that didn't die with Claire. It lived on in Alice. 'You knew, you always knew, and you didn't tell me?'

Alice wept.

'Did you think for a minute about Jane?'

'You know I did.'

Lizzie gathered her bag and coat and stood to go.

'Please don't leave,' said Alice. 'Not like this.'

Lizzie's ears thrummed, the room blurred, her legs like rubber beneath her. Ed was Jane's father. Jane was his daughter.

'Let's go somewhere quiet, have a coffee, talk.'

Lizzie didn't want to go for coffee, she didn't want to talk. 'There's nothing more to say.'

'You shouldn't be alone, Lizzie, not tonight.'

'You betrayed me, betrayed our friendship.'

Alice stared grim-faced. 'It's not that simple.'

Did Alice really think she could justify a deception that affected so many lives?

Lizzie fled as she had always fled when life became too much. She shunned those who had hurt her, saw only her own pain. She would go home, she would close the door, she would retreat into her anger and grief, eventually emerging to find years had passed.

'Lizzie, please, don't go.'

Lizzie dissolved into the crowd and for a moment their worlds stopped turning.

CHAPTER 15

ALICE RUBBED HER EYES, SMUDGING black into the sockets.

She dropped her head into her hands, rueing again that she'd stopped by Lizzie's on that Friday afternoon all those years ago.

She'd been heading home after an appointment in the city and, on a whim, decided to drop in on Lizzie and take her to lunch. Alice hadn't phoned ahead, expecting Lizzie would be home from Canberra for the weekend.

It was a gorgeous day, the sun a buttery yellow, feathery clouds in a hazy blue sky. Alice turned up the radio. God, she loved Madonna. She sang along to 'Holiday'. She would have taken Lizzie on a holiday if it would have done any good.

She missed her old friend, the nights out, the nights in, the three of them heading off on weekends. Tom's death had cast a pall over everything.

Work was Lizzie's only solace. Alice had occasionally caught a glimpse of Lizzie on the news, standing behind the prime minister during one of his press conferences. It surprised her that she was so composed, even laughing at his lame jokes. Lizzie had said when she was at work there was no time to think, no time to feel.

When the three of them came together, they did their best to lift Lizzie's spirits, but it was as if their friend had died, too. She would sometimes join in, a rare glimpse of the old Lizzie, but mostly she was terribly still, staring at something in the distance only she could see.

When tears erupted, as they so often did, Alice was left wondering what tactless words she might have spoken, what thoughtless thing she might have done. Being around Lizzie was like treading on eggshells. She always floundered, usually over-egging it. Claire would simply offer a tissue and put an arm around Lizzie, often not saying a word.

The last time they had met, Lizzie, without warning, doubled over, shoulders shaking. Alice had been telling them about the sweet couple next door, baby on the way, who were moving out of their apartment to something bigger.

Claire had helped Lizzie from the room, made her a cup of tea, returning to say it was probably better if Alice went home. Didn't Claire realise she was Lizzie's friend, too?

When Alice grumbled, wondering aloud if Lizzie would ever be the same again, Claire told her she was being selfish. It wasn't that Alice didn't feel for Lizzie. She did, tremendously. For ages. And ages. But—and she hardly dared admit it to herself—grief, over time, did become a trifle boring.

Still feeling the sting of Claire's rebuke, Alice decided that time alone with Lizzie would be just the thing. After all, Alice was famously entertaining. Even in her early forties with work dropping away a little, she was still invited to every opening, every soirée, every everything. She bought glamour and fun to gatherings, everyone said so, and she almost always got a mention in the gossip mags, which had recently started calling her colourful.

Alice flicked off the radio and turned into Lizzie's driveway.

Wouldn't you know, Claire's car.

She didn't ring the doorbell. On a day like today they'd be in the garden, the one place that still gave Lizzie some pleasure.

Following the path that led the length of the house, her eyes were taken by the jacaranda, branches heavy with lavender blossom. The tree reminded her that Tom had been gone almost a year. However long she lived, she would never see a jacaranda without thinking of that little boy.

It wasn't until Alice turned the corner that she saw them beneath the large old vine that covered the back of the house, their arms around each other.

She knew immediately they were lovers.

Ed stepped back, his hand touching Claire's face, with a tenderness Alice hadn't seen before. He was talking, almost as if he were pleading, Claire shaking her head but her body still straining towards his.

Ed was the first to see Alice, his face initially disbelieving, then horrified. Claire followed his eyes, almost collapsing when she saw her friend. They looked at each other for what felt like hours before Claire broke away from Ed and ran to Alice, wailing. She took her by the shoulders, shaking her, begging her not to tell Lizzie, saying again and again: *It's over, it's over.*

Claire, who had stayed with Lizzie in those first weeks after Tom's death, who visited almost every day after that. All the love and kindness and sacrifice that Alice had begrudgingly admired was a lie.

It took a moment for the enormity of what she'd stumbled upon to hit her. 'You . . . Ed? Have you completely lost your minds?'

Claire gripped Alice's hands, begging her to understand. She was babbling on about how it should never have happened, how she had come to the house that very day to end it.

Alice shook her hands away.

For years she had withstood the patronising look, the raised eyebrow, the imagined whispers: poor lamentable Alice, her life strewn with broken relationships.

And now here was Claire, crumpled and hysterical, terrible in her fear and guilt and thinking only of herself. In Alice's chest swelled a feeling of revenge, a feeling she misinterpreted as justice. No longer would she need to compare herself to the incomparable Claire.

Ed stood helpless, arms hanging loose beside him. Alice saw his own face was tear-stained.

'How could you do this . . . do this to Lizzie?'

'We didn't mean it to happen,' Ed said, eyes cast down.

'*It* seems to have been happening for some time.'

'Lizzie can't find out . . .'

'Of course she'll find out.'

Claire dropped to the ground, hands covering her face, sobbing.

'It would kill Lizzie,' said Ed.

'You should have thought about that before—' Alice looked towards Claire '—before you had an affair with her best friend.'

Claire's sobbing grew louder.

He wasn't thinking of Lizzie, he was thinking of himself because that's what Ed did. 'It's not Lizzie you want to protect, it's your career.'

Beads of sweat had broken out on Ed's upper lip. 'She's my wife, of course I want to protect her.'

Alice shook her head. 'Are you seriously that delusional?'

'Alice . . .' Claire, her face red and swollen from crying, clambered to her feet. 'Please listen to Ed, please.'

'Claire is going away, we won't be seeing each other again,' he said, as if what they were asking was quite reasonable. 'No one need ever know.'

'I'll know,' said Alice.

Ed's eyes hardened. 'How many affairs have you had, Alice? Quite a few, by my reckoning.'

'You, preaching your family values,' said Alice, regarding him with contempt.

He paused as if calculating what to say next. 'What about Margot?' he replied. 'Have you thought about her?'

'I've thought a lot more about Margot than you obviously have.'

'She's been through so much already,' said Claire.

'I can't talk to you now, I can't even look at you,' said Alice, walking away.

'Alice!' Ed was chasing after her. 'You won't tell Lizzie. Swear you won't tell her!'

Alice turned to face them: Ed, arms outstretched, almost as if he were pleading; Claire staring after her.

'You fucked up, you both fucked up.'

She didn't bother with goodbyes.

'Is there anything else I can get you? asked the waiter, keeping more than the usual distance.

'No, nothing,' said Alice. 'Thank you.'

The burden of the secret she'd carried, carried for decades, hadn't died with Claire. For years, she'd practised forgetting.

Sometimes when she woke, she almost believed it was something she'd dreamed in her sleep.

What story, she wondered, had Claire told herself? Did she consider Alice, her unwilling lifelong collaborator, trapped and complicit?

Claire had known she was soon to die. She could have confessed, sought forgiveness. But she'd taken the cowardly way out. *Damn you, Claire. Damn you, for not sorting things out.*

She was weeping again.

Double-damn you, Claire Reid.

The two women sat either end of Alice's sofa, Claire so wilted and defeated that Alice felt a momentary stab of compassion.

Claire had phoned Alice that morning, asking if they could meet before she left for the UK. Alice reluctantly agreed.

'I was hoping that once you'd slept on it, you'd realise—'

'I have slept on it, and I haven't changed my mind.'

'It was a horrible dreadful mistake, but it's over.'

Alice was unmoved. 'If you don't tell Lizzie before you leave, then I will.'

'I can't.'

'Can't or won't?'

Claire left the sofa to stand by the window. 'You've always been jealous of my friendship with Lizzie.'

Alice's eyes widened. 'You honestly think . . . ?'

Claire turned to look at her. 'Perhaps you also need to examine your conscience, Alice. And your motivations.'

Alice hesitated. 'My conscience is clear.'

The two women regarded each other.

'Look,' said Claire, 'we both know what Lizzie has been through, we both love her. As her friend, I am begging you not to tell her.'

'Is it Lizzie you care about or yourself?'

'I can't believe that you would even ask that question.'

Alice raised an eyebrow. 'Given recent history . . .'

'You won't reconsider?'

'You're a human rights lawyer, you don't need me to remind you about right and wrong.'

'There's something else, something I haven't told you,' Claire said, sitting back on the sofa, hands resting on her tummy.

For a minute Alice had the absurd thought that Claire, who had tried for years to have a baby, was going to say she was pregnant.

'I'm having a baby.'

Alice was aghast. 'Holy hell, Claire.' Jeremy had only just returned from a three-month sabbatical, so obviously . . .

'I couldn't believe it at first. I've never been regular and lately my cycle . . .' She shrugged helplessly. 'So when I missed a couple of times—'

'Tell me you're not going to keep it?'

Alice saw in her face that she was.

'It's not an *it*.'

Alice leapt from the sofa and stood in the middle of the room. 'Jesus. Does Ed know?'

Claire shook her head. 'It will be Jeremy's baby.'

Alice closed her eyes, trying to make Claire's words make sense. 'Jeremy knows?'

'I've told him everything.'

'I can't believe what I'm hearing.'

Claire sat taller, her voice stronger. 'Ed must never know.'

'He's the father, for God's sake.'

'He wouldn't want the baby. He'd much prefer not to know, that way he is excused of any responsibility.'

'How can you possibly explain away a pregnancy when Jeremy's been away?'

'In a few months I'll write Lizzie a letter telling her I've just learned, unbelievably, that I'm pregnant.'

'And lie again about the date of birth?'

'I'll say the baby was prem.'

'My God.'

'We won't be back from the UK until after the baby's born.'

Alice paced. 'How long after?'

'A year, maybe two.'

'Which is when you will tell Lizzie? And Ed?'

'What do you think might happen if I was to tell Lizzie now, in three years? Five?'

'Have you considered what might happen if you don't?'

Claire pressed a hand to her forehead. 'I've been through every possible scenario.'

Alice glared at her friend. 'I think you wanted this baby, the baby you never thought you could have, and no matter who you hurt, you made a decision to keep it.'

Claire looked directly at Alice. 'I've told you the truth, whether you believe it is up to you.'

Alice shook her head and sat again on the sofa. 'I'm realising that you and Ed are actually very alike.'

'What do you mean?'

'Charming when you get your own way, which is most of the time, also mendacious and cowardly.'

'Don't be cruel, Alice, it doesn't become you.'

'Then why involve me, why make me part of your lie?'

Claire returned Alice's icy stare. 'You're the only one who might have guessed the truth when you heard.'

Alice's head ached, her tongue felt thick in her mouth. 'Have you any idea what you are asking of me?'

'I hope in time you can forgive me,' said Claire, hands reaching out to Alice. 'I hope we can still be friends.'

Alice's hands stayed firmly clasped in her lap.

She would be living with Claire's lie for the rest of her life.

When Lizzie later asked Alice if she knew anything about Ed and Claire's falling-out, Alice shook her head, certain her face would give her away. Something to do with politics, Lizzie said. She hoped it would blow over. Alice said she was sure things would work out.

That following week, Claire and Jeremy retreated to the UK. When they returned, Lizzie and Ed were divorced, and Claire and Jeremy had a baby daughter they'd named Jane Elizabeth.

Things took up much as they'd left off except that Ed had departed the scene. Lizzie was over the moon that Claire had had a little girl, whom she and Margot doted on. Claire and Jeremy were wonderful, loving parents. The three friends met just as they always had; it was as if the conversation Alice had had with Claire before she left for the UK had never taken place.

Claire and Lizzie were closer than ever.

But the secret hung over Claire and Alice's friendship. The dynamics had shifted, Alice often sniping at Claire who never gave Alice the satisfaction of retaliating. Claire was the first at Alice's side when she was diagnosed with breast cancer, visiting her often, always with gifts that delighted, but couldn't buy the forgiveness Alice knew Claire sought.

Alice rang Lizzie.

Her call, unanswered, rang mournful and guilty into the night.

CHAPTER 16

STEPPING BLINDLY INTO THE TAXI, Lizzie almost fell onto the back seat. She mumbled her address to the alarmed driver observing her in the mirror. He probably thought she was drunk.

Claire. Claire and Ed. Her phone rang. *Alice.* She turned it off.

Clinging to the strap above the passenger door, she felt if she could just hold on, she would make it home.

'I am sorry, can I help?'

He was just a boy, if in your early twenties you could still be a boy. She shook her head and managed a thank you, staring out the window as the world flashed past, neon signs pointing heavenwards, the baubles they spruiked, promising this way happiness lies.

Her thoughts raced, a confusion of emotions circling and tumbling over each other. Claire, whose conscience had troubled her until her last breath, had confessed and, in turn, wanted forgiveness. Her fate, regardless of all her planning, was a frightening and lonely death.

Claire's confession at the last minute was nothing more than a desperate attempt to save her soul. Her unburdening coming too late for Lizzie.

Their friendship, the intimacies they'd shared, the things they'd faced together, the secrets they'd kept for each other, meaningless.

Claire, who performed many good deeds, deeds she made sure came to public attention; Claire the schmoozer, the networker, the faker. The woman who fought for justice, who modelled courage and determination, a hypocrite, someone who deserved her pity.

Lizzie felt no pity.

Away from the city, warm-lit houses hemmed suburban streets. Families and friends and lovers going about their evening, sharing food and stories, laughing at something inane on TV, playing their favourite music, pets at their feet.

Lizzie thought about the days immediately after Tom died, sedated and out of her mind with grief. It was Claire who supported her, staying those first days, watching over what was left of Lizzie's family.

Lizzie and Ed, unable to comfort each other, mourned alone, Lizzie spending her nights on Tom's bed, Ed lying lonely in theirs. She couldn't quite recall when Ed started blaming her for Tom's death. Filled with remorse and recrimination—*if she hadn't been in Canberra, Tom might still be with them*—his condemnation was no less shocking to hear. As the weeks went on, Ed's anger grew, his words becoming more and more cruel.

'He was sick, he begged you to stay . . .'

His accusations were accusations already playing on a loop in her head. Too ashamed and crushed to defend herself, she escaped, returning to work, working long hours and home less than ever.

Later, she asked Ed if they could have another baby. He shook his head: there could never be another Tom. 'And that,' he said, 'is my last word on the matter.'

In the months following Tom's death, Lizzie had known that Ed, despite all the promises he had made, was having another affair. She hadn't bothered casting around, as she had often done, to identify the woman who'd attracted his attention. They were most often young and easily impressed. They were never *Claire*.

Feeling as though she might be sick, Lizzie asked the driver if he could turn down the heater and open the windows. Gulping icy air, Lizzie leaned back in the seat thinking about the day she told Claire she was leaving Ed.

They were in Claire's garden early one Saturday morning, hoping to finish a mid-spring tidy-up. They'd been working, mostly in silence, unusual for them; Lizzie meditating on her future, Claire uncharacteristically withdrawn.

Lizzie paused, secateurs still in her hand. 'I'm leaving Ed.'

Claire, who was on her knees weeding, fell back on her haunches. 'Lizzie, you can't be serious?'

Lizzie managed to disentangle a dead cane from an old rose. 'Only months since Tom died, and he's already fucking around.'

Claire grimaced.

'He promised last time . . . I believed him. I really thought that losing Tom . . .'

Claire tugged her hat low. 'I don't know what to say.'

Lizzie had expected Claire to put her arms around her, tell her she shouldn't make life-changing decisions so soon after

Tom's death; that she loved Ed, Ed loved her. That after all they'd been through, they just needed time.

Claire was back on her hands and knees weeding.

'I tell you I'm leaving Ed, and you carry on weeding?'

Claire looked up, eyes hidden beneath the brim of her hat. 'I know things are still raw for you, and I don't want to say the wrong thing.'

Lizzie saw the exhaustion in Claire, her shoulders slumped, her head bowed. She dropped the secateurs and knelt beside her friend. 'Sorry, I shouldn't have blurted it out like that.'

Claire was crying.

Lizzie rubbed Claire's back. 'Don't take any notice of me.'

Claire swiped at her tears with a gloved hand. 'Have you told Ed?'

'Not yet.' Lizzie stretched and lifted her face to the sun. 'I've thought about it for weeks, but being out here,' she gestured to the sky, the garden, 'has helped clear my head. Ed's never going to change.'

Claire pressed on with her task. 'How do you think Ed will take it?'

'Badly,' said Lizzie. 'I know it sounds silly but he still loves me.' In many ways, she loved him, too.

Claire stabbed the fork into the bed, stood up and pulled off her gloves. 'It really is getting warm. Would you like a drink?'

'I wouldn't say no to a glass of water.'

Lizzie went back to her pruning, guilty her emotional roller-coaster had so worn Claire out.

Claire returned with long glasses, ice clinking. She'd washed the smear of dirt from her mouth and donned a pair of sunglasses. They took a seat in the shade of an old gum, its honey-scented blossom sweetening the air.

'Does Ed know you know?'

'I don't think so.'

'Well,' Claire squeezed a wedge of lemon, pale juice trickling down the inside of the glass, 'if you've thought about it and you think it's the right thing . . .'

'I don't want to be one of those women who stay, hoping that one day he'll change.'

'Any idea who he's seeing?'

'No.' Lizzie shook her head. 'Whoever she is, she's lasted a lot longer than anyone else.'

'Could you be imagining things?'

Lizzie shook her head. 'I know the signs.'

'What sort of signs?'

Lizzie laughed in spite of herself. 'He sings in the shower, leaps out of bed in the morning, pays too many compliments, that sort of thing.'

Claire stood suddenly, her hip striking the corner of the table.

'Madam. Madam?'

Lizzie sat up with a start.

'We have arrived.'

Lizzie rummaged through her bag for her wallet. She added a generous tip to the fare. 'Thank you.'

He lowered his eyes and wished her well.

Lizzie stumbled along the path, found the key, hands shaking as she opened the door. Claire suggesting she was imagining things when all along she was sleeping with Ed.

An affair with your best friend's husband was unforgivable enough, an affair when that friend was mourning the death of her son, the most unforgivable sin of all.

She stabbed the key into the lock.

When exactly had Claire started her affair with Ed?

Lizzie let Fred in, collapsing beside him on the rug. How long she lay there, she wasn't sure. She eventually willed herself up and turned on the lights, tearing off the dress and discarding it on the floor. She put on something warm, sensible. Everywhere she looked she was reminded of Claire. Gifts given, mementos, that time they'd painted the sitting room blue, Claire smiling at her from photos, little misses standing to attention in monogrammed blazers, white socks folded at the ankle, polished black shoes. Claire's great big grin. A photo taken when they were at uni, pouting and posing, hair teased into matching beehives, white-stockinged legs and too much eyeliner, wedding photos, baby photos, travel photos.

Tears stung as she was reminded of their last bushwalk—backpacks, sturdy shoes, stunning views—Claire determined never to put Jeremy in respite again after he returned home distraught and more confused. She ripped the photo from the frame, tearing at it until it lay like confetti at her feet.

Grabbing Fred's lead, she fled the house. Fred forged ahead, as much as an old greyhound could forge, wild with joy everything was back to normal.

Smoke curling from terracotta chimneys smudged the night sky, street lights cast long shadows. Lizzie didn't notice in which direction they went, little awareness of turning left or right with no sense of how long they'd been walking.

She was crying—no tears, just furious sobs. She'd forgotten to put on her coat. It didn't matter. Nothing mattered. Fred pulled up, long nose buried in grass as he sniffed his way around a telegraph pole. Throwing back her head, she breathed deep breaths.

The night was still, streets abandoned for firesides and central heating, the odd bike flashing past, headlights floating somewhere in the distance, one or two rugged-up dog-walkers smiling politely, murmuring *good evenings*, breath steamy and moonlit.

Fred had taken over the walk, leading her down side streets, around dark corners, stopping to snuffle and scent. She came to a standstill, tugged on Fred's lead. Where had she ended up? She vaguely recognised the street name. Lord, kilometres from home. Turning quickly, she tripped on the lead, tumbling forward.

Someone caught her.

'Goodness, are you okay?'

'Thank you.' She stood her tallest—grey hair led people to judgement far too quickly. 'I'm perfectly fine.'

'Poppy has a habit of tripping me up, too.'

He was also walking a greyhound. 'Adopted?' she asked, catching a glimpse of green collar beneath the fleecy tartan coat.

He nodded and smiled.

She'd seen him around the neighbourhood, though it wasn't him she remembered but Poppy's beautiful brindle coat. 'Best be getting back.'

'Looks like we're headed in the same direction.' He hesitated. 'Would you mind if I walked with you?'

She minded terribly. 'By all means.'

'It's not often Poppy meets another greyhound.'

The dogs were certainly hitting it off, ears pricked, tails whirling.

'I'm Anthony, by the way.'

'Elizabeth. And this is Fred.'

They fell into step, dogs trotting ahead. Lizzie, choking back tears, lied about not feeling the cold when he asked why she wasn't wearing a coat, *not even a scarf*.

'I've seen you about, you and Fred.'

'I've seen you about, too.'

'Have you lived here long?'

'Going on forty years. You?'

'Ten, give or take. You must have seen some changes.'

When she and Ed first moved into their street, tomatoes and zucchinis filled front gardens, Greek and Italian women, sweeping their swept footpaths, always making time to stop and smile indulgently at babies and toddlers, shake their heads at the weather.

'Not all for the better, I'd wager.'

'Unfortunately, not.'

'Are you a winter person?' he asked.

This man was quite a chatterbox. 'Sometimes I think it's my favourite season.'

'Me too,' he said. 'But then spring comes along . . .'

'A beautiful spring so far.' She quickened her step. She wasn't in the mood to make small talk with anyone, certainly not a stranger. She wanted to scream at the sky. And sob and beat her fists and curse Claire. They walked on, the occasional sound of someone enjoying themselves a little too much, a budding pianist practising scales, a train rattling in the distance.

'Do you always take Fred on such long walks?'

'We got a little carried away tonight.'

They crossed over the creek, bridge suspended in mist, a squawk from a startled bird piercing the thick silence.

They walked through Lizzie's local shopping centre. 'The Village', real estate agents called it, although it had begun to feel less like a village over the years, as the greengrocer, the butcher and milk bar made way for beauticians and yoga studios.

Couples in cafés leaned close over candlelit dinners, happy

chatter as people poured from the cinema, a homeless man and his dog sitting by the art deco doors.

During the day, the same man set himself up outside the organic grocer's, likely hoping the hippie generation hadn't lost their compassion and the hipsters had discovered theirs. Out early on an unseasonably cold morning the Christmas before, Lizzie, noticing the man's dog had the best of the bedding and a lovely warm coat, had taken pity on him and bought him coffee and a fancy French version of pizza. She'd felt uncom-fortable about how good it made her feel, the do-gooder feeling lasting all day.

'Dreadful state of affairs,' said Anthony.

Lizzie hoped he meant dreadful for the homeless man, not cinema-goers.

'It feels wrong just to walk past,' said Lizzie. Yet she did. Every day.

'What's his story, do you know?'

Lizzie had never thought to speak to him, caring limited to one hot meal and the giving of gold coins. 'I haven't asked.'

They walked the last few minutes in silence.

'Here we are,' she said, stopping at her gate.

He peered at her garden, the street light spilling over him. Lizzie guessed he was around her age, maybe a little younger, with a thick head of hair, perhaps a little too thick at the temples, grey streaked with charcoal. He wasn't exactly handsome but his face was open and friendly. Uncomplicated, she thought.

'Lovely garden.'

'A bit wild around the edges,' she said.

'There's the charm of it.' He pulled Poppy to heel. 'I'll be on my way then.'

She pushed through the gate.

'Do you know that fenced-off area where the dogs run off lead?' he asked.

'Attracts quite a crowd.'

'I'm there at eight most mornings. Perhaps the four of us could meet up, go for a coffee afterwards?'

'Perhaps,' she said.

He patted Fred's head and smiled. 'I'll look out for you.'

'The comfort of strangers,' she said to Fred, unlocking the door, grateful for the silence that greeted her.

Lizzie dropped into a chair without turning on the lights or the heating.

If only Claire hadn't written that note, if only she hadn't questioned Alice, if only there hadn't been an affair, a baby . . .

She fell forward, head in her hands.

Oh, Claire, what have you done?

CHAPTER 17

MARGOT AND JANE WERE HANGING out in the front room of Jane's house, clothes drying on a rack, coffee table cluttered with books and stuff, shoes chucked by the front door. There was always something going on in the kitchen, someone bread-baking or marmalade-making, leaving half the mess behind. Beds, strewn with clothes, were never made.

The house, a Californian bungalow, sat on a slight tilt, cracks flowed like tributaries across the walls, and the bay window sagged a little, maybe a lot.

Margot removed one of the too-many cushions from the armchair and made herself comfy. She couldn't stand a thing out of place at home, anything asymmetrical made her anxious; she couldn't settle unless everything was picture-perfect, even a crumb and she'd vacuum. And yet, she loved Jane's place—the messiness, the freedom of kicking back, no worries about putting feet on furniture or coasters on tables.

Jane was on the sofa, no makeup, hair short—low maintenance was her motto—wearing one of her comfy pairs of jeans, jumper sourced from the op shop.

Margot sipped her too-strong coffee. 'You're going okay, then?'

'Yeah, you know . . . some days are better than others, just taking it as it comes, not expecting too much of myself.'

Margot nodded. 'You have to go with it.'

'I keep thinking if I could just see them one last time . . . say all the things I should have said, thank them for all the things I never thanked them for. Say goodbye.'

'I know,' said Margot.

'See ya,' called Jess, rushing past, door slamming behind her.

Jane laughed and shook her head. 'What's news?'

Margot filled her in on Molly and Jack, told her about Julian wanting to be away less and home more, asked Jane about her travel plans, wanted to know the latest gig she'd been to and how her job was going. She drank the last bitter mouthful of coffee, reminding herself to ask for tea next time. 'Do you ever feel like something's missing?'

'Yeah, because, you know . . . patriarchy, capitalism.'

'I mean like missing in your actual life?' Margot could talk to Jane about anything. She trusted her more than her therapist, who listened, too, but always with her eye on the clock. She was more herself with Jane than she was with anyone.

'Sometimes—doesn't everyone?' replied Jane, tucking her feet under her. 'But work helps, getting out of the house helps.'

'That simple?'

'What about picking up that abandoned camera of yours?'

'Now that you mention it, I did a shoot for a friend of a friend a few weeks ago—a vintage clothing start-up.'

'Sounds fun.'

'It sort of got me wanting to get back into it . . . like back into photography.'

'Total waste if you don't.'

'Anyway, I dropped Jack off at day care a couple of days ago and spent the day in the city with my camera.'

Jane looked pleased. 'About time.'

She didn't tell Jane that her plan had been to take photos in and around her neighbourhood. Which she did. Flowers and picket fences, lattice-framed shops, and divinely dressed people ordering coffee and being generally divine.

Bored—she might as well have been taking pics to post on Instagram—Margot was about to head home, when she found herself driving into the city, to the places she'd go with her camera before Julian came back from the UK and gave her a call. Which was when she dropped everything because here was her chance, a second chance . . .

She had been drawn to the streets then, she still was: the elderly couple sitting at a tram stop eating meat pies, the carnage of the butcher shop window, a girl in over-the-knee boots giving attitude and the finger to a bunch of pervy tradies.

'So, plans?' asked Jane. 'Comps, freelance . . . ?'

'Don't know, we'll see.' For the moment, it felt like enough.

'What about setting up that darkroom you've been talking about?'

Margot shrugged. 'That'll do about me? How are you? Sam?'

'Yeah, good.'

'Are you going to . . . like, you know . . . ?'

Jane looked amused. 'Like, move in together?'

'Yeah.' Margot grinned. 'S'pose.'

'Tying yourself to one person for the next fifty years?' Jane shook her head. 'Monogamy's a stupid idea. It's never worked, it's never going to work.'

'Okay, marriage, whatever, doesn't always work out, but when it does, I mean, look at your parents.'

Jane unfurled and stretched her legs. 'More coffee, biscuits, homemade?'

'Maybe one,' said Margot. Her phone buzzed. A message from Charlotte. She had tickets to *Gone Girl*. Ed would babysit if Julian was away.

Jane put a plate of biscuits on the table. 'I made too many so eat up.'

Margot broke a biscuit in half.

'Live dangerously and have a whole entire biscuit to yourself.'

'I could eat every last one on the plate,' said Margot. 'Addictive personality, remember?'

'Do you still think about it—heroin, I mean?' asked Jane.

'Sometimes.'

'Ever tempted?'

Margot took little bites of her biscuit. 'Every now and then . . . think anyone who's had a habit is.'

'I thought I was going to lose you.'

'I thought I was going to lose myself.'

She had wanted more. Every day, more. She had liked its routines: the syringes, the swabs, the spoons, the anticipation. The hit. Once in her veins, she felt cocooned. She floated, she dreamed.

She loved the altered state; the edge taken off things. She didn't care about her studies or her complicated fucked-up family. She was happy to just be.

Patrick started hassling, said she was developing a habit. She liked it best when they used together, the sex afterwards. Dreamy hours of pleasure. But he still only used on weekends. He'd become boring. She began hanging out with a different crowd, using most days. She reassured him, reassured herself. Always in total control, she said. Hadn't she done all sorts of shit? Like cocaine. How addictive was that stuff? She'd given that up, hadn't she? And when she was ready, she'd give up heroin, too.

Her father's monthly allowance covered her rent and bills. Nice to have a rich old man, Patrick said. Her father was rich and guilty, she said. Guilty parents were always trying to make up for stuff they couldn't make up for.

She started dipping into the allowance her father provided to cover her living expenses with a little left over. For the nice things in life, he'd said. The little bit left over soon wasn't enough. One night she raided Patrick's cupboards, eventually finding his weekend stash tucked into a shoe. She hardly noticed when he packed up his things and left. And when she did, she didn't care.

She was soon stealing from her housemate, Elle; stuff she could pawn like a pair of vintage earrings, things it would take ages for Elle to miss. The more she got away with, the more brazen she became. Elle came from money, nothing Margot stole from her couldn't be replaced. Everything, Margot discovered, could be justified.

It wasn't long before Elle asked Margot to leave. She was nice about it, said she knew the other Margot would always pay her rent, the other Margot would never take her things. She gave her two weeks to find another place. Margot called Elle all sorts of names before storming out.

She wandered the streets, more anxious about how she'd get the money to score than where she'd spend the night. She kept to the main drag not far from where the street girls hung out. Safety in company, she reckoned. The icy wind blew about her bare legs and made her ears ache. And suddenly she wanted her mother, to hear her say, *My dear darling girl*, with arms around her promising everything would be all right.

Margot was searching in her bag for her phone when a man pulled up alongside and asked for a head job. He was wearing a suit, there was a baby seat in the back, and he looked totally harmless. She asked what it was worth. He told her.

She got into the car.

What she most remembered were the smells.

Bodies, breath, semen, sex.

In front seats, back seats, in laneways, dark corners. They came quickly, mostly, the taste of latex in her mouth. Occasionally, she was called a slut or a no-good junkie. She'd laugh—whatever—so lacking in imagination they couldn't come up with anything other than a cliché to insult her.

She had been sleeping in her car or couch-surfing mostly at Jane's house. Jane, or one of her housemates, would turn on the shower, feed her and make up a bed.

But after a bout of pneumonia put her in hospital, she got lucky when the nurse screening her for sexually transmitted nasties told her about a brothel that was looking for new girls. It was legal, clean and had a good reputation. Margot fronted up and got the nod. The place wasn't much to look at but, hey, a bed instead of the back seat of a car; a shower instead of a tissue or hankie; a panic button and a security guard.

With money coming in every week, Margot soon had enough to rent a grimy little flat behind a strip of run-down shops. It wasn't much, an open space that included a tiny kitchen in one corner, room for a bed, couch and television in the other. The toilet was separate, so separate you had to go out the back door where you'd find it along with a laundry, in a lean-to that had almost keeled over.

Her mother scrubbed the place clean, and, with her father's help, bought a bed, a couch, table and chairs. She hung new blinds, filled her cupboards with food and put meals in the freezer. She was grateful-not grateful. *The caring mother she'd longed for.*

Jane, now in her late teens, called by a few times a week, dropping in for coffee or taking her out to dinner. Popping in for a chat, she'd say. She got Margot onto a methadone program, the first of many. When she was at her lowest, Jane would appear with food and clean clothes and a sensible word.

She had listened when there was no one else to listen. She didn't judge when everyone else was judging; she remained her friend when all her friends had gone.

Jane had saved her life.

CHAPTER 18

ALICE WAS ON THE BALCONY with a cup of coffee—trees bare only days before now dusted with blossom, everywhere the soft veil of green. She'd be long gone by autumn, when those same leaves would, on the slightest breath, pirouette and fall to earth.

She thought again of Lizzie and the situation in which they found themselves. She had phoned her she didn't know how many times. She'd even, against her better judgement, knocked on Lizzie's door, calling her name when she didn't answer. She wanted things smoothed over, sorrys said, anything difficult or unpleasant hurried away.

Maybe she should contact Margot. Lizzie was always saying how close they were.

Why hadn't she insisted all those years ago that Claire tell Lizzie she'd had an affair with Ed, that there was a baby? And that the baby was Jane. It was unthinkable, what Claire had asked of her. Foolish and wrong that she'd agreed. She could see now it wasn't only Lizzie she had wanted to protect. They were three, not two. She had wanted to preserve their friendship, too.

Alice swiped at a tear. How could Lizzie accuse her of an affair with Ed? How could she? Tears had been replaced by anger, though a therapist had once told her that tears and anger were much of the same.

It had been a difficult few days, that very morning selling two more of her pieces; this time a dressing table with Bakelite handles, along with a huge circular mirror she had discovered in an op shop. They'd been with her almost as long as she'd been in the apartment. As each piece was ferried to its new home, her apartment became an echo chamber of all she had lost.

She had never forgotten how broken she had been when she first moved in. In just a few short months, Christopher had taken all her confidence, as well as most of her money. But it had been much worse than that.

The doctor had been shocked when he examined her, asking what on earth had been going on. *Nothing*, she told him. For who would believe her? She must not let it continue, he said, her internal injuries needed rest if they were to heal.

But refusing only made Christopher more angry, more determined to have his way. It was as if his desire for her caused him to hate her. When it was over, and he was asleep, she'd lie in bed planning how she might escape.

The next day he would transform into the man she fell in love with, his tenderness inexplicable. Desperate to make up for his 'grumpy mood', he would go on his knees, there was nothing he wouldn't do for her, nothing he wouldn't do to keep her. It wasn't his fault that he loved her so much that she sometimes made him crazy.

And then it would start all over again.

Terrified he might carry out his threats if she left, she stayed.

Walking back inside, she turned to enjoy the view for a moment longer. Although he occasionally came to her in nightmares, Christopher was long gone. She never need fear him again. She rinsed the dregs of coffee from her cup and gazed long and lovingly at her apartment. Her little piece of LA in Melbourne.

She glanced at the time. Alice was to do her very first pose that afternoon. The studio was as lovely as the online description. Light and airy and surrounded by ancient trees, their branches filled with birdsong. And only a short walk from her apartment, too. She just hoped that none of her neighbours were artists, emerged or emerging. It wasn't her potential for embarrassment, but theirs, that made her smile.

Alice approached the stage. It was bare but for a floor cushion, a small wooden box to one side, if required. She let her robe fall. The teacher, Marcus, helped her set the pose: on the floor, cushion beneath her bottom, right hand to rest on the box, left leg curled in front of her, just so, relax the shoulders so they sit softly, look to the side, a little more, yes, that's it.

The artists, poised behind easels, were gathered in a horseshoe shape facing the stage.

'Today,' said Marcus, 'we'll be concentrating on proportion, so really think before you put down a line.'

The artists murmured and nodded. He adjusted the lighting, someone pointing out there was too much light on the chest area, tweaking until everyone was satisfied.

Marcus set the timer. 'Okay, let's start with some five-minute poses to warm up.' The artists took up their pencils.

Alice concentrated her gaze on the view of parkland outside the window. It was strange being naked—though life models were said to be nude, not naked—in a room full of strangers. If she thought about it, the only times you were naked were in the shower or when it had something to do with sex, maybe in bed on an airless summer's night.

What would her life be now, she wondered, had she stayed in journalism, had she not sacrificed the long term for the short term? Had she been more like Lizzie?

As suited her bohemian sensibilities, her career had been an exciting patchwork of bits and pieces, of this-and-thats: she'd popped in and out of morning television, their go-to person for vox pops and advertorials; she was co-host—sidekick to male hosts—on reality TV and game shows; she made regular appearances on panels and chat shows as zany older woman; and worked as an extra, the most recent parts more often involving a walking frame or wheelchair. She did whatever ads came her way, but not many had come her way lately. And now, life modelling.

'Okay, longer break,' said Marcus.

Alice slipped into her robe. She wandered the room, a chance to meet the artists and see their work in progress.

They sketched on sheets of paper, bulldog clips securing the paper to a board, boards resting on easels, most artists using pencils in various degrees of blackness, one or two with charcoal. They had so far, only the basic contours down, but already there was a sense of the human form.

After the break, Marcus re-posed her, chalk marks guiding where the feet should go, the hand, so that the exact same pose was replicated. Other than for the scratch of pencil against paper, the room was silent. Time ticked slowly. She tried not to fidget. *Stillness*, she chanted to herself. Stillness.

Eventually, an itch behind her ear she longed to scratch. Her wrist, where some of her weight rested, began to ache. Alice could see, out of the corner of her eye, the artists, their focus shifting from her to the work in front of them, then back, foreheads creased in concentration, eyes thoughtful. What did they see when they looked at her? she wondered. What did her body tell them about her life, what did they hope to capture?

They stopped for another short break, she stretched and flexed and made herself a coffee. She chatted to one or two of the artists, interested to see how they had interpreted her, many of them looking at each other's work, some commenting, others asking questions.

Back on stage for the longer of the poses, her thoughts wandered to Claire. She had been the only one of her friends who knew about Christopher. How, Alice could not fathom. She had a wardrobe of long sleeves and clothes that covered her back and chest, a scarf she wore when necessary. No one must know. And yet somehow . . . It was there in Claire's eyes when she looked at her, in her voice when she asked how she was. Then the day she had pressed into Alice's hand a piece of paper. *Ring this number*, she said.

The phone number had been for a battered women's support group. The leaflet said they offered information and advice. Alice resisted going at first, for who wanted to be identified as a battered woman? Particularly as it was widely agreed that if men beat their women, the women must deserve it. When she did eventually get up the courage, she met women who suffered as she did. In silence. Those who had attempted to speak of what was taking place inside the four walls of their home were not believed. Their stories were as awful as Alice's. But they were trapped by the threat of an even greater violence should they leave. And so, they stayed. And submitted. Priests advised them to pray, hospitals patched them up, police told them to stop their nagging.

Alice had lost all sense of time, impossible to chart how long she had been in the pose. In her peripheral vision, she could see a tall erect woman around her age, perhaps a few years younger, working intensely. A corner of the cushion poked uncomfortably into her groin, but still she held the pose, her eyes unwavering on the outside view.

'Time,' called Marcus.

Alice stood, reached for her robe and had a little stretch. She would go for a short run when she got home. She wandered again between the easels, a few artists thanking her, conversation about how the hand needed work, how pleased they were with the shapes.

The sketches were as individual as handwriting, with more freedom in some, more play in others, the skill and craft of the more accomplished artists on show. She liked all their renderings.

The woman she had noticed earlier was still at her easel, standing back and adding final touches. She looked up as Alice approached. 'Thank you for holding the pose so beautifully.'

'My first time,' said Alice, feeling pleased. 'I'm Alice, by the way.'

'Ursula.'

'Hello,' said Alice, joining Ursula in front of her easel, anxious to see herself through this woman's intelligent eyes.

'Oh.' Alice was too moved to speak. Sketched onto a rectangle of paper, her body was all lines and planes, a landscape rising and falling. Her face, in profile, spoke of resilience, her expression of grace and graciousness. In her eyes, a humanity, something melancholic, a hint of a smile on her lips. Alice, for the first time, saw that she was beautiful, an inner beauty there if only you looked. Ursula had looked.

She had brought Alice to life.

CHAPTER 19

LIZZIE'S EMOTIONS WERE ALL MIXED up, love and hate colliding. She was missing Claire, horribly, longing to pick up the phone and hear her voice, to feel her arms around her in welcome. Almost in the same moment, she was burning with anger, wanting to confront her, witness her shame and guilt, turn her back when she begged forgiveness.

It occurred to her that most of her wrath had been directed at Claire, not Ed. She was furious with him, too, but she had long ago learned that when it came to Ed, you could never set the bar too low.

Lizzie rolled onto her side, pulling up her knees, wrapping her arms around them so they rested against her chest. Should she tell Jane about Ed? Tell Margot? Would she confront Ed? Or should the lie be left well alone, where it could do no further damage?

Shivering one minute, sweltering the next, she tossed off the doona.

Alice could no longer be her friend; she had never been her friend, just a facsimile thereof. A friend could never, would never, do as she had done. An accomplice after the fact, an accomplice to a terrible travesty.

Lizzie locked herself away, cancelled her dental appointment, put off the plumber coming to fix the washing machine, and ordered in groceries and anything else she needed, venturing only to the letterbox with a restless Fred.

With curtains drawn, she moved in a twilight world. She hadn't spoken to a single soul for days. The only person who could have coaxed her from her self-imposed exile was Margot. Lizzie had thought when she left a message cancelling her day with Molly and Jack, something she had never once done, that Margot might have called to check on her.

Alice phoned every day for the first few days, worrying half to death about her, frantic to explain, ready to answer all her questions, desperately sorry. She always finished by saying she missed her, that life was too short.

What you might say after a tiff, not a deceit that had lasted a lifetime.

To keep such a betrayal from her for not one year or two, but more than thirty years. Alice and Claire must have met on at least one occasion and discussed what was to be done. The lies they'd conceived, the deceptions they'd played out, a cover-up she and Claire had conspired to take to their graves.

Eventually Alice came to the house, as Lizzie knew she would, ringing her doorbell, peering through the window, calling her name. Fred confused when she didn't answer.

*

It was days before Lizzie vacuumed up the photo, fragments of Lizzie and Claire swirling in dirt and dust and dog hair. She emptied the cleaner, the tiny flecks of colour disappearing into the bin, along with the picture frame she no longer had use for.

The red dress, discarded on the floor, lay bleeding like a wound into the white rug. It was pretty and, for her, expensive. But she could never wear it again. Folding it neatly, Lizzie slid the dress into a plastic bag. Someone else would get great pleasure from it.

Exhaustion overwhelmed her, everything an enormous effort. She'd hardly eaten, she should, she couldn't; even sitting close to the fire, she felt cold. She spent most of her time in bed, staring into the darkness. When sleep did eventually come, it wasn't for long, waking at the same time each morning, a metallic taste on her tongue.

When had the affair begun? Was it a clandestine meeting when Lizzie was away in Canberra? Was it when Claire moved into their home in the week after Tom died? Did their treachery start with a friendly kiss, an empathetic arm slung over a shoulder, a whispered compliment? Had they slept together in the bed she and Ed had shared, heads close, laughing, teasing?

Ed had got away scot-free, as men so often did. Had he had an inkling when he'd heard about Claire's pregnancy? When he met Jane for the first time, did he look into her eyes and wonder? The olive complexion, the curly hair. No resemblance to Jeremy whatsoever.

Why hadn't she seen what had been right in front of her? The nuances passed from parent to child, that fleeting something in the smile, a certain swing to their arms as they walked, an expression?

She had, for days, been weighing up whether to tell Jane. How to tell her? When to tell her? Not now, now wasn't the right time, not after what she had been through, the loss of two parents, the whole awful tragedy.

Fred jumped onto the bed, the length of his body warm against hers.

'Lovely old boy,' she said, stroking his dear old head.

She would leave things for a while, tell Jane later? But when? A month, a year? What possible good would it serve? Heartbreak for everyone with no resolution. Would Jane even want to know? Would she wish, like Lizzie, that she hadn't been told? And who should tell her? Ed, surely. No matter what, didn't everyone have the right to know who their parents were? Oh God, she was back where she started.

And then, an epiphany. Her dilemma had also been Alice's dilemma—to tell, to not tell, to tell who and when. It had been an impossible choice, one that Claire should never have asked Alice to make.

She pulled the doona over her head, wished sleep would come, if secrecy was a burden to carry, so was truth.

Whatever she decided, she would be playing God with people's lives.

When Lizzie lost Tom, she had turned to work and to Claire, but this time she didn't know where or who to turn to.

Once again, she rugged up and sat outside. There she could see Tom and Margot playing under the tree. On the day Lizzie discovered Ed was having an affair with his media adviser, she took refuge in the pantry where her children wouldn't see the tears. Tom came to her holding out a handful of blooms, his little eyes filled with concern. 'For you, Mummy, from the jacanda tree.'

Lizzie's fingers felt for the notch she had cut into the trunk to record Tom's height, his name carved next to it.

'Make Margot's name, too,' Tom insisted. 'And Penny's.' Penny had been their border collie, long gone now.

She laughed, telling him that one day he would grow as tall and strong as the tree. He was gone before she could make the second notch.

Tom died when the jacaranda was in full flower. In his tiny white coffin, he floated on a lavender cloud.

Lizzie was in bed when the doorbell rang. Alice didn't give up easily. Tenacity had been one of the things Lizzie liked about her.

She had been thinking about those traits she'd once admired, admitting now that perhaps she had tired of Alice's quirks, the way, over a lifetime, one tires of many things.

How often Alice irritated her, frivolous and superficial, her narcissism undimmed by age. Yes, she had grown tired of her. Quite fed up, if she thought about it.

The bell rang again, one, two, three times. She glanced outside expecting to see Alice's old Renault parked haphazardly on the nature strip, bird poo all over the duco.

But it wasn't Alice's car, and it wasn't Alice ringing her doorbell.

Lizzie opened the door in such a rush it flew back, hitting the wall with a bang.

'Mum?'

Margot's eyes skimmed unforgivingly over Lizzie, coming to rest on her exposed breasts. Lizzie drew her dressing-gown around her.

Margot rattled the door, flywire unleashing a cloud of dust. 'Are you going to let me in?'

Lizzie, still clutching her dressing-gown with one hand, managed to use the other to undo the snib.

Margot stepped inside, eyes searching the hallway before returning to Lizzie. 'You look terrible.'

Margot, wearing a leather jacket with jeans, did not look terrible.

'I'm only just out of bed.'

Her daughter walked purposefully towards the back of the house, boots adding authority to her stride. 'It's nearly midday.'

'Give me a moment,' Lizzie said, detouring up the stairs to her bedroom.

Groaning silently, she looked in the mirror—an old woman stared back. Hair not washed for days, the once determined jaw dissolving into the concertinaed folds of her neck, dressing-gown spattered with heavens knows.

She washed her face, pulling on a pair of pants and a blouse missing one of its buttons. A smudge of lipstick and she was ready to face her inquisitor. She practised her brightest smile and disappeared from the mirror.

'Darling.' Lizzie swept starlet-like into the lounge room, opening curtains on her way through, dust motes taking flight. 'If this isn't the loveliest surprise.'

Margot, who was patting Fred, looked at her mother suspiciously. 'You're not sick or something?'

'A virus, I think,' said Lizzie, seizing the opportunity to explain the disarray. 'Turning the corner today, though.' She removed newspapers from the couch and half-empty cups from the coffee table, with a silent prayer Margot wouldn't see the bottle she'd meant to retrieve after it rolled under the couch. 'I'll make you a coffee?'

'Alice phoned,' Margot said, watchful eyes on her mother. 'She's worried about you.'

How dare Alice involve Margot. 'Well, as you can see, she was worrying about nothing.'

'Mmm,' said Margot, eyes still scanning.

God, she'd seen the bottle. The empty bottle. She'd think she'd been on a bender.

'It's not like you to drink alone.'

How would Margot know whether she drank alone or not? 'A glass before dinner stimulates the appetite.'

Margot looked unconvinced.

Lizzie's foot scuffed at the furred edges of the rug, annoyed that at her age, in her own home, she needed to make excuses. 'What did Alice say exactly?'

'She wanted me to check on you, make sure you were okay.'

Margot followed Lizzie into the kitchen, where Lizzie added dirty cups to a sink already overflowing with dishes, including a wine glass or two.

'Why is there a spanner on the tap?'

The spanner had been in place so long, Lizzie no longer noticed it. 'The plumber's coming this week.' She had every intention of replacing it, but plumbers and taps didn't come cheap.

'Ask him to find out what's causing the water hammer while he's at it.'

Lizzie had also stopped noticing the bang and knock of the pipes, the old house shuddering every time she turned on the water. 'She. My plumber is a she.'

Margot rolled her eyes.

'I can't remember the last time you visited,' said Lizzie, wiping away spills and crumbs in-between making coffee.

'I can't stay long.'

She couldn't stay long last time either. 'I could make lunch or we could go out. There's this little place up the road.' Lizzie's voice was hopeful. 'They say it's very good.'

Margot flicked her hair so it fell long over one shoulder. 'Another time.'

Lizzie wasn't sure how many 'another time's' she had left.

'Have you thought about moving into something smaller, more manageable, one of those units with a nurse on call?'

A horrified Lizzie imagined a beige room, a small settee and coffee table, one or two treasured photos. No pets allowed. She pushed the vase of dead flowers to one side. 'This is my home.'

'A renovation, then?'

Lizzie had seen the before and after photos of renovations. She preferred the befores. 'I've let things go since Claire . . . then this darn virus. If you'd come any other time.'

'It's an old house, Mum. It needs work.'

Lizzie ran her hand over the timber benchtop, every dint and scratch familiar. *Never* was she giving up her home. She knew every corner of every room—where, behind an armchair, the wallpaper peeled, where the roots of the liquidambar made a slight bulge in the floor; at what time of day the sun bathed the study in winter; how each room of the house held a different view of the garden. Her life had been here, the house a witness to all her gladness and grief. She understood its idiosyncrasies, it understood hers. They had grown old together. Leaving would be worse than death.

'Three bedrooms, two bathrooms, the garden to look after. It's way too big for you.'

'I've managed so far.'

Margot raised a beautifully groomed eyebrow. 'You can't stay here forever.'

'That's exactly what I intend to do.'

Margot took her coffee and claimed the chair that once was hers. 'Haven't you ever wanted to get away from all those memories?'

'Memories of Tom?'

'Tom,' Margot's voice drifted. 'Everything.'

Lizzie sat across from Margot, hands around her cup to warm them. 'Everything?'

Margot dropped her eyes. 'Tom, you and Dad breaking up . . .'

The cup was suddenly heavy in Lizzie's hand. 'Is that why you don't visit?'

Margot shrugged.

'I hardly see you.'

Margot put down her mug with a clunk. 'We see each other every week.'

'It would be nice to go on outings together, have Molly and Jack come to stay.' Something spontaneous, not in the diary, not 'I'll get back to you' but never does.

'You know how it is when you've got kids.'

'I'd like to have you and Julian and the children over to dinner once in a while.'

'Life gets busy.'

'Not too busy for dinner at your father's.'

'That's different.' Margot's eyes flashed. 'Our children are the same age, Charlotte and I are friends . . . not that I should have to explain.'

'This was your home. It's still your home.'

Margot swung one long leg over the other. 'Mum, I hardly lived here, and when I did, you were locked away in the study or on the phone.'

And what about your father? Lizzie wanted to ask. He had rarely been home, never there for bathtime or stories or meals, away most weekends.

'I pretty much lived at Claire's.'

'You stayed here when Claire was in the UK . . . this is where you came to recover from your illness.'

'Illness?' Margot laughed a hollow laugh. 'I was a junkie, Mum. But that's not something we talk about, is it?'

Lizzie didn't dare speak of that time: the years of waiting and worrying; her beautiful daughter selling her body for a few dollars; the drug that turned her into a liar and thief; the terrible dead-eyed state of her.

'You still blame me?'

'It's not about blame, Mum.'

'Then what is it about?'

'I didn't just lose my brother, I lost my home, my family, my school. Everything.'

Lizzie pressed a hand to her chest. 'I thought you were happy living at Claire's.'

'We'd only just lost Tom and then you sent me away.'

'Sent you away?' She wanted to run from her daughter's words, words she could not hear, a past she could not bring herself to face. 'No, no, it wasn't like that, you must know it wasn't like that.'

'I grew up thinking you wished it was me not Tom . . .'

'I had no idea. If only you'd said . . . if only I'd known.'

'Mum, I was Molly's age!'

Lizzie reached for her usual justifications. 'I wasn't coping after Tom died and then your dad and I . . .'

Stop, she told herself. *Stop*.

'I had to work, and my job . . . the hours . . . Living with Claire seemed like a perfect solution.'

Margot shook her head. 'Perfect? Perfect for who?'

Lizzie cast around for an answer.

'Did you even think about me?'

'I never stopped thinking about you.'

Margot stood to go. 'I didn't come here to talk about this stuff.'

'Please stay. Don't go. Not yet.'

'We've got enough going on without raking over the past.' Margot slung her bag over her shoulder, pecked Lizzie on the cheek. 'Ring Alice. She's worried about you.'

Lizzie followed Margot out the door and watched her drive away, staring into the distance long after her car had disappeared.

CHAPTER 20

MARGOT FOUND A PARKING SPOT across the road from Jack's kindy. Too early for pick-up, she leaned back in the seat and closed her eyes hoping it might help ease the pounding in her head.

She should never have gone to her mother's house. Never. She ought to have known the feelings it would give rise to, the memories it would resurrect. Those feelings were impossible to separate, a great tidal wave of loss and remorse, of love and longing.

The call from Alice the day before had come as a surprise. Could Margot check on her mother, something vague about her not answering the phone, that she seemed out of sorts. Alice still making too much of things, she decided. But the call had played on her mind. Like it or not, she was the only family her mother had.

Margot had wanted to turn the car around the minute she arrived. The house, her old home, looked run-down, and the garden, which she had always thought of as wild and beautiful, seemed chaotic and untended. Tom's bedroom window, glinting in the low sun, drew her eyes reluctantly upwards. She caught her breath. *Tom.* She could see Tom at the window, smiling and waving. She had shaded her eyes thinking the light was playing tricks. And then he was calling, *Margot, Margot.* She tried to call back, *Wait, Tom, wait.* She wanted to say goodbye. She'd never had the chance to say goodbye. But he had already gone. She imagined his feet hurrying on the stairs as he rushed to tell her all the wonderful things that had happened since they last saw each other.

Transfixed, Margot waited, longing to see him one last time. Around her bees hummed, butterflies floated. Had she imagined him, her little brother so much like Jack? She was sure she hadn't. He had been waiting to see her. To tell her he had forgiven her for hating him, hating him because he had taken up so much space in her mother's heart.

After Tom had died, how guilty the six-year old Margot had been, that she had blamed him for her mother's absence in her life.

On the few occasions Margot visited her mother, she avoided the bedrooms where once she and Tom and her parents slept. The beds were empty now, but for her mother's. Shaken, she made her way up the front steps, the smell of daphne, heady and claustrophobic, beginning a headache that would last days.

Dear God, her mother when she'd opened the door, dressing-gown gaping, her dishevelment framed by a cloud of dust released when Margot rattled the flywire. The flight of emotion across her mother's face—disbelief, pain, shame—when she saw Margot, reminded her of Molly when she'd been naughty and needed loving arms about her.

Her mother had finally covered herself and unlocked the door. The house smelled stuffy and moth-eaten, and the blinds were closed. The deep gloom couldn't conceal the dirty dishes strewn about the room, the empty wine bottle forgotten beneath a chair, the trail of crumbs leading to the stairs. In the kitchen, a festering bin overflowed, and everywhere paint was peeling, rugs fraying, taps gone missing.

Alice hadn't been exaggerating after all. She felt a twinge of guilt remembering the message her mother had left cancelling her afternoon with Molly and Jack. She'd thought it unusual; her mother never missed a visit. She'd meant to phone but put it off, and then when a few days had passed . . .

Perhaps her mother really had had a virus. She might even be in the early stages of Alzheimer's. It's what happened if you lived long enough, didn't it? Perhaps she was having another breakdown? She shook her head. Her mother was grieving, and grieving had a way of undoing you.

Seeing Tom, being in that house, the feeling time had stood still, Tom haunting every room . . . it was as if she were that same six-year-old, who didn't know what death was, or what it meant, until the morning Tom didn't wake up.

She wished she hadn't brought up Tom, or her parents' breakup, or how it had been for her. Her mother had always been too fragile to hear her truth. She would crumple, she would dissolve.

Margot hadn't been unhappy living with Claire. Claire, Jeremy and Jane had been more like a family to her than her own parents. But they weren't her family. She had promised herself then, that when she grew up, she would have her very own family, a family no one could take away.

Margot couldn't remember ever talking with her mother about her addiction. For what mother wanted to talk about their daughter being a junkie, a smackhead . . . ? And what daughter wanted to tell her mother she had found in a needle and spoon the mother she had been looking for?

Nothing was resolved. It would be as it had always been, an unspoken agreement not to revisit their latest spat, as if they were both fearful of what might be said if they had it out. Her mother would visit the children as she always did, they would be courteous, as strangers are courteous, the coolness between them more chilly and, eventually, a slight thaw.

Margot's phone rang. It was Jack's kindy teacher concerned Margot was late. Was there someone who could pick up Jack? God, she'd never once been late for pick-up. She sprinted across the road, dodging traffic. The usual entourage of children, cherished artworks held in tiny hands, had well and truly departed. Jack was waiting, his teacher beside him, little face creased with worry. His mummy was always on time. Always.

'Jack!' Margot called. 'Jack.' She couldn't bear him to feel lost or deserted, not even for a second.

'Mummy, Mummy, where were you?'

'Right here, Jack.' She swept him into her arms. 'Mummy's right here.'

CHAPTER 21

LIZZIE WOKE TO FRED WHIMPERING. His nose was pressed to hers, eyes unblinking and pleading. He made a clicking noise with his teeth. *Walk me.*

For the first time in days, she didn't stay in bed, she didn't flick on the television or radio or open a book. She texted Margot to let her know she'd be along to see Molly and Jack, usual day, usual time. Margot messaged back that perhaps she'd forgotten they would be interstate visiting Julian's mother.

Lizzie had, since Margot's visit, seen the house through her daughter's eyes and decided not just to clean, but to relieve it of its sad past, starting with Tom's room. She would ring Ed. He would be puzzled, intrigued. Why did she want to see him? She would give nothing away. But first she must speak to Alice.

*

Lizzie heard Alice's car pull into the driveway. They had things to discuss, understandings to reach.

She opened the door, Alice's arms wide open, too. Lizzie smiled. 'Old friend.'

Alice threw herself at Lizzie, tears falling unabated. 'I thought I'd never see you again.'

Lizzie wrapped her arms around Alice.

They laughed at each other then, at themselves, and closed the door behind them.

Lizzie waved Alice into a chair, Alice adding a bottle of wine to the offerings on the table.

The conversation, long overdue, began.

'I phoned, I emailed, I even called round. But I suppose you know that,' said Alice.

'I needed time,' said Lizzie.

'Not being able to see you, to speak to you, has been very upsetting.'

'Did you think about what it's been like for me?'

'That is all I have thought about,' said Alice. 'Not just these past weeks but, like, forever.'

'Didn't you once in all those years think I had a right to know?'

'I didn't set out to deceive you.'

'Nevertheless . . .'

'It's complicated.'

Lizzie conceded that it was. 'Claire put you in an impossible position, the same position I'm in now. If I should tell, who I tell? When? The consequences if I do, if I don't.'

'All Claire's making,' said Alice.

'How did you know about Ed and Claire?'

Alice glanced anxiously at Lizzie. 'Where to start.'

'At the beginning.'

Alice crossed and uncrossed her legs. 'It was a Friday, around midday, lovely and sunny—I don't want to upset you.'

'Keep going.'

'I dropped by your place thinking you'd be home for the weekend. Claire's car was in the driveway, which wasn't so unusual. The side gate was unlocked so I just assumed you'd both be in the garden.' Alice gave her head a little shake. 'As soon as I saw them, I knew.'

Everything in the room was as it had always been, the furniture arranged around the fireplace, the blinds a little dusty, the rug soft beneath Lizzie's feet, its swirls familiar. But everything was changed.

Lizzie asked the question that had been on repeat in her head. 'How long was this after Tom—?'

'Lizzie, ask yourself how much you want to know.'

'How long?'

Alice stared at her feet, tiny in their pointy witchy shoes. 'About a year.'

Lizzie felt time slipping and merging, the loss of Tom, Claire gone, Claire and Ed . . .

'Do you know when it started? Their affair.'

'I can only tell you what Claire told me.'

Lizzie's face was burning, the rest of her ice cold. 'What did she tell you?'

'That it began about three months after you lost Tom.'

Sunlight pressed through the window, a halo of light filling the room only to retreat as if it had changed its mind.

'What else did she say?'

'Lizzie . . .'

'Tell me.'

'She'd gone to your place with plans to cook a meal and give the house a tidy before you got back from Canberra. She wasn't expecting Ed to be home, but when she let herself in, she heard him weeping.' Alice paused. 'She went to him, put her arms around him. She was crying, too. And before she knew it . . .'

Before they knew it, comforting arms extended to an embrace, a hug to a kiss, they kissed again, a deep kiss this time, not the way you kiss the husband of your dearest friend. Bodies pressed close, buttons undone, breath coming in hot gasps, neither willing to stop and ask themselves or each other what they were doing. And slowly, or quickly, their clothes came off, they looked into each other's eyes and saw the wrongness of it. And kept going.

'Her emotions were all mixed up,' said Alice. 'Everything must have been so intense. Claire spending all that time with you and Ed, everyone so sad.'

'There are no excuses for what she did, what they did.'

Alice nodded. 'I never fully forgave her.'

'And the baby?'

'She was going to England. She wasn't sure for how long, other than she wouldn't return until after the baby was born.'

Alice's voice faded; the room blurred.

Lizzie was back in Claire's kitchen. Claire was telling her she and Ed had had a falling-out; she was not herself.

'I haven't wanted to say anything, but really, it's been brewing for months,' said Claire. The knife she was using to slice the cake slipped from her hand and clattered to the floor.

Lizzie was mystified. 'But you and Ed get on so well.'

'It wouldn't be the first time politics ruined a friendship,' said Claire.

Claire was vague about the specifics of their argument, saying she was furious that Ed had helped pass welfare cuts she'd lobbied months to prevent. He'd become insulting, she said, saying he pitied Jeremy having to live with such a difficult woman and that perhaps she should go back to Legal Aid where her limited abilities wouldn't be noticed.

Lizzie almost laughed. 'Ed's never been good with strong women.'

'I don't care what Ed thinks,' Claire said, 'as long as it doesn't come between *us*.'

Lizzie didn't tell Claire she'd already asked Ed to leave. However irrational, it had hurt that he hadn't tried to talk her round as he had done—successfully—in the past. He asked if he could have a few weeks to organise things. They agreed it would be best to keep it to themselves until it was a fait accompli.

Lizzie put her hand on Claire's. 'Of course, it won't.'

'That's all that matters.'

'I don't know what I would have done without you.'

'We both loved Tom.'

Lizzie felt the tears burning behind her eyes, saw they were in Claire's eyes, too.

Claire passed Lizzie a slice of cake, knocking her cup flying, coffee dripping down the side of the bench. Lizzie had never seen her in such a state.

'We should organise a weekend away,' said Lizzie. 'The Lizzie and Claire antique roadshow in Tassie.'

'Speaking of *Antiques Roadshow* . . .' Claire busied herself cleaning up the spill. 'Jeremy and I are going to the UK for a while, can't say for certain when we'll be back.'

Lizzie was completely thrown.

'Jeremy's been away for so long we thought it might be nice to have some time together, a white Christmas—one of those spur-of-the-moment things.'

Since when did Claire do anything spur-of-the-moment?

'That's as clearly as I can remember it,' said Alice.

Until that moment Lizzie had clung to the tiniest of hopes that something might explain or excuse Claire. Since that night long ago, when Claire had reached out to her at boarding school, Lizzie had loved her. And now she didn't know what to do.

Alice looked at Lizzie. 'You're not still cross?'

Lizzie smiled, Alice maddeningly endearing. 'You had my back. You've always had my back.'

Alice poured the wine. 'We have each other's backs.'

They had forgiven each other. They would heal.

'To friendship.' They raised their glasses.

They were like an old puzzle, thought Lizzie, edges worn and familiar, each knowing where they fitted, each a part of the whole.

CHAPTER 22

MARGOT WAS ON INSTAGRAM, NOT posting this time but stalking. In a good way. There was something about Eloise; always the right word, the funny line. Margot liked all her posts, left flattering comments and regularly tapped out three *hearts*.

Eloise had followed her back but otherwise ignored her: not a *like*, not a *smiley face*, no *hearts*, no *rainbows*. It hurt in the most unreasonable way.

She put Eloise's popularity down to location, which was, in a word, beachy. She had come to realise there was more to 'beachy' than a glittering ocean and Instagrammable sunsets: think golden tans, windswept hair, friends meeting beachside, designer towels. And children. Not one or two, but hordes. Four of them belonging to the impossibly slender Eloise who, like their mother, had beachy hair, sun-kissed skin and the whitest—but not too white—of smiles.

If Eloise and her children didn't have the cutest socks, the dearest little hats, the most adorable shoes, all tagged with the names of makers who were at least as exclusive as their clientele. They wore slouchy knits and ecru linens and gathered around environmentally approved fires, cooked together, ate together, had fun together. Did every bloody thing together. Eloise's photogenic husband appeared to play non-stop with their children; he read to them at bedtime, and seemed always to have his hands around his precious Eloise's tiny waist.

Together, Eloise and her children and their equally beachy friends built Instagrammable sandcastles and played cricket, constantly shouting *Howzat*. And no matter how many sun-filled hours they spent frolicking on the beach, they seemed never to get sunburnt. Children were forever clustering around Eloise as she served homemade culinary delights—refer to Instagrammable kitchen—always vegan, always organic.

Molly's seventh birthday party was coming up and Margot was working her way through Eloise's posts in search of inspiration. She was thinking fairy lights and pastel-pink balloons. *Understated.* The birthday cake, a ballerina—Molly did so want to be a ballet dancer—all creamy pinks. Molly's dress would be softly pink and diaphanous, satiny ballet flats to match.

Margot's mother hadn't believed in birthday parties—all that consumption, spoiled children who wanted for nothing given stuff that would eventually be discarded to landfill. There was some effort made, a birthday cake, vanilla or chocolate, which, in later years gave way to carrot cake—no icing—and her mother running around at the last minute for candles. And there'd be a present, two when her parents separated. Always something thoughtful and expensive from her father, a voucher from her mother. Margot came to dread the singing of 'Happy Birthday', her mother always ending up in silent tears, all of them thinking of Tom: his missed birthdays, how old he would be, how good-looking, how funny, how kind, how very talented. She eventually told her mother no more parties, and instead went out with friends, drinking until she passed out.

Laughter rippled happily down the stairs. Margot, who was in the kitchen stirring stock into the risotto, smiled to herself. No one read a story with as much abandon as Jane. *More, Jane, we want more!* If she wasn't down soon, she would have to go and rescue her. Julian was in New Zealand, work again, and Jane's partner, Sam, was on tour, so it was, very happily, just the two of them.

Margot had looked forward all week to seeing Jane, dinner at a grown-up time and, for a few hours, being Margot not *Mummy.*

They'd only seen each other a couple of times since Claire and Jeremy's farewell. Jane had sounded okay when they spoke on the phone, but people could sound any way they wanted on the phone. Social media, same. Not that Jane was on social media. She thought it a waste of precious time.

She waited for the rice to soak up the last little bubbles of stock before adding more. She liked to cook; it occupied her head and her hands. Everything else in the house was taken care of; a cleaning lady came twice a week, a gardener once a month. Margot liked her life, she really did. Her days were busy. If Julian was home, she'd go for an early-morning sprint, hard and fast around the manicured streets of her neighbourhood, back in time to make the children breakfast and take Molly to school, often dropping in on Charlotte on the way home. Later a workout in the home gym and, if he wasn't at kindy, an hour or two pottering with Jack before his afternoon sleep.

Although it was difficult finding time between kinder and school drop-offs and pick-ups, she'd been on a couple of excursions with her camera, too. Margot felt guilty if she put Jack in day care, even if only very occasionally: doing something without her children at the centre of it somehow felt irredeemably selfish.

Even before Claire's loss, she hadn't been feeling quite herself. Her doctor ordered blood tests which came back normal. She took her blood pressure, listened to her heart, and noted down her weight. After Margot answered *no* to questions about low mood and diminished appetite, her doctor wondered if she was feeling a little adrift now that Molly was at school and Jack had started kindy. Margot had shaken her head and hurried away from the knowing look and intrusive questions.

Margot took the peppers from the oven, inhaling their fragrance as she scraped the sticky golden mess into the risotto, setting aside a few caramelised slivers for garnish. She aimed her camera.

'Please don't tell me my dinner is going to be consumed on Instagram,' said Jane, observing Margot from the doorway.

Margot laughed and put down her phone. 'You sound like Julian.'

'Listen to Julian.'

Margot laughed again and poured Jane a wine, herself a mineral water; a glass of wine would have been nice, she missed it, but she had years before decided not to risk replacing one addiction with another.

Jane sipped her wine. 'Those kids of yours crack me up.'

'You're so good with them,' said Margot, grating extra parmesan into a bowl.

Jane wandered around the kitchen. 'Anything I can do?'

'Sit down,' said Margot, 'and tell me how you are, how you've been.'

Jane pulled up a stool and leaned her elbows on the cold marble of the benchtop. 'Okay, I think. But those first few weeks . . . God. Waking up every morning and remembering that both of them are gone.' She shook her head. 'It's like being dumped by a huge wave. But yeah, I'm okay.'

And when you surface, thought Margot, you're winded and gasping for air. 'You must miss them terribly.'

'I sometimes listen to Mum on voicemail. Those long messages . . . She'd always start by saying: *Now Jane* . . . An hour later . . .'

They laughed and cried a bit, too.

'How's Lizzie?'

Margot told her about the state of the house, the state of her mother.

Jane looked vaguely amused. 'Lizzie's never been one for housework.'

Unwaged domestic labour, her mother called it.

Margot chopped the parsley. Jane disappeared to put on some music. Margot heard her shuffling through the vinyl, hoping to find something Jane would consider listenable.

Back in the kitchen, Jane, shaking her head, topped up her drink. 'Thank goodness one of you knows something about music.'

'I have eclectic tastes.'

Jane laughed and leaned against the bench. 'Ms Molly has been telling me all about her birthday party.'

'You know then that everything, I mean everything, has to be pink,' said Margot. 'God knows what her grandmother is going to make of it.' *Some of the children's mothers were coming, too,* she said. *Not her tribe.* Thank God Jane would be there, for how else would she survive?

Jane told her about an interview she was hoping to snag with a well-known writer who kept a low profile, and caught her up on some radio goss.

Margot ladled the risotto into bowls; Jane ferried them to the table.

Early twilight filled the room, Philip Glass played in the background. 'This is lovely,' said Margot. And it was.

'Mummy.' Jack was calling Margot from the top of the stairs.

Margot waved away Jane's offer to settle him. She carried him back to bed and tucked him in. He was asleep in a minute. She tip-toed out of his room.

'He's such a beautiful boy,' said Jane.

Margot smiled. 'He reminds me so much of Tom.'

'Oh, Margot.'

'If I tell you something . . .' Margot shook her head. 'Maybe not.'

'You have to tell me now.'

Margot hesitated for a moment. 'I saw him . . . I saw Tom when I visited Mum—'

'You saw Tom?'

'He was in his bedroom standing at the window, waving and calling to me. But I couldn't move, couldn't speak. And then he was gone.'

'A beautiful haunting,' said Jane.

'You don't think I'm crazy?'

Jane shook her head and poured herself a glass of water. 'Did you tell Lizzie?'

'She'd say there was a logical explanation.'

'Maybe Lizzie sees Tom, too.'

Margot hardly heard—unwanted memories flooding back.

*

Jane was sitting on the edge of Margot's bed, eyes not missing a thing. Margot sat up and pushed a pillow between her back and the wall, hoping Jane wouldn't see how unwell she was.

'Friday nights are the worst,' she said. 'End-of-the-working-week celebrations with the mates, a Fozzie and a prossie thrown in.'

Jane shook her head. 'I'm trying not to laugh.'

Margot was joking but it really had been a rough night, one client after another, hardly time to shower between them. She knew how she must look, her face bleached white, pupils pinpoint, hair wild with too much product and sex.

Jane pulled back the doona. 'Come on, it's midday, you've been in bed long enough.'

Margot caught the flash of concern in Jane's eyes when she helped her up. She'd lost more weight, so much that she hadn't had a period in months, and the concealer she'd applied to hide the marks tracking her arms had mostly worn off.

She plonked back down. 'I look pretty shit, right?'

'Yeah,' said Jane, sitting beside her. 'You do.'

'Great friend you are.'

'Best friend you'll ever have.'

'I forgot you don't do lies, not even tiny white ones.'

Jane looked amused. 'How about I rustle up a toastie? Or we could go out—my shout?'

Jane always shouted.

Margot shook her head. 'Later maybe.'

'You have to eat. Don't want you getting sick again.'

Margot hadn't long recovered from pneumonia, discharging herself early because, like, obviously . . .

Jane wasn't the only one to visit Margot in her little bedsit. Her mother came once a week, sometimes with Claire; her father, occasionally. Unlike Jane, they weren't good at hiding their feelings, their expressions ranging from devastated to disbelieving. They always seemed agitated, fidgety, constantly glancing at their watches as if they were counting the minutes until they could go.

Jane took Margot's face between her hands. 'Look at me.'

Margot blinked. 'Jane?'

'Listen. No, don't look away, listen.'

'Okay, okay, I'm listening.'

'If. You. Don't. Stop. Using. You. Are. Going. To. Fucken. Die.'

Margot fell back against the pillow. 'I'm tired of trying.'

Jane squeezed Margot's hand. 'Give methadone another go.'

Margot shook her head: methadone, rehab, she'd even tried going cold turkey.

'I can go with you if you like, and if you want, you can come hang out with me and my housemates for a few days, a few weeks, whatever.'

'You do know you should never trust a junkie.'

'Me, Jane, trust you, Margot.'

Margot didn't move into Jane's. She didn't last more than a week on the methadone program, but she never forgot, that even when she was the worst version of herself, that Jane was there.

A few months later when Jane found Margot so ill she couldn't get out of bed, she rang an ambulance. Margot recognised the doctor who admitted her, he'd been one of Julian's friends at uni. She had pneumonia again; she was malnourished; she hadn't had a period in over a year. She would die if she didn't stop using, said the doctor whose name she couldn't remember. It wasn't so much his ultimatum that frightened her, but the shock in his eyes when he examined her. She wondered for the first time in a long while what she must look like.

She hadn't been clean for three years.

CHAPTER 23

LIZZIE HAD ARRANGED TO MEET Ed on her side of town. She needed to be somewhere knowable and predictable, not in their old family home, certainly not at his, and not in a café where they might be overheard.

She sat at one of the few unoccupied tables, surrounded by groups of friends who'd gathered to enjoy the sunshine and a glass of wine, families running wild with dogs and balls, canoodling couples wherever you looked.

She had given some thought to what she'd say, how she might say it. She'd even rehearsed her lines. She *would not* cry, she *would not* lose her cool. Rational, restrained, responsible. As to how Ed would react . . . ? She didn't have to wait long to find out.

He was striding down the path, looking equal parts curious and annoyed. 'Lizzie,' he said, leaning in to kiss her.

She tolerated it.

He dug his hands into his pockets, looked around. 'We used to come here with Penny and the kids. Remember?'

She remembered like yesterday. They'd often walk there— Penny off-lead, Margot helping supervise Tom on the slide and swings that had long ago been dismantled. Dismantled, taken apart, pulled to pieces. Had they walked there after Tom? She didn't think they had.

It was those remembered moments that she often longed to share with Ed: laughing about that time Tom squirted shampoo in the toilet bowl, shaking their heads about the ridiculously expensive red sneakers that Tom grew out of in five minutes, Margot riding high on Ed's shoulders.

'Hard to believe we're so close to the city.'

'It is.'

He sat opposite Lizzie, the precaution of the table between them. 'What's this all about, Lizzie?'

Long limbs flashed past, ticks of approval on an endorphin-inducing sports bra here, an aeronautical heel there.

'Everything all right with Margot?'

'Margot's fine.'

'For fuck's sake, Lizzie, I don't have all day.'

Better just to come right out and say it.

'I know about you and Claire.'

His mouth tightened, eyes darting as if searching for an excuse, a lie, a putdown, one that would mock the foolishness of her allegations. 'I've no idea what you're talking about.'

He was nothing if not predictable. 'You and Claire had an affair.'

He stared, not at her but at something distant and forgotten, emotions flitting across his face. A rare unguarded moment.

'Jesus, Lizzie. What a goddam dreadful accusation to make.'

'What a goddam dreadful thing to do.'

'I've told you—nothing happened between Claire and me.'

She had, over the years of their marriage, come to know when he was lying, the beginning of a frown, a disengagement in the eyes, the slightest flutter of the fingers, an almost indiscernible shift of expression, all of which she was seeing now.

'Claire said it did.'

Ed's arms fell slack beside him, all pretence falling away. 'Claire told you?'

'She wrote a letter before she died.'

'What did her letter say?'

'She asked me to forgive her.'

'Have you forgiven her?'

He was really asking if Lizzie had forgiven him. 'In our home, in our bed?'

He flinched. 'I never meant it to happen, nor did she.'

'You never meant . . .' She shook her head in disgust.

'If you hadn't been such a hopeless wife, such a hopeless mother.'

She didn't want his stupid words to hurt. It pissed her off that they did.

A young couple wandered past, arms slung around each other, laughing in that intimate way lovers do.

They had once been in love, too. Their first few years together had been some of her happiest. They'd argued, of course they did. But then they made up. Passionately. He had been her first love. Her only love.

She missed them, those young lovers, no matter her mood Ed had always made her laugh. How every day he had told Lizzie she was beautiful, coming home to the house filled with candles— forever the romantic, wanting always to be madly endlessly in love.

What would their younger selves make of this couple at war, who, at that very moment, were thinking up the next hurtful words, the next poisoned barb?

'What sort of person has an affair weeks after their son dies?'

'It wasn't an affair.'

'What would you call it?'

His eyes were distant again. 'We loved each other. I was leaving you. She was leaving Jeremy.'

In the background, kids on skateboards whooped as they rolled the ramp.

'It was all planned . . . she'd even told Jeremy.'

He's lying, lying to you the way he always did, messing with your head.

'We were going away for a while, let things settle. The flights were booked, everything arranged. Once I'd told you, we were heading straight to the airport.'

Somewhere in the distance, a child shouted *mark*.

'The day before we were due to fly out, she came to see me. As soon as I saw her face, I knew she'd changed her mind. I won't lie: I did everything to persuade her. Everything.'

How had she not known? 'She couldn't leave Jeremy?'

'Or you.'

A moment of empathy for Claire, whose guilt and regret had lasted a lifetime.

'She was going to the UK with Jeremy, she wasn't sure for how long. I was still pleading with her when Alice—'

'Alice told me.'

He looked at her. 'You knew all along?'

'She filled in the gaps after I read Claire's letter.'

He recovered himself. 'None of it matters now. Claire's gone.'

'It does matter,' said Lizzie. She'd put off the moment long enough. 'There was a baby . . .'

Ed stared at her, his face blank before he fully grasped the enormity of what she'd said. 'A baby? You can't possibly be saying . . .' He stood up, sat down again. 'You're lying.'

'Claire told Alice she was pregnant before she left for the UK. Jane is your daughter.'

His face collapsed. 'Jane.'

Lizzie took no pleasure in that moment, no feeling of victory that Ed, at last, had his comeuppance. Perhaps if he had been the only one affected, but he was not. There was Jane to think of, Margot, Charlotte, his children.

'Absurd. Jane is Jeremy's daughter.'

'Jeremy had been away for months, something I'm sure you'll remember. It's impossible for him to have been Jane's father.'

Ed composed himself, clearing his throat, adjusting the carefully rolled shirt sleeves. The politician was back. 'What if Claire was lying?'

How dare he resurrect that old furphy. 'Why would she lie?'

'Or Alice . . . Wouldn't put anything past that woman.'

She scanned his face searching for a shred of guilt or remorse. 'I wouldn't judge others by your standards.'

'Does Jane know?'

'No.'

'Margot?'

'No, but when you tell Jane, you'll need to tell Margot, too.'

He shook his head. 'They mustn't ever know. No one must know.'

'They're your daughters,' said Lizzie. 'You're going to have to tell them. Not just yet, not after what Jane's been through, but soon.'

'She's not my daughter until a paternity test says so . . . and I've got no intention of doing a paternity test.'

'You feel no obligation, no duty, no care?'

'Claire didn't give me that chance.'

'That's hardly Jane's fault.'

'I've met her once, maybe twice. I can't even think what she looks like.'

'She has your curly hair.'

He laughed in that deprecating way. 'So does my neighbour.'

'When you heard Claire was pregnant, didn't you wonder . . . ?'

'That was months after she'd left.'

'Does Charlotte know about you and Claire?'

'God no.'

'Will you tell her?'

'Charlotte would prefer not to know.'

'I see,' said Lizzie, unconvinced. She screwed the top back on her water bottle. 'If you do decide to tell Jane, you will let me know?'

'That won't be happening.'

'You might think about it and change your mind.'

'You won't say anything to Margot?'

'It has to be you who tells her.'

Ed looked relieved. 'You know this comes at a very bad time. The media's been snooping around, trying to find dirt on me. I'll need you to be discreet.'

She tried not to hate him. 'I think we've said all that needs to be said.'

He pulled on his jacket. 'I'll walk with you.'

Lizzie picked up her water bottle. 'We're going in different directions.'

They walked away from each other, shoulders hunched, eyes blind to the cloudless blue sky. Lizzie remembered another time, their first date, that long goodbye; Lizzie turning to watch Ed's departing figure, only to discover he had turned, too.

CHAPTER 24

ALICE SAILED INTO THE LIFT, the thrill of the afternoon she'd spent with Emilio making her almost light-headed. The love-making had been exquisite. He was never in a hurry, tiny kisses to her fingertips, the back of her neck, the inside of her wrists, tender, teasing, coaxing. He held her tightly. She was beautiful, he said. And she truly felt she was.

Later, they talked shop. He'd had a couple of small roles since they'd last met and the excitement of a call-back for a part in an ABC miniseries that, ultimately, he didn't get. It was a relief, he said, to talk with someone who understood the courage required to turn up and audition when behind you stretched a long line of talent who wanted that same role. She gave him wise counsel, telling him, telling herself, how necessary it was for anyone leading a creative life to silence the heckling voices in their head.

If he had rushed her out the door, she forgave him, a call from a friend in need, something Alice understood better than most.

So absorbed was she in reliving each moment, she didn't notice how cold the wind, how threatening the grey skies. Alice Miller was on a high. She usually walked past the art gallery without giving it a second glance, but today she stopped, smiling at the children pressing little hands flat to the Waterwall, the wonder in their faces. Today, everything brought joy.

It wasn't until she was about to tap on at the train station, that she realised she'd left her jacket behind. She'd slipped it off when they were enjoying drinks and a short burst of sunshine on the balcony. It was her favourite jacket, an op-shop find, the green striking against her red hair.

The door to Emilio's apartment was slightly ajar. Alice called his name. No answer. She pushed through the doorway. Ah, there was her jacket, hanging on the back of the chair almost as if it were waiting for her.

She heard his laugh, a woman's laugh, too. They were on the balcony. Tears welled. She knew she was being ridiculous. It was how he made his living. 'You are amazing,' she heard him say. She should leave immediately. But she wanted to see this other *amazing* woman first.

Alice couldn't see her face, only the silver hair falling long down her back, Emilio kissing kisses along the length of her scrawny arm, a glimpse of his polished brown body gleaming against the cold grey sky.

Alice Miller hooked the coat over her arm, composed her face and walked through the door of Emilio's apartment never to return.

*

Alice held out the tray to a passing customer. 'Brie or blue?' she smiled.

'OMG, so creamy,' said the lady returning for seconds.

'Isn't it?' replied Alice, wearing a frilly red and white apron that tied at the back in a large bow. 'On special, today only.' She swept her hand to indicate the brie's position in the fridge, the same fridge that was slowly turning her into an ice block.

'Mmm, maybe just one more. Don't want to overdo it.'

When the company offered her the job, her only success from thirty interviews, she'd thought, How hard can it be? Offering trays of free dairy to customers. But it was hard standing for hours next to fridges and freezers, hard standing in a draughty doorway, hard smiling all the time when she had little to smile about.

Her legs ached, her back ached, her heart broke.

'Weren't you . . . ?' The lady surveyed her, cheese on toothpick halfway to her mouth. 'Didn't you used to be . . . ? You are! That weather girl, what was her name? It's on the tip of my tongue.'

'Alice.' Her name was Alice.

'Used to watch you when I was a kid. Bloody hell, getting old, ay. Hey, Darl,' she pointed her toothpick in Alice's direction, 'do you remember her?'

'Yeah,' said Darl, 'now you mention it. What was her name?' They wandered off, a couple of samples in the handbag for later.

Alice had been hoping for a bit of workplace chit-chat but soon discovered she was more of a nuisance than anything, always in the way when staff were stacking shelves, causing traffic jams in the aisles. She was also old enough to be their grandmother, great-grandmother in some cases.

Nevermind, the elderly liked her, often wanting a chat. Some said she was the first person they'd spoken to in weeks. Alice always gave them extras.

'Mummmyyyy, I want more. The lady won't let me have more.'

Mummy appeared, looking slightly miffed.

'We have a limit of three per customer,' explained Alice, who used to be the weather girl.

'One more can't hurt. Surely?'

Surely not, smiled Alice, handing out toothpick number five.

If she hated cheese days, she hated bickie and dip days more. People loved something for nothing. They'd mosey on past four, five, more times, to chow down as many samples as they could fit in, surprised when they discovered she'd been counting. Unfortunately, enjoying the product didn't all that often translate into a purchase. This was particularly worrying, as they'd been clear at the interview that if there wasn't a bump in sales on free-sample days, she would be retrenched. If you could retrench someone who worked casually for an abysmal pittance per hour.

'If you wouldn't mind using the toothpick provided, sir.' Her sweetest smile. 'And one at a time. Thank you and enjoy.'

She was working between four jobs: handing out samples in supermarkets, a day here and there as an extra, modelling—one success out of ten auditions—and life modelling.

Soon, a new address, a home of sorts, one she never could have imagined, but somewhere to sleep, a place to return to. Shelter.

Marcus helped Alice re-pose. 'Okay, everyone, back to work.'

Alice had quickly understood the necessity of strong lines and shapes, light and shadow, and stillness. The quality of

stillness was so much more than the absence of movement—
a stillness that Alice, so unstill, so unmoored, somehow conjured
in every pose.

She became increasingly confident, striking her own poses,
stretching, reaching, folding. Stripped of clothing that flattered,
that covered, that restrained, she had never felt so liberated.

'Okay, people, take ten.'

Alice enjoyed wandering among the artists and easels during
breaks. Always she liked Ursula's work the most, fluid lines, confident, enigmatic.

Back after the break, Alice adopted reclining pose, leaning
back on her arms, one leg over the other, head thrown back, hair
loosely pinned and coming adrift. Good geometry, she thought,
and something she could hold for fifteen minutes.

What would her mother make of it all? she wondered. Alice
was relieved she had died before age had made her daughter
unemployable. It would have broken her heart to know that
Alice, in her Third Act, was in even more parlous circumstances
than she had been.

A single mother without family to support her, she had raised
Alice on her own. Her whole life taken up with her daughter, she
never married, cleaning houses to support them. With no one
to babysit, Alice went with her, wandering rooms, looking at,
but not daring to touch, photos of the families who lived there,
making up stories about their lives.

Her back was beginning to ache, her bottom had gone numb.

Alice wasn't always welcome, some concerned *their* cleaning
lady wouldn't get anything done with a child under her feet. Her
mother, with no other choice, would leave Alice at home, radio
on, a little stack of books from the library on the table, a plate of
sandwiches and a piece of fruit for lunch, a little treat for afters.

Alice could still see her face, white and worried, as she closed the door, Alice promising she would be very good and never ever open the door or leave the house.

She had underestimated the demands of the pose—neck, elbows, back.

Alice hadn't missed having a father. Too many of the fathers she'd known came home from work via the pub and took out their torments on the wife and kids. Her mother had been vague about paternity, the story changing over the years. As Alice became more worldly, she wondered if there'd been an affair with a married man who, she convinced herself, was impossibly rich and terribly famous.

There was energy in the room today, she thought. Whether it was the pose or the mix of artists, perhaps even the light, each class had its own personality.

The instructor called time.

Alice, with some relief, reached for her gown, gave her arms and legs a good shake, the instructor extending a hand so she might rise elegantly.

'Beautiful pose, thank you,' said one of the artists.

'You held that pose with such poise,' said Ursula.

'Thank you. May I take a look?' asked Alice, as she joined Ursula behind the easel.

'Be my guest.'

'Oh.' Alice felt quite overcome: Ursula had seen inside her sad, sad heart.

'It's beautiful. I'm very moved.'

'That is the nicest compliment,' said Ursula.

'Would you like to go for a coffee?' Alice couldn't believe herself. It wasn't like her to make the first move, and really, the chance of making new friends at her age . . .

'I absolutely would,' said Ursula, packing up.

They discovered they both liked the same café, a neighbour-hood meeting place where patrons were as cool as their chilled glasses of wine.

'Tell me about yourself,' said Ursula, after they both ordered cappuccinos, refusing to be tempted by the lemon tart.

'Oh, I wouldn't know where to start.' But start she did, begin-ning with her career in journalism, breezy anecdotes that covered her many different roles, rueing that the old boys' club was as old and as white and as clannish as ever.

Ursula laughed. 'I shouldn't be laughing,' she said. 'Nothing's changed.'

Alice asked Ursula if she was a professional artist.

'Amateur,' she said. 'My first love is community theatre.'

'You mean like amateur theatre?'

Ursula shook her head. 'I work with communities who are marginalised in some way. Most of the performers have never appeared on a stage before, English is often their second language. They perform their own stories, stories of migration, of violence, of racism and poverty. It's theatre that gives people who are rarely heard a voice.'

Alice wasn't quite sure what to make of Ursula's plays. She loved the theatre, she quite enjoyed amateur theatre, but she'd never heard, and certainly hadn't seen, anything like Ursula was describing.

'I did do other theatre,' said Ursula. 'Never on a grand scale but I had some success. But after a few years, I got weary of stories about privileged white people pondering the meaning of life.'

Alice laughed. 'They're my favourite plays.'

Ursula laughed, too. 'God, it all sounds terribly worthy, but it's actually wonderful theatre and tremendously uplifting for the performers and the audience.' She handed Alice a leaflet. 'Come along. See what you think.'

Alice took the leaflet. 'I'd love to.'

Coffee somehow turned into lunch. They had in common giving up stable careers to live a creative life. Ursula had been an actress, though nothing of note to boast of, she said, tried her hand at directing but you know, boys' club again. She'd bought an old cottage in Melbourne's west yonks ago. Who knows where she'd be otherwise?

Where I am, thought Alice. She told Ursula she was soon to move, dodging questions about where. 'Still working that out,' she said, as if there were any number of options.

Neither had married nor had children. The more they talked the more they found they had in common.

'I could chat with you all day,' said Ursula. 'But rehearsals beckon.'

'I'll see you at the next sitting,' said Alice.

They shook hands and said goodbye.

Not too old to make a new friend after all.

CHAPTER 25

'JANE, THIS IS THE NICEST surprise,' Lizzie said, opening the door.

Jane had phoned earlier that morning; she was in the neighbourhood and wondered if she could drop by.

'So good to see you, Lizzie.'

'I've been thinking about you,' said Lizzie, enveloped in one of Jane's big hugs.

'Oh, wow,' said Jane, stepping back and looking around. 'You've done stuff to the house.' She sounded surprised.

'I'm halfway through a once-in-one-hundred-year spring clean. New rugs, new curtains . . .'

'Looks great,' said Jane. 'So do you.' She sounded surprised again.

Lizzie laughed. 'You've been talking to Margot.'

Jane laughed, too. 'She might have mentioned something.'

'Come on, I'll make you a coffee—white, no sugar, right?'

Jane wandered while Lizzie made coffee. 'I can see why you don't want to leave,' she said.

'I've thought about it, and Margot could be right, that it's better for me to have something smaller, leave the past behind, but I'm quite happy as I am. I have Fred and the garden and a car to tootle around in, and everyone in the neighbourhood knows me.'

'Now that you've done all this work, it would be a shame not to enjoy it.'

Lizzie had a feeling there was something on Jane's mind. 'Talk to me, tell me how you are.'

'Some days, yeah, well; other days, fine. Keeping busy works for me. Not dwelling too much. I talk to them you know, every day. Silly, I guess . . .'

'Not silly, not at all silly.'

'Lizzie?' Jane put her mug on the table.

Lizzie smiled hesitantly. 'Sounding very serious?'

'It's just that . . . and I hope you don't mind me asking . . . what did Mum say in her letter to you?'

Lizzie was caught completely off guard. 'She wanted to say goodbye, asked me to understand . . .'

'Nothing about me?'

Lizzie folded her hands in her lap to still them. 'I know she was thinking of you.'

Jane regarded Lizzie for a moment, Lizzie sure she could see straight through her.

'Did she say anything about Ed?'

Lizzie took a deep breath. *She knows, Jane knows.*

Jane held Lizzie's eyes. 'Lizzie, do you know?'

'Oh, Jane.' Lizzie felt almost relieved. 'You know, too.'

The two women, decades between them, held each other.

'I'm sorry, Jane, so sorry.'

'I'm sorry, too.'

'Claire told you in her letter?'

Jane shook her head. 'She spoke to me a few months before she died. Probably when she first had her diagnosis. If I'd known she was ill, I wouldn't have said the things I did. I was more shocked than anything. Upset for Dad. It haunts me the way she just sat there, she didn't try to make excuses or defend herself, said that I had every right to be angry and that she hoped in time I would forgive her. It must have been so hard for her.'

How awful those last few months of Claire's life must have been.

'Hard for you, too, Jane.'

'I did forgive her, like almost straight away, but I never said sorry for the things I said. And now it's too late.'

'She would have known—mothers have a way of reading between the lines.'

'I hope you'll be able to forgive her, too.'

Lizzie didn't want to shatter Jane's already broken heart, she didn't want to lie either.

'I have so many feelings at the moment . . .'

Their eyes met. They had both loved and lost Claire, they were both mourning in their different ways, they would each find their own peace. No more, for the moment, needed to be said.

Lizzie heated up their now-cold coffees in the microwave.

'Lizzie,' Jane cleared her throat, 'does Ed know about me?'

'We spoke yesterday.'

'How did he take it?'

'I wish I could tell you differently, Jane, but not graciously.'

She nodded. 'It's okay. He might be my biological father, but Jeremy's my dad. I'm so grateful that he was, that he still is.'

'And you were his daughter, his adored daughter.'

'Someone will have to tell Margot.'

'You know how much she looks up to her father . . . and to Claire,' said Lizzie.

'It's big,' said Jane.

'Now that you know, it would be wrong not to tell her.'

'Might be better leaving it until after Molly's birthday, though.'

Lizzie agreed. 'How do you think Margot is?'

'Yeah, okay, I think.'

'Losing Claire has raised a lot of things for her, and now her father . . .'

Jane sighed. 'Yep.'

'Once it's out in the open we'll all be able to breathe again.'

'How are things between you and Margot?'

Lizzie didn't often talk to Jane about Margot—it made her feel that she was talking behind her back—and then only in the vaguest terms. But she felt a need to unburden, also a feeling that everything had shifted.

'We argued last time she visited. We were both upset. But at least she opened up, told me a few home truths.'

'Home truths hurt the most.'

'Sometimes you need to hear them.'

Jane grinned. 'Maybe if you weren't so alike . . .'

'What?' Lizzie laughed. 'We're nothing alike.'

'Oh, Lizzie.' Jane was laughing, too. 'Both perfectionists, both bloody-minded, both a little touchy . . . Am I right?'

'I'm not sure what Margot would have to say about that,' said Lizzie, hearing the truth in Jane's words.

'She'd agree with you.'

'You know us too well,' said Lizzie, smiling and shaking her head. 'Anyway, back to Ed. Should I tell him that you know?'

Jane thought for a moment. 'No reason why not.'

'How will you feel if he ignores you or just denies the whole thing?'

'I'll feel like the rest of Australia.'

They laughed their heads off at that one.

'I've asked Ed to speak to Margot.'

'Good luck with that.'

'If he refuses, we'll tell her together.'

Lizzie's heart jolted. Her mother was slumped in a chair, feet not quite touching the floor. She'd phoned the nursing home a few days before, asking them to let her mother know she wasn't well and would be in as soon as she recovered. How could she have been so selfish?

'Mum,' she knelt beside her, 'it's Lizzie.'

She'd lost more weight, her head seeming much too large for her tiny body.

Her mother opened her eyes and clasped Lizzie's hand. 'Darling girl.'

Lizzie smoothed back strands of hair from her mother's face. 'You got my message?'

'They said you weren't well.'

'A virus,' said Lizzie kissing her forehead and avoiding the searching eyes. 'I didn't want to pass it on.'

'You look a bit done in.'

'Recovered now,' said Lizzie sliding a footstool under her mother's dangling feet. She pulled back the curtains, wound the window open and turned off the light. 'You should tell them you like to look outside.'

'They flit in and out so fast . . .'

Lizzie could complain but she'd complained about so many things. She looked over at Grace's bed, empty and stripped down to the mattress. 'Oh goodness. Not Grace?'

'Her boy came in. They must have called him. Never come by before. He cried and cried.'

'Was he here in time?'

'I'm thinking he was, but whether she was too beyond to know . . .'

She waited for him, thought Lizzie, waited until he was there beside her.

Lizzie arranged roses picked from the garden, positioning the vase next to a photo of her father.

Her mother's eyes filled with tears. 'I miss that man.'

Lizzie squeezed her hand. 'I do, too.'

Lizzie's father had died suddenly in his sixties. He had been sitting next to her mother reading the paper when he fell forward and, without a word, was gone.

Lizzie moved the roses a little closer so her mother could enjoy their fragrance.

'Look how lovely they are. Oh, wouldn't it be something to be holding a bunch like that in my coffin. What a fine last impression. Wrap them stems up well though, else those thorns will have my fingers bleeding.'

'What's all this talk . . . ?'

'I want to exit this world in style and enter next the same way.'

Smiling, Lizzie shook her head and investigated her mother's tray. 'You haven't eaten a thing.'

'That mush.'

'You have to eat, Mum.'

'And I will, come dinnertime.' She smiled, the paralysis caused by the stroke, tugging her smile into a grimace.

'There must be something I can tempt you with?'

'Wouldn't mind a cup of proper coffee, white with a bit of froth. Two sugars. Nice and hot is how I like it.'

Lizzie laughed out loud. 'Mum, you don't drink coffee.'

'A latte's top of my bucket list.'

'Let's get you into the shower so I can give that hair of yours a wash.' Lizzie placed the four-point stick within reach and helped her mother slide her bottom to the edge of the chair. 'On the count of three . . .' She placed one hand around the belt of her mother's dressing-gown, the other beneath her elbow. 'There.' Her mother gripped the stick, and slowly, they made their way to the bathroom.

After slipping off the dressing-gown and removing the nappy, Lizzie sat her mother on the shower chair. She positioned the shower-hose so the warm water flowed over her mother's neck and down her back, little knobs of spine poking skeletal through transparent skin.

'Ooh, there's lovely.'

'Warms the bones,' said Lizzie.

'Can we talk about matters serious?'

'We can talk about whatever you like.'

'I got to thinking when you didn't come in . . .'

Lizzie squirted shampoo into her mother's hair, her mother protecting her eyes with a face-washer. 'Thinking about what?'

'That there were things unsaid that needed saying.'

Lizzie paused. 'What sort of things?'

'I should have spoken of it years ago.'

'You haven't been worrying yourself again . . . ?'

'I want them said before I die.'

Goodness. 'Mum?'

'I wasn't the mother I ought to have been.'

The hose almost swivelled out of Lizzie's hand, water spraying the mirror and basin. How many times had she accused her mother of just that, hot angry words said through floods of tears? 'What's brought all this on?'

'We both know the truth of it.'

What point now, raising the past. It was done. However long her mother had left, she wanted it to be peaceful and free from regret. 'You mustn't go upsetting yourself.'

'It was the sadness, it filled me up.'

'Oh, Mammy.' Lizzie rinsed away the shampoo, soapy water eddying around the plughole.

'All them doctors I went to wanting to find out what was ailing me. Perhaps a little outing, they'd say. A new lipstick or a pretty dress, that'll fix you.'

Lizzie put an arm around her mother's naked shoulders.

'Missed half your life, I did.'

Those years they rarely saw each other, strained phone calls in-between. The demands of Lizzie's work and geographical distance much relied-on excuses to explain why they didn't visit more often. After Margot was born, Lizzie made more of an effort, with Margot and her mother bonding in a way that surprised her. More lost years after Tom died, Lizzie eventually re-establishing contact for Margot's sake.

'Wakes me up at night all those years gone and nothing good to come from them, can't get that time back.'

Margot patted her mother's face with the towel. 'You're not to go blaming yourself.'

'It's praying I am that it's not too late.'

'Too late for what?' asked Lizzie.

Her mother clutched Lizzie's hand, their eyes meeting in the mirror.

'It's sorry I want to say.'

'Mum.' Lizzie laced her fingers through her mother's. 'I'm sorry, too.'

Lizzie knew, then, what she had to do.

CHAPTER 26

ALICE HAD SO FAR BEEN able to hide her changed circumstances from Lizzie. Keeping up appearances. She should have confided in her, but she'd blame Alice for always being too extravagant— extravagance when you were poor was impulsive and chaotic, when you had means, a well-deserved indulgence, some much-needed pampering—and was too embarrassed to confirm she was, sometimes, exactly that. She would be sympathetic, concerned, certainly, but there would be judgement.

Although Lizzie also had to be careful with money, she owned her own home, falling down, but a house, nevertheless.

She wondered again where it had all gone wrong. She'd made bad choices: lovers, career, real estate. Was it, as Lizzie said, that women were a casualty of patriarchy? Or was it just her own stupid fault?

She could have married, preferably for money, borne children, lived a sensible life. She could be a loving and beloved grand-mother, babysitting grandchildren, whipping up gourmet meals in her neat-as-a-pin home, her biggest worry choosing which countries to visit on her next sojourn overseas.

Who was she kidding: she'd never owned a cookbook—not even a Margaret Fulton. Housework had wasted enough women's lives without laying waste to hers, and she would rather have a knee replacement than drift the ocean with elderly strangers in a glorified test tube. As for motherhood—she was much too selfish for martyrdom.

Since Claire's passing, Alice had been contemplating how lonesome she would be if she were to outlive Lizzie. Given her youthful outlook and, with the heart, doctors said, of someone half her age, it seemed the likely scenario. Outliving her friend was one of the few contests she didn't want to win.

Lizzie loved her, she knew that. She also knew she wasn't blood; her family would always come before Alice. Which was as it should be. But it was sometimes lonely, this island she lived on.

It wasn't that she didn't like solitude, those evenings with a book, something nice delivered, a glass or two of wine, that on hot summer evenings she enjoyed on the balcony. But lately, loneliness seemed always to be waiting, a drift of laughter or a glimpse through a window of people gathered, but it was in a crowd Alice felt most alone. Their bustle, their purpose, their eye to the future. Perhaps it was that her life was nearly over, oppor-tunities all in past tense.

The world of coupledom had only reinforced her aloneness; unpartnered, she felt excluded from their world. Married friends had drifted away. What to do with a single someone at a dinner party or couples' weekends away, and why, they'd wondered, often out loud, had she not been able to find someone to settle down with? It was as if being single made her deficient in some way. Unloved, unlovely, unlovable.

And then there were the assumptions. If one more person asked Alice about her grandchildren ... When she informed them there were no grandchildren by virtue of the fact there were no children, they became immediately flustered casting around for the right thing to say, most usually *I'm so sorry*, accompanied by a sad shake of the head. A barren woman, a thing of pity.

Alice walked through the rooms, fingertips trailing the curve of the wall. She didn't know how she could leave. Like a death, she thought, the denial stage when she'd fallen to the floor and beat her fists, furious at fate, more furious with herself. Then had come the sleepless nights, the endless weeping.

She'd waited until the last minute to bundle up her few remaining belongings. Her clothes she packed into a suitcase, unpacked it again when it wouldn't close, and made difficult decisions about what she could live without and what she could not. Most of her books she would leave to the new owner.

The landlord didn't even wait for her to vacate the apartment before putting it on the market. Though she disappeared during open-for-inspections, strangers striding through her home with aspirational eyes for weeks on end, felt like the ultimate humiliation.

The neighbours, who'd already had a good squiz during those same open-for-inspections, had laid bets on what price *the comfortable apartment with boundless potential*, would attract. Alice avoided auction day.

The new owner, the agent said, was a lovely young woman— why was it that young women were always described as lovely, what were older women, if not lovely—a professional. Head screwed on the right way. Recognised the value of good real estate. She'd done her research, all right. Couldn't wait to see what she'd do with the place.

The lovely young woman with her head screwed on the right way would likely update the kitchen with European appliances and replace the hotch-potch of tiles in the bathroom. Not satisfied, she would sand away the imperfections in the floorboards and paint the walls in whatever was that year's trending colour.

Alice told her friends in the apartments adjoining hers when they wondered why on earth she would leave, that offers overseas beckoned. And then thrown a lavish party befitting someone whose talents were of international renown.

Timing her departure for when those same friends were at work, Alice made her way carefully down the flights of stairs, boxes precariously balanced in her arms. She thought again of her mother, who, in her last days, had pleaded with Alice to help her escape her hospital bed so she might see her home one last time. Only now did Alice understand.

It was awful, the leaving. But hadn't she long ago made a choice not to surrender to the drudge of regular work and a mortgage? Just as she had chosen not to tie herself to one person for life or bear children. She hadn't just let life happen.

Back in her apartment she gathered her suitcase and the last of the boxes, a final glance over her shoulder. Life, as you grew older, was about letting go, she thought. She had let go of many things and survived. Even when she had been sure she could not.

She closed the door behind her and said goodbye.

CHAPTER 27

THE PARK WAS LEAPING WITH dogs of all shapes and sizes, every colour and breed and temperament, doting owners, arranged in a semi-circle, keeping an eye on their Oscars and Chagalls, watchful they weren't bullied by a Minnie or Beethoven.

Fred was yelping excitedly, tail whirring. Kneeling beside him, Lizzie unclipped his lead, reminding him he was the new boy on the block and to behave accordingly. He tore off, galloping and spinning, pink tongue lolling, clearly not having heard a word she said. His speed took the other dogs by surprise, the smaller ones barking their disapproval, the larger ones competing. Fred, who had given over to the joy of flight, was oblivious to the excitement he'd created.

Lizzie glanced around. No Poppy and no Anthony. Foolish to feel disappointed. For the best, really. Now wasn't the time for new friendships, certainly not male friendship. She'd make for poor company and her life was already much too complicated. And she really wasn't an early morning coffee sort of person.

The sun soon shed its wintry shroud, raindrops from an overnight shower still clinging to branches, a shiver of crystal. A church spire glittered in the distance. Children ran and called and played. An elderly couple held hands, smiling into each other's eyes as if they knew something no one else did.

Stepping forward, Lizzie joined the exclusive dog-owner circle. People introduced themselves, proudly pointing out their dogs, who, at first glance, looked a little too like their owners.

Snippets of overheard conversation included the Kathmandu sale and complaints about the fifteen-level apartment block being built close by. Someone slipped a pamphlet into Lizzie's hand and asked if she'd join them at their next meeting. She wasn't a joiner but nodded and thought vaguely that she might.

'Elizabeth.'

She turned. 'Anthony.'

He was wearing a beanie, scarf tied in a jaunty knot at his throat. At their age, scarves were a necessary part of the wardrobe.

'I'd given up on you coming.'

'Fred insisted.'

'Good on Fred,' he said, releasing Poppy from her lead. 'Off you go.'

A little more timid than Fred, Poppy took her time, watching the melee from a safe distance. Fred quickly spotted his new friend, Poppy the only other greyhound at the park, racing over to greet her. They sniffed and nuzzled, Fred hurtling about in full show-off mode, Poppy chasing after him, a cocker spaniel bouncing behind.

Lizzie glanced at Anthony, interested to see him in daylight. Unpretentious, she decided, mild of manner, a lopsided smile and a good straight back.

'How have you been?' he asked.

'Well,' she said. 'How are you?' If he was going to go on about aches and operations—past and forthcoming—she would be making a quick exit.

He smiled. 'No complaints.'

No complaints was a very good start.

Dog numbers were beginning to dwindle, people drifting away, Beryls and Brunos in tow, Fred and Poppy still gallivanting.

'Always a mass exodus around now—work, getting kids off to school. Can't say I'm sorry those days are over.'

It had been Claire, not Lizzie, who'd packed Margot's lunch, Claire who checked Margot's homework was in her bag, Claire who made sure Margot got to school on time.

'How about we grab a coffee?'

Hesitating, Lizzie ran through a number of excuses she could make. But it was just a cup of coffee. And the dogs were getting on so well.

'Please don't feel obliged.'

'Anywhere you'd recommend?'

They took an outside table, Fred and Poppy lazing at their feet. He saw her leaflet and grumbled about plans for another development a little further up the road, twelve storeys of Stalinism, he said, and chatted about the dogs and the weather.

Mothers with babies snuggled into slings gathered at one of the tables, fat little packages snoozing contentedly between milky breasts.

Lizzie having coffee with a bloke—what would Alice say?

'It's nice here,' she said. It was.

From behind her sunglasses, Lizzie observed a strong brow above inquisitive eyes—hazel, possibly. His hands were a gardener's hands—dirt ingrained in the cracks that age had opened up—moving in gentle rhythms as he spoke.

He leaned down and stroked Fred. She patted Poppy.

'Are you on your own?' he asked.

Down to the nitty-gritty before their coffees were even on the table. 'If you mean, am I married? No. Are you?'

'My wife died five years ago. It feels like forever and yet it feels like yesterday.'

'You must miss her.'

'Terribly, at first, but it gets easier.'

She nodded. 'Grief can't be hurried away.'

The young woman who'd taken their order returned, stating, with volume turned up, that Lizzie's was the latte, Anthony's, the long flat white.

They were quiet for a moment, blowing and sipping and watching commuters pile onto the tram, faces, when they looked up from their phones, set in resignation.

'Is it long since your husband . . . ?'

'We divorced years ago.'

'Shame,' he said.

'It would have been more of a shame if we hadn't.'

Anthony's eyes assessed her over the rim of his cup, Lizzie wary of long-term couple smugness: *staying together through thick and thin, weathering the ups and downs, being in it for the long haul*, when it was more likely they were trapped in a dreary, sexless marriage.

'What about children?'

'A daughter, Margot.'

'What would we do without daughters?' he replied. 'My two are very good to me, phoning and dropping by. Their fussing gets on my nerves sometimes, but I shouldn't complain.'

Lizzie changed the subject to their dogs, what couch potatoes greyhounds were, how gentle and shy and silly. They discovered they both loved gardens and gardening; surprised, not surprised, that they had acquaintances in common.

She finished her coffee. 'Well, must get a move on.'

'I'll walk with you.'

'Shopping and other bits and pieces to do.'

He stood. 'Perhaps I'll see you tomorrow?'

'Perhaps,' she said.

Perhaps not, she thought.

CHAPTER 28

ONCE UPON A TIME, THOUGHT Alice, as she was swept along in a rush through the train doors, she would have been paid the courtesy due her age, commuters stepping aside to give her first dibs on a seat. No longer. She did, however, conveniently forget that the last time she had been offered a seat, she had fixed the young man with a frosty stare and shaken her head. Did he think she was old or something? Like manners, train travel wasn't what it used to be.

The carriage filled quickly, passengers, phones in hand, earbuds in situ, plugged into endlessly entertaining digital worlds, took their seats without taking their eyes from their (infernal) devices. Alice managed to snag a window seat. For what that was worth. Windows from which you should be able to glimpse the passing world in all its glory and confusion, hazed with the breath of countless commuters. Surely whoever it was who now owned public transport could invest in a bit of newspaper and vinegar.

For most of her life, Alice had managed to avoid the challenges of train travel—Europe the exception, of course—but in the last little while the train had become a necessary form of transport. A group of school kids, breathless and smelling of cigarettes and hormones, piled in just as the doors slammed shut. A warning blast of the horn, a shudder and the train was on its way. She wriggled her bottom, trying, without success, to make herself more comfortable, bag positioned beside her to signal the seat was taken.

The train emerged from the tunnel into pale sunshine, streaking past leafy parks filled with workers enjoying their lunchbreak. Glimpses of graffiti slid past, long-ago messages of protest and revolt traded for tags that said not much at all. Rickety clotheslines and chimney pots soon gave way to highways heaving with cars, cavernous malls replaced shopping strips and dimly lit bars were lost to pubs filled with pokie machines, their Mardi Gras of lights and colour lucky for some.

The train journey to the place she now called home had at first filled her with remorse, crying for days about the way things had turned out.

The train swayed, passengers lurched and grabbed for the straps that swung like nooses above their heads. Someone dropped their phone and swore. In their tired windcheaters and cheap runners, the people on the train, people who delivered food and parcels to front doors, who worked in abattoirs and who, late at night, cleaned office blocks, had until recently, been as invisible to Alice as she, in her older age, had become.

Suburbs flashed past, tiny treeless blocks, streets empty of people. The train slowed, pulling into a station one stop before the end of the line. This was where the carriage emptied, the drawcard a huge shopping centre that sprawled for kilometres. A teenage girl loaded with shopping bags slid into the seat opposite Alice, arranged her bags into some sort of order, peeking into one or two like an excited child.

Dark-haired, voluptuous, lips a swollen pink, every man in the carriage had noticed her, some gawking, others glancing. Pulling a phone from her bag, the girl used it as a mirror to guide the addition of more mascara.

What was her story? Alice wondered: daughter of a single mother was her guess. More calculation than guess—that part of the world had the highest number of single mums in the state. Dad had nicked off. Probably to Darwin. Didn't pay child support or whinged when he did, terrified his ex might spend a few dollars on a lippy from Kmart. Alice ran a knowing eye over the girl: she'd likely already left school, worked in some dead-end job. Wooed by the myth of romantic love, she would be planning an escape from the humdrum of her life with a boy not much older than her. They'd marry young, children soon after, she'd work the double-shift, unpaid slave at home, paid slave at work. She and her partner would rent, they'd daydream for a while about owning their own home, reality soon taking over. Love would fly out the window. There'd be an affair. A marriage ended. Another relationship, not so different from the first. Who would she be, this girl on the train, when youth and beauty had fled?

If not for her mother . . . Alice remembered her insistence that she stay on at school. Although her mother eventually found full-time work as a ward clerk at the local hospital, they lived on a tight budget. Somehow though, there had always been money for whatever Alice had set her heart on: music lessons, tennis tuition, ballet classes.

It wasn't until her mother's funeral that Alice discovered how little she knew the woman who had devoted her life to her. She had been oblivious to the Mildred her mother's very dear friends spoke of: the hilarious mimic, the talented singer, the wonderful story-teller; nor did she know there'd been a long line of disappointed would-be suitors. It wasn't until then Alice saw that it had always been about her: the beautiful, the talented, the fabulous Alice.

The girl gathered her bags as they pulled into the station, Alice following her through the gates before losing sight of her. Waiting for the bus to ferry her home, Alice spotted her again, running towards a car, a young man behind the wheel, blasting the horn impatiently. He took off before she closed the door, wheels screeching their disapproval.

CHAPTER 29

LIZZIE STOOD IN FRONT OF the mirror. The long skirt and blouse with sleeves that dangled were all wrong. Flinging the skirt on the bed, she proceeded to try on half her wardrobe. How it had happened she did not know, but it seemed that every one of her blouses had dangly sleeves of one description or another, and so similar were her skirts, it was almost impossible to tell them apart.

If only Alice were here . . . she would pull something together in moments. Oh God! Alice? She had meant to offer her a lift, pick her up on the way to Molly's party. Molly had insisted that Alice be invited: Alice was funny, she liked playing with Barbie dolls and her favourite colour was pink.

Lizzie rang. No answer. She left a message: *There within the hour!*

Even if Lizzie missed her, it was only five minutes out of her way.

Jane would be at the party, too. And Ed. He still hadn't contacted Jane, though he knew now that Jane had known he was her father for some time. He didn't want to force things or make her feel uncomfortable, he'd said. He would leave it up to Jane.

I'll be fine, Jane told Lizzie. Nothing had changed. Anyway, it was Molly's day, and the adults could put their shit aside for a few hours.

Lizzie finally settled on the first skirt she'd tried on. It was colourful and happy and Molly would like it. A last look in the mirror did not reassure her, the red face and fly-away hair adding to the misfortunes of her appearance.

She jumped. The shrill ring of her landline. She must turn down the volume. Alice? No, it wouldn't be Alice. The very idea that anyone still had a landline . . .

'Lizzie.' The voice was vaguely familiar. 'It's Pete, long time no speak.'

The journalist Lizzie knew from her days in Canberra, sounded a bit croakier—she remembered the pack-a-day habit—and more weary, but yes, it was Pete. 'Pete, my goodness. It's been I don't know how long.'

'Found this phone number of yours from years back, thought I'd give it a go.'

Lizzie laughed. 'I knew there was a reason I'd hung on to my landline.' They'd been mates, one of the few journalists she trusted. She'd met him when he was a cadet, green about the gills but with a good nose for politics.

'Where did that time go?' he said.

'Had we but known . . .'

They chatted for a few minutes—the promises broken, the lies told, the principles lost.

'Outta here just as soon as the super ratchets up.'

'Young Pete talking about retirement?'

'Not so young anymore, Lizzie.'

'So, why's Australia's best investigative journalist ringing me?'

'I'm doing a piece on your ex.'

'Ed?'

'Just between you and me. Right?'

'Of course.'

'You've heard there's going to be a spill?'

What did he want? 'I have.'

'It's looking like Ed has the numbers.'

Ed had been working towards this moment for the last forty years. 'Only a matter of time.'

'An old rumour's resurfaced.'

'I'm sure there're plenty of those.'

'It involves your friend Claire, who just passed.'

Lizzie sat down. 'What about Claire?'

'The rumour about Claire having an affair with Ed not long after you lost your little boy.'

She closed her eyes. Had she been the only person who hadn't known?

'Lizzie, you still there?'

'Yes, sorry . . . I . . .'

'I . . . I assumed you knew?'

Lizzie recovered her voice. And her mettle. 'I heard those rumours, too.'

'Sorry to raise it again especially so soon after . . . You and Claire remained friends, so I put it down to scuttlebutt.'

'I thought you were above hatchet jobs.'

'The public has a right to know what the aspiring PM has been up to.'

'The public doesn't care.'

'He's not fit to be in government, Lizzie, and he's certainly not fit to run the country.'

'You're not just talking about his affairs, are you?'

'No, I'm not.'

'I'm still not sure what this has to do with me?'

'Questions will be asked if I don't make mention of something that's common knowledge. Conclusions drawn. I need you to confirm or deny.'

'When will this piece be published?'

'Still undecided, but no more than a day or two.'

'What is it you would like me to say, exactly?'

She drove off, head full of her conversation with Pete. Distressing enough for Margot to find out about her father and Claire, but to hear without any warning in the media . . .

Lizzie would take Ed aside, tell him they needed to talk. Either she would phone him later that night or they could meet early the next day? She had a plan, she felt better when she had a plan.

Shit. She turned the car around. She'd forgotten Molly's gift.

And now she was running late.

Lizzie pulled up outside Alice's apartment, one in a block of four, half-expecting her to be waiting on the footpath tapping a booted foot impatiently or engrossed in a book on her second-floor balcony. But there was no Alice waving madly or calling *Come on up*. Running late, thought Lizzie, a last-minute touch-up—hair, makeup, wardrobe.

She liked driving across the river to that part of town. It had been months since she'd visited Alice in her lovely apartment, the owner undertaking a restoration that seemed never to end. It was a perfectly-Alice apartment—what Claire used to say— with its sinuous curves and gloriously ornate ceilings and glowing floorboards, a tiny balcony floating in the treetops.

Lizzie reflected again that their friendship had survived Claire. They had been seeing more of each other, as if they realised in their time apart, that friendship was precious and not to be squandered. Not on one of those occasions had they mentioned Claire, but every now and then, Lizzie had the uninvited thought that Claire had drawn them closer together.

Buzzing apartment four, she noticed Alice's name had been replaced by another. Perhaps it was a security measure or one of Alice's fancies.

She waited. Tried again. Still no answer.

'Hey.'

Lizzie turned, a twenty-something exposing the bits a seventy-something covered up. Pushing at the glasses poised precariously on the tip of her nose, she tried not to give in to feeling old, unbeautiful and irrelevant. 'I was looking for Alice Miller?'

'Alice? She moved out a few weeks ago.'

Lizzie was sure she'd misunderstood. 'Moved? Out of her apartment? Permanently?'

'She. Threw. The. Most. Awesome. Goodbye Party.'

Of course she did. 'Did she leave an address?'

She shrugged sculpted shoulders. 'She was heading off overseas—work, I think.'

Lizzie thanked her, promising to pass on hugs and kisses and to tell Alice they all missed her *like* so much. She sat a few minutes in her car feeling slightly unnerved: Alice no longer in her apartment, Claire gone.

The next stage of life, that stage . . .

She fished in her bag for her phone. Alice had texted: *dont pick up on way c u there*

Lizzie responded: *I'm at your apartment?*

Cars filled Margot's driveway, Lizzie eventually sneaking her old Mazda, ding in the passenger door, between a Porsche and an Audi. She left it clinging haphazardly to the nature strip, regretting she hadn't made time to go to the carwash.

Lizzie rang the doorbell. A young woman, camera around her neck, answered and asked if it was possible Lizzie had the wrong address. After Lizzie assured her she was an invited guest—the adored grandmother, no less—she was granted entry.

The house had been taken over by little girls a-flight in gossamer wings and pink tutus, magic wands granting their every wish. Lizzie stopped to watch them posing like rock stars for the lady with the camera. She shook her head. Childhood didn't last five minutes these days.

Molly zoomed down the hallway, leaping into her arms. More of a tomboy than a fairy, thought Lizzie, spinning her around and kissing the top of her head. 'Happy Birthday, Miss Molly Newman.'

'You can put your present over there,' Molly pointed to a table piled high with glitter and ribbon. 'Mummy says we won't be opening family presents until everyone has gone home.'

Lizzie gave her another twirl.

'I'd be careful after what she's eaten,' said Margot, pecking her mother's cheek.

Lizzie looked at her lovely daughter, knowing that her life was about to be upended, wishing there was some way she could protect her from the past.

Molly wriggled down and joined her friends who were arranging furniture in an enormous pink Barbie house. Lizzie couldn't see inside Barbie's home without getting down on her knees, but she was in no doubt it would be filled with labour-saving devices and a walk-in wardrobe overflowing with designer handbags.

'Yes, Mum,' Margot whispered, 'it's a Barbie house—perpetuating gender stereotypes and all that.'

Lizzie returned the kiss. 'Sorry, I'm late—roadworks.'

'You missed the Fairy Godmother.'

'There'll be plenty more birthdays.'

Margot glanced at Lizzie's sandals, eyes flitting to her hair. 'Well, you're here now.'

Lizzie smoothed her hair and wondered if her toenails needed attention.

'Girls,' called Margot, 'Olivia's mummy is doing pass-the-parcel in the cinema room.'

A dozen or so fairies, ringlets tumbling down tiny backs, deserted Barbie's dream home and fluttered upstairs.

'I'll get you a drink,' Margot said, heading into the kitchen, silky pants swishing around slender ankles, lacy top hugging her petite figure, Lizzie trailing behind like so much flotsam.

'Lizzie, lovely to see you.' Charlotte slid cool and elegant from her seat, kissed Lizzie and indicated the chair next to hers.

'Hey,' said Jane, throwing an arm around her.

Lizzie was grateful for Jane's presence—an ally in a sea of pink. She thought perhaps Jane might be as grateful to see her.

Margot introduced Lizzie to her friends—Tiffanys and Victorias who appeared to have watched the same three-hour YouTube makeup tutorial—milling around the marble benchtop sipping champagne and ignoring both the children and the hors d'oeuvres.

Lizzie felt the sweep of their eyes (and eyelashes). They would be wondering how such a dishevelled creature gave life to the immaculate Margot.

The topic under intense discussion was private schools, the woes of deciding which school their daughters would attend post-primary. A girls-only school, an absolute must, they agreed.

They were also in furious agreement about fees, an outrage when you added uniforms and overseas jaunts and who knew how many fundraisers to the cost. But then, you get what you pay for.

Had they not heard of the many excellent public schools? wondered Lizzie. Had they not followed the research? Didn't they know that kids from public schools did better at uni? Did no one read the newspaper anymore?

Jane had once said that Margot only met and mixed with people like her, white and wealthy, and although she didn't say, they were both thinking, entitled. But then, Jane had said, wasn't that true of them, too? Would they read that publication, watch that channel, listen to people who had opposing views? Didn't they also live in their own reinforcing enclave?

'There's a public school not far from us, has a great reputation, apparently,' said Sarah. 'Not quite the right fit for Harry, unfortunately.'

'The thing is,' said Monique, 'you don't know who they might meet if they go to just any old school.'

The young women blinked agreement and sipped thoughtfully. 'Yes,' said Isabelle, who knew what to expect of children whose parents weren't prepared to make an investment in their education.

They moved on to the problem of nannies. Live-in or forty-hour-week contracts? Discuss.

'Alice is here, Alice is here,' announced a beaming Molly, dragging Alice through the door. Alice, hair in a long plait, was wearing turmeric-coloured pants and a beautifully arranged pink shawl. Buckles shone at her feet.

'Sorry, I'm late.'

Margot dutifully kissed her hello, she shook hands with Jane, and gave Lizzie a hug, whispering, 'Don't say anything, explain later.'

Margot introduced Alice as a friend of her mother's, Margot's friends exchanging amused glances.

'Alice is my greatest-aunty,' Molly said. 'And she likes Barbie dolls.'

Victoria looked at her phone, looked at Alice, again at her phone. She let out a little squeal. 'You are, I knew I'd seen you . . .' She waved her phone in the air. 'That ad . . . You know when you need your grandson to show you how to turn on the computer. My dad was like, didn't she used to be that weather girl? Wait till I tell him.'

'Say hi to your dad from Alice who used to be the weather girl,' said Alice, reaching for a champagne.

'What's a weather girl?' asked Molly, dragging Alice out of the kitchen.

'A meteorologist,' said Alice.

Lizzie saw Ed out of the corner of her eye, talking to the other men who'd gathered around the barbecue. She glanced at Jane. She'd seen him, too.

Male laughter and the slapping of masculine thighs drifted through the open window, men hovering, artisan beers in hand. Julian was basting whatever sacrifice was on the spit, and Ed was playing Everyman, impressing the younger men with one of his many practised anecdotes.

Jane left the table, gave Lizzie a look that said *here goes*, and headed outside. Lizzie watched her approach Ed, who for a moment, looked taken aback. Jane smiled, held out her hand for a handshake. Ed's face when he took her hand: overwhelmed and quite emotional. He quickly recovered, handing Jane a beer. They appeared to chat amiably. Ed would be relieved, thought Lizzie: Jane wasn't going to threaten his career, she wasn't going to make a fuss.

Margot glanced at Ed and Jane a couple of times, a quizzical expression before she disappeared with a tray of fairy bread.

Lizzie's phone pinged. A message from Pete: the article would be posted online later that arvo.

CHAPTER 30

WHEN THE BEDRAGGLED FAIRIES HAD gone home clutching their thank-you-for-coming goody-bags containing lip gloss and sparkly nail polish, Margot organised the grandparents around the table so they could give a tired Molly their presents.

Alice, who had spent most of the afternoon with Molly, steadfastly refusing to meet Lizzie's eye, was laughing about something with Jane.

Lizzie glanced anxiously at her watch; she would have to wait until presents were given before taking Ed aside.

Jack wanted to sing 'Happy Birthday' again. Molly squirmed with happiness as she blew out another seven candles and made a second wish; Tom blowing, too. Lizzie wondered what he would have looked like had he lived to be seven or seventeen, any age older than three-going-on-four.

Ed smiled at Lizzie over the birthday cake, or what was left of its three pink tiers, the ballerina long demolished. She returned his smile, imagining thrusting a nearby knife down his throat. Something she would have told Claire, had Claire not had an affair with her husband, had she not been dead.

Molly tore open her presents; the first from Ed and Charlotte—a necklace, its silver locket engraved with Molly's name.

Margot beamed at her father. 'It's beautiful, Dad. Thank you.'

'Thank you, Grandpa.' Molly flung her arms around his neck. 'Thank you, Charlotte.'

Lizzie passed Molly her gift, Molly tearing excitedly at the paper. 'A book.' Molly looked at the cover and laughed. 'Princesses don't wear black, Grandma, they wear pink.'

'She wears pink, too,' said Lizzie. 'But when she is saving the world, she wears black.'

'Mmm,' said Margot, busying herself clearing the floor of wrapping and ribbons.

Molly flicked through the pages. 'Mummy, look, the princess is wearing a cape.'

'I like the sound of this princess,' said Alice. 'I'd like to meet her.'

'We can sit over there,' said Molly, tugging at Alice's hand.

'You don't think Molly is a little too young to be reading this book?' asked Margot, her arms full of discarded wrapping paper.

'It's recommended for five-to-eight-year-olds.'

'I don't want Molly having nightmares.'

'Mummy, Mummy,' Molly was back, still holding Alice's hand, 'can I take my new book to Show and Tell on Monday?'

'Of course, you can,' said Lizzie.

*

'No, I won't.' Molly's face was all scrunched up, blue eyes filled with unshed tears.

They were in Molly's bedroom, Margot wanting to post a photo of Molly wearing the locket her father and Charlotte bought for her birthday. 'Molly, you will do as I say.'

'I don't want any more photos. You're always taking photos.'

Molly was overtired. 'Molly, you're setting a bad example for Jack.'

Molly stuck out her bottom lip. 'You're mean.'

Margot felt suddenly exhausted. The day, the preparation, wanting everything to be perfect, had caught up with her. 'Mummy is not mean.'

'You're mean to Grandma, too.'

Margot was completely thrown. 'Mummy is not mean to Grandma.'

Molly stamped her foot and clutched her princess book to her chest.

'Molly, what did I just say.'

Jack jumped up and down on the bed. 'Mean, mean, mean—'

'Jack, stop it!' Margot could hear herself shouting. She jerked him across the bed. 'Right now!' She never shouted.

Jack burst into tears.

'Okay.' She grabbed Molly by the arm. 'Time out for both of you until you calm down.'

Molly started sobbing. 'I hate you, I hate you.'

Margot raised her hand, remembering another birthday, another raised hand.

It would have been Tom's fourth birthday. The house in terrible mourning for the little boy lost. Margot's father hadn't been home for days. She was sure he would be back, the family together for Tom. Her mother was in his bedroom. If she listened at the door, she could hear her crying.

Margot sat outside Tom's room in her prettiest dress, her arms around her knees rocking and waiting. Mummy wished she'd died instead of Tom; she loved Tom more than she loved her; it was her fault Tom was dead. Lunchtime came and went. No sign of her father, her mother still in Tom's room. She started to get angry. Angry with the world. Angry with her mother. Angry with her father for not being home on Tom's birthday. Angry with Tom for dying. Angry and sad.

She threw open Tom's door. His room was exactly as he'd left it, posters on the walls, toys scattered on the floor, books piled haphazardly on shelves. Her mother was lying on Tom's bed, his pillow crushed to her chest, her face all squashed up, her eyes swollen and red. She didn't look like her mummy anymore. 'You're always in Tom's room,' she screamed. 'You never come to my room.'

Her mother sat up. 'Margot, darling—'

'I hate Tom. I'm glad he's dead. I hate him, I hate him.'

Her mother's hand lashed out, striking Margot's face. 'Get out,' she screamed. 'Get out of Tom's room.'

Margot ran sobbing to her bedroom, a red welt blooming on her cheek.

Margot's hand fell into her lap. Had she really been about to hit her own daughter? 'Molly, come here, sit with Mummy.'

Molly's sobs subsided. She wiped a runny nose on her sleeve. 'I didn't mean it, Mummy.'

'Sometimes we say things we don't mean when we're angry.' Margot sat Molly on her knee. 'Of course, Mummy loves Grandma.'

Molly rested her head on Margot's shoulder, fingers playing with the locket Margot wore around her neck. 'Did Grandpa and Charlotte give you your locket, too?'

'No, I bought it a long time ago.'

'Is there a photo inside?'

Margot hesitated. She had put away all photos of Tom when Molly was born. How to tell her children that the happy, smiling boy in the photos, died in his sleep? For years after his death, Margot had been afraid that when she went to sleep, she too might not wake. She didn't want her children growing up with that same fear. She kept a photo of Tom close to her heart instead.

'Can I see?' asked Molly.

Margot reluctantly opened the locket.

'A little boy.' Molly clapped. 'What's his name?'

'His name is Tom. He was my little brother.'

Jack wanted to look, too.

'Tom, Tom,' he said.

'That's right,' said Margot. 'Tom-Tom.'

Molly looked at the photo more closely. 'I saw a picture of Tom in Grandma's bedroom. Sometimes he sits on her knee when she reads a story.'

Margot sat very still. 'Do you tell Grandma you see him?'

'She already knows.'

Did her mother see Tom, too?

'Where is Tom now?'

'He died a long time ago.'

'Is he in heaven?'

Margot nodded.

'Oh, Mummy.' Molly hugged her. 'It's all right to be sad.'

Margot buried her face in Molly's curls.

Molly slipped from her knee. 'I want to find a photo to put in my locket.'

Margot smiled. 'Whose photo would you like?'

'Grandma's.'

CHAPTER 31

WHEN THE CHILDREN WERE PLAYING outside, Charlotte and Julian supervising, Lizzie told Jane that an investigative piece on Ed, including an alleged affair with Claire, was about to be posted online. They agreed: she had to talk to Ed.

Lizzie eventually found him scrolling through his phone on the verandah. 'Have you got a few minutes?'

He nodded, barely acknowledging her.

'In the study where it's private.'

He looked up from his phone. 'If this is about Jane, we're good.'

'It's about Margot.'

He sighed, slipped his phone into his pocket and followed her into the study. She closed the door behind them.

The room was dark and sombre, masculine, thought Lizzie, where important men's work was done.

'What is it this time?'

'You must tell Margot. Now. Today.'

He looked confused. 'Now? At our grandchild's birthday party?'

'Yes, you have to take her aside and tell her.'

'What's the rush?'

'She's your daughter, she has a right to know.'

He offered Lizzie a cognac, poured one for himself. 'Why upset her needlessly, what possible good can come from it?'

She refused the drink. 'We've already spoken about this.'

She saw the build-up to nasty in his eyes, heard it in his tone. 'You want to turn Margot against me. Is that it?'

'This isn't about me, it's not about you either, this is about Margot.'

'You never could leave things alone, could you?'

'No more secrets, Ed.'

He stood behind the desk as if he was already prime minister. 'I know what you're up to.'

She laughed at him. 'Stirring my witch's brew?'

'You can laugh,' he said. 'But it's me Margot comes to for advice, me she trusts. It's me she wants in her life. Not you.'

He knew how to hurt her, but this time she didn't give him the pleasure of her tears, this time she saw the fear behind the bluster.

She glanced at her watch. Pete had warned her about the risk of Ed knowing before publication—he'd bring in the silks, try to shut the story down—but she couldn't stall any longer. 'A reporter rang asking me about your affair with Claire.'

He slammed down his cognac. 'What the . . . Jesus fucking Christ. Who? What's his name?'

'I can't give you the name, Ed. I'm only telling you, so you understand the urgency.'

He took a step towards her. 'I want the name of that fucking journo.'

'You'll find out soon enough,' she said.

His mobile pinged, then pinged again. And again. He snatched the phone from his pocket, eyes panicked, hands shaky.

He stared at the screen. 'Fuck,' he said. 'Prying into my fucking private life . . .'

Yeah, and the rest . . . 'It's going to be all over the media which is why you have to speak to Margot.'

For a moment she thought he was going to throw the phone in her face. 'Margot is the least of my worries.'

'For God's sake, Ed.'

He was already on the phone to his media adviser, screaming at her to find out where the story was coming from, what was he bloody paying her for.

'This isn't about your political career, it's about your *daughter*.'

He blundered about the room. 'One thing at a bloody time.'

'Your daughter is not a thing!'

He stared at his phone. 'Shit.'

'Going viral?'

He advanced on her, face all twisted. 'This is all your doing.'

'No, Ed, it's all your doing.'

'You ruined everything.'

'No, Ed, you ruined it a long time ago.' She walked away, stopped and turned. 'Oh, and by the way . . .'

He looked up from his phone.

'You're not going to be PM, Ed. You're never going to be PM.'

Margot pushed through the door, looking from one parent to the other.

'Your father has something to tell you.'

*

Their faces when she opened the door: her father guilty, her mother, shaken. How dare they argue, no matter how quietly, in her house on Molly's birthday? She'd hoped they'd grown older and wiser. But they'd just grown older. They were as temperamental, as impulsive, as selfish as they'd always been.

Her father looked somehow dishevelled, and there was a splash of something syrupy on his very nice jacket.

'What did you want to tell me?'

Her father stared in fury at her mother.

Cancer, thought Margot. He's been diagnosed with cancer. He has months left to live. 'Dad . . . ?'

'Margot.' He raised his arm almost as if in salutation, then let it fall beside him.

Margot moved from the doorway into the room. 'Do we need to sit down?'

'Yes, let's sit down,' said her mother taking Margot's arm, asking where the children were, what they were doing.

'Julian's with them,' said Margot. 'He's set up the tee-pee in the garden.'

'And Charlotte? Where's Charlotte?' asked Ed.

'Making Jane and Alice a coffee.' Jane and Alice were enjoying each other's company so much they hadn't noticed Margot slip past.

Lizzie looked at Ed. Ed looked away.

'So . . .' asked Margot.

'Margot, I . . . You know I love you very much,' said Ed.

A little knot tightened in Margot's tummy.

'A long time ago, decades ago, I had an affair, a stupid affair that shouldn't have happened. I should have known better.'

Margot looked from her mother to her father. 'Why exactly are we talking about something that happened eons ago?'

Her mother said nothing, her face gave nothing away.

'When Tom died, well, it was a very difficult time . . . I wasn't thinking straight.'

The knot tugged a little tighter. 'An affair after Tom died—like, you mean, years after?'

He kept glancing at the door as if he might make a run for it. 'A few months, I think.'

'You think!'

He looked at her mother, almost as if she were to blame. 'I can see now that it was a way of coping with my grief, a distraction. I was in a terrible way, and Claire . . .'

Margot thought she'd misunderstood.

'Claire?'

'Claire and I became close.'

'*Close?* What the hell does that mean?'

Her mother was like a statue beside her.

'You had an affair? With Claire?'

He dropped his head.

'Jesus.' Margot was speaking quietly, but there was no controlling the fury in her voice. 'My God, how could you, how fucking could you?'

Her father's face crumpled.

Lizzie shifted closer to her daughter.

'I didn't know. If I had . . .' He was mumbling almost incoherently. 'I thought she couldn't have a baby.'

A baby? What was he even saying?

Margot ran her hands over her face and through her hair. Surely, she'd misheard. 'Claire was pregnant?'

'I didn't know, she didn't tell me.'

'She had an abortion, right?'

He was silent, her powerful father, slumped and pathetic in his chair.

Lizzie put an arm around her daughter. 'Claire gave birth to Jane when she was in the UK.'

Her father was Jane's father, too. The realisation came on a surge of anger and grief, and she began to sob. She cried for Tom; she cried for her mother; she cried for the little girl whose parents didn't see that she'd lost something precious, too. And she cried for Claire, who she had so loved and looked up to, flesh and blood and as fucked up as the rest of them. And Jane. She even cried for her hopeless father. She cried more than she thought it possible to cry, her mother's arms around her.

When finally she looked up, Julian was kneeling beside her, his face full of concern. Jane was in the doorway; Charlotte, too, one hand on her tummy, an expression Margot couldn't discern, Alice's arm around her. Her father had his head in his hands.

'The kids?' Margot asked.

'Watching The Wiggles,' said Julian.

'Dad?'

He looked up. 'Margot, I—'

'Please leave.'

'If we could just talk . . .' He looked at Lizzie. 'In private.'

'No,' said Margot. 'I want you to go.'

'It's not just me here . . .'

'Get out.'

'I'll ring—'

'Don't ring, don't text.'

As soon as he stood, Charlotte left the room, Alice following. Jane sat beside Margot.

Her mother offered to bring coffee.

'I'm sorry,' Jane whispered.

'I'm sorry, too,' Margot whispered back.

As if their parents' transgressions were their own, as if it were somehow their fault that the adults who were supposed to care for them had had a terribly timed affair.

'Mum told me before she died. I wanted to tell you so many times.'

'Oh, Jane, keeping it all to yourself, I can't imagine . . .'

'I was sick about it at first,' said Jane. 'But, you know, it's a long time ago, things happen, people mess up. I wish I could put my arms around her. Tell her not to feel bad. But I can't; she's gone.'

How Margot loved Jane's common-sense goodness.

'Your dad—must be tough. I'm sorry.'

'Your dad now, too.'

They laughed and shook their heads, arms around each other. *Sisters*, they said.

'Are you okay?' Jane asked.

'Are you?' asked Margot.

'Let's be wiser than our parents,' said Jane.

CHAPTER 32

IT WAS LATE AFTERNOON AS Alice, arm in arm with Lizzie, walked to Lizzie's car. 'You did the right thing—it's all out in the open, which is where it should have been in the first place.'

'Margot will need some time,' Lizzie said.

Alice searched for the silver lining. She was good at silver linings. 'But a sister, Margot has a sister.'

Lizzie smiled. 'That's the nice bit.'

'Nice for Jane, too.'

'I'll be needing to keep an eye on her, an eye on both of them.'

Lizzie found her keys. She'd insisted on driving Alice home, as Alice knew she would.

'I insist,' said Lizzie, taking her elbow.

'Drop me in the city and I'll catch a train.'

'Is that how you got here?'

Alice nodded.

'Where's your car?'

Alice couldn't afford the repair until pension day. 'Out of action until they source a part.'

'Honestly, Alice. All this pretending—isn't it time you stopped living in this fantasy land of yours?'

Alice sighed. Did she point out Lizzie's flaws to her? No, she did not. She chose to see the best in people even when they didn't quite deserve it. 'Don't talk to me like I'm a child.'

'Then stop acting like one.'

'Give me one instance . . .'

'You're not twenty anymore, you're seventy-five. You might look young for your age, but no younger than late sixties; you spend money like you have lots of it, and now you move and don't bother telling me.'

Lizzie's words hurt. Late sixties, that just wasn't true. Everyone said she didn't look a day over sixty. 'If you knew what these last months have been like for me, you'd realise how grown up I am.'

'Oh, Alice,' Lizzie draped an arm over her shoulder. 'I'm sure that's true. I'm tired and cranky, and I shouldn't have said any of it.'

'That's all right,' said Alice, in an it's-not-all-right voice.

'So,' Lizzie said unlocking the door, 'where is home these days?'

'An hour's drive, give or take.'

Lizzie put on her seatbelt. 'Plenty of time then for you to catch me up on the last few months.'

Oh, excellent, thought Alice arranging herself in the front seat. An hour of interrogation to get through. 'Do a U-ey and turn right at the roundabout then straight ahead.' As if there hadn't been enough excitement.

Lizzie waited for a car to pass before making the U-turn.

'Alice?'

Alice sighed. 'I was going to tell you . . .'

'What? That you've moved into a commune?'

Alice fell over herself laughing. 'No, Lizzie, not a commune—once was enough.'

'Taken up residence with someone you met on Tinder?'

Alice scrolled distractedly through Instagram, wondering why Margot never posted pictures of Lizzie with Margot and the grandchildren. 'You're hilarious.'

'An old beau, or—' Lizzie took her eyes off the road '—a young lover?'

'I wish.'

'For God's sake Alice, why all the secrecy?'

'I live in a caravan in a caravan park.'

'You? In a caravan?'

'Keep your eyes on the road—yes, me in a caravan. On my own.'

'One of those gorgeous glampy things parked somewhere with glorious views?'

They had been friends all their lives and yet Lizzie hadn't ever considered how things might be for someone who had never had the financial security of marriage or the luxury of permanent work. 'No. Not gorgeous. Not much that's glamp. But I do have views, of a fence, if that counts.'

'Why didn't you tell me?'

'Your tone is exactly the reason I haven't told you.'

'What tone?'

'That *ugh, living-in-a-caravan-park* tone.'

'It's a lot to take in, that's all,' said Lizzie, eyes darting between Alice and a road filled with grunting trucks and impatient traffic.

'I hung on as long as I could, but the rent kept going up.' Alice dropped her phone in her lap. 'No one wanted to live there thirty years ago. And then, overnight, everyone's into art deco and landlords can charge what they like.'

'You could have stayed with me,' said Lizzie.

Alice waited for a truck to pass, the roar of its wheels filling the car. 'I'm too old for couch-surfing. Left at the lights.'

Factories loomed either side, traffic was stop-start.

'I have two spare bedrooms, a spare bed.'

'I don't want charity.' She remembered her mother saying those exact words.

'Not charity, Alice. Friendship.'

'How do you think Ed is?'

'I don't care how he is and don't change the subject.'

'He looked sort of shattered.'

'Consequences,' said Lizzie. 'I know all about them.'

'Doesn't everybody at our age?'

They sat quietly, the silence comfortable between them.

Alice pointed right. 'Turn here.' She unbuckled her seatbelt ready to make a quick exit. 'End of this street and we're there.'

A picture of older couples enjoying a spa framed the entrance. 'You can drop me here.'

Lizzie continued through the gates. 'It's been a long drive, I could do with a cup of tea.'

'Another time.'

'I need to see where you live.'

'No, you don't.'

Lizzie pulled into a parking bay.

'You can't park here—these bays are reserved for residents.'

'Is there a visitors' carpark?'

Alice pointed behind her. 'Back there—five-hundred metres.'

'How annoying.'

Yes, how annoying that the people who lived there took precedence.

Lizzie looked around. 'Goodness,' she said, double-checking the car was securely locked. She chased after Alice who had taken off. They passed a flurry of red umbrellas, people lolling about in deckchairs enjoying the mild evening and the last rays of sun. 'Are they residents, too?'

Alice gestured to the four-wheel drives parked on squares of oil-stained concrete. 'Holiday-makers.'

She led Lizzie behind a row of identical cabins each clad with grim plastic weatherboards, mean strips of verandah home to solitary chairs, the odd pot of geranium or daisy clinging to life.

'Here we are,' said Alice, stopping at a cluster of caravans, the steady roar of traffic in the background. She unlocked the door, cream duco flecked with rust, the once jaunty green trim, faded and peeling. Standing in the doorway, she made a sweeping gesture with her hand. 'Welcome.'

Barely big enough for one, the caravan was lined with dark timber veneer, a bunk bed at one end, vinyl-covered seating encircling a built-in table at the other.

'Perfect for someone who doesn't like housework,' said Alice, leaving the door ajar and opening the window as far as it would wind.

'What did you do with your furniture?'

She'd had enough shaming for one day. 'A friend is storing it for me.'

'How long have you been here?'

'A while.'

Lizzie sat down. 'You can't stay.'

'Where do you suggest I go?'

'You could find a cheaper apartment or perhaps a run-down single-fronted, what about one of those dear little mobile homes I keep reading about?'

'Lizzie, I have the tiniest bit of super, virtually no savings . . .'

'Oh, Alice.'

The kettle whistled, steam beading the ceiling.

Alice organised cups and saucers, her pretty china out of place on the cracked laminate. 'I hated it when I first came here, but I'm getting used to it and I've made friends.'

She didn't tell Lizzie she had cried for weeks, how terribly she missed her little apartment. How she thought she might die. But it was in this desolate place she had also discovered the purpose that had been missing from her life.

'Pack your things and move in with me.'

'We tried that once—you'll remember it didn't go well?'

Lizzie, apparently easily persuaded, nodded. 'We'll figure out something.'

CHAPTER 33

BRIBERY, BRANCH STACKING, BULLYING, MISLEADING *parliament, dirty deals done*. The list was long. Margot looked at the screen again. She closed her eyes, held her head in her hands. Her father was not a good person.

She read on. So many accusations, so much evidence.

Though no complaints of sexual harassment were alleged, his *womanising* was said to be legendary. There had been multiple liaisons over multiple years, including rumours of a scandalous relationship with his wife's lifelong friend in the weeks following the tragic loss of his son.

Her mother was quoted.

Ed Windsor's ex-wife, Elizabeth Kavanagh, lifelong friend of Claire Reid, categorically denied the rumour that her then-husband had had an affair with Reid shortly after the death of their three-year old son. 'Appalling and absurd,' Kavanagh said, that the character of her dearest friend, a friend who had supported her during a tragic and terrible time, and who had been a wonderful and generous advocate for so many, had been besmirched in this way. 'Disgusting gossip that has no basis whatsoever.' There hadn't been an affair. She would say no more on the matter.

More secrets, thought Margot, more lies.

She opened Instagram. She no longer needed to keep secrets, she no longer needed to participate in her father's charade. It was time for the truth. Her truth.

The words, when they came, flowed.

I've realised that when I post, I always try to show a perfect life. The perfect children, the perfect house, the perfect family. I want to believe that this is my life, I wanted you to believe it, too, but in reality, it's far from perfect.

My mother lied to the media about an affair my father had with my mother's best friend, a woman I loved and respected, to protect me, to protect her family and her friend. I can't speak for anyone else, but I'm no longer ashamed of my past. I'm ready to tell my own story, to tell the truth of my messy, tangled life.

This is a photo of me in the depths of my heroin addiction. I'm shocked at how vulnerable I look. I was spiralling from the unaddressed trauma of my brother's death as a child. After his death, my family unravelled. We were never able to put us together again.

I'm not without fault, far from it: I've blamed and punished and kept people who cared for me at a distance. I'm learning to forgive myself and live a more authentic life. It isn't perfect by any means. But I want to share these snapshots to let you know that things can get better *#authenticity #addiction #recovering #lovingmyselffully*.

Journalists—so-called—trawling through social media, searching for anything salacious about her father, would quickly find her post. Her father would be not only politically accountable, but accountable to his family.

Her finger hovered ready to post.

As well as being truthful, was she being vengeful?

Her concern was not for her father but her mother who had protected her and Jane, even protected her father. She'd protected the memory of Claire. And now her lie would be exposed. Her mother's life would be picked over: the bad mother, the woman who wanted it all, who sacrificed her husband and daughter, and ultimately, her son, for her career. That woman. She would be mauled by the media, as women who don't conform are always mauled.

And before you knew it, her father would be the victim, the man deserted by his wife in his hour of need, a woman who put ambition before her grieving family. Her father would play to the role. He would relish it. She could see him now, standing beside a pregnant Charlotte, Hamish hanging on to his leg, Amelia holding his hand. A man reformed, the loving father, adoring faithful husband, his beautiful family. Surely, it would be implied, this man, a family man, deserved a second chance. There would be an outpouring of affection, men remembering him as a good bloke, a best mate . . . He would be contrite;

his life had been upended when his wife abandoned him and their daughter. He'd made mistakes. Stupid mistakes. But he was not that man anymore. He would be redeemed.

And what of Jane, who had always avoided the media, her mother constantly in the news. She was a private person, she disliked attention. Margot's confession would also expose her to media scrutiny. She would be tailed by journalists, cameras in tow, hoping to catch her with her recently discovered father, an unguarded moment that hinted at her trauma. Her unconventional relationship with Sam would be attacked, she and Sam becoming fodder for the tabloids; her *lifestyle* perhaps even considered dangerous.

Charlotte's life would be laid bare for public consumption, endlessly photographed; she would be harangued with questions, her decision to stand-by-her-man admired or condemned, her privacy violated. Her humiliation for all the world to see. Little Hamish and Amelia would lose their innocence.

Claire's reputation would be in ruins. The woman who had had an affair with her best friend's husband while his son was still warm in his grave (her poor father, too grief-stricken, of course, to realise what he was doing). Claire, the same woman who murdered her poor demented husband rather than care for him. The selfish hypocrite, the woman who wrecked every life she touched. More distress for Jane, for her mother, for Charlotte. Everyone.

Margot would not be able to shield Molly and Jack from the photos she was about to post. Frightened and confused, they would hear over and over again that their mother was a druggie and a prostitute; Molly would be teased at school, hear the slut-word, the word that degraded and shamed women.

And overnight, their much-loved grandparents would become people not to be trusted. Their little lives would be turned upside down.

Julian, who would support her, would be scrutinised, too. What sort of man would want to marry a woman with her background? Another poor man duped by another conniving woman.

There was one person she hadn't thought of: herself. The photos taken in the depth of her addiction, looking ill and damaged, would inevitably make their way into newspapers and be shared online. The spoiled little rich girl prostituting herself for drugs. Attracted by notoriety, people from her past might come forward. She would have to live it all over again.

Margot knew the media would quickly lose interest and move on to the next story. But every detail of her life and the lives of her family and friends would live forever online, their darkest and saddest moments, only a name search away.

When Molly and Jack were old enough, she would tell them the truth of her past. In her own words.

Her authentic life didn't start with a confession on Instagram, with *likes* and emojis from people she'd never met. Authenticity began with being true to herself and to the people she loved. She counted among those people her mother.

She hit delete.

Julian came to her and wrapped his arms around her. Holding her while she wept.

CHAPTER 34

WITH A STORM FORECAST, LIZZIE had been in two minds about taking Fred for a walk. She grabbed his lead. He needed a run. And fresh air might clear her head. She had woken early, Margot on her mind. They'd spoken, but only briefly. Margot had slept badly, she said, she shouldn't have read the article about her father before bed. She needed a few days to think things through.

Lizzie checked her watch. Anthony had said he was usually at the park at eight. She packed her umbrella, put on their water-proof coats and hurried out the door. It would be a shame if Fred missed his chance to have a run with Poppy.

They walked at a clip, cyclists gliding past, polite tinkles of the bell, high-vis vests neon under the stormy sky. The wind was picking up, the smell of rain on its way. There was something exhilarating about the hours before a storm, the air filled with portent, a feeling anything could happen.

In the distance she heard barking, high-pitched and excited. Fred seemed especially eager, pulling her along the path until she was almost running. By the time they arrived, she was quite out of breath. The park was rushing with dogs, many clad in fashionable coats. She released Fred from his lead. He bounded off to join the commotion, hurtling from one dog to another. He stopped and looked towards Lizzie as if to say *no Poppy* before being distracted by a red labradoodle.

There was no Anthony to be seen, either. Lizzie felt almost as disappointed as Fred seemed to be. She gave herself a shake: it really didn't matter a jot whether Anthony was there. Fred loved the run, she liked the park and the canine antics. He had seemed nice, but a little too chatty for her liking, possibly nosey. She hated nosey.

Perhaps he was as relieved not to have run into her again, one of those fellows frightened by any woman who wasn't his mother. Men so often thought women were out to trap them, lure them into domesticity—which deep in their heart they yearned for—or take them down financially. He hadn't given that impression, though. The description that came to mind was affable, easygoing.

A relationship was the last thing on her mind; she wouldn't know how to be in a relationship or what it would even mean. Still, he was pleasant company and Fred and Poppy got on well.

The sky grew darker, clouds threatening. It would have to be a short run for Fred and a sprightly walk home. With any luck, they'd miss the rain. She could hear Fred barking when he almost never barked. It took a moment to realise he was barking at Poppy. She spotted Anthony. It was her turn to surprise him.

'Elizabeth.'

It was ridiculous how pleased she was to see him. 'My friends call me Lizzie.'

'Lizzie—Lizzie suits you,' he said. 'You're well?'

'Very,' she said. 'How are you?'

'Hale and hearty last time I checked.'

Had he seen the story about Ed and Claire? About her? If he wasn't going to mention it, she wouldn't either. 'I think I owe you a coffee.'

'You do.'

Her attraction to him took her by surprise. It also felt exactly as it had always felt: a little overwhelming, somewhat disconcerting. It wasn't just the kind intelligent eyes and sense of humour. There was a sexual energy, too: heart beating a little faster, the feeling of wanting to kiss and be kissed. Did he feel it, too? she wondered.

Lizzie searched her memory: how long since she'd been with someone? Somewhere in her late sixties—a man she'd met through a dating app. She hadn't wanted a relationship, she wasn't interested in a romance, she wanted sex. Only clean, attractive, intelligent men without underlying medical conditions need apply. She eventually found someone suitable. Things turned out quite well until he started talking firesides and walks on the beach and wanting to introduce her to his children.

She wondered again if her interest in Anthony coincided a little too conveniently with the loss of Claire. Or perhaps—and she had been thinking about this—was it that she was free to pursue friendships without feeling disloyal, free to be her own person, free to do whatever she wanted.

She had, Lizzie realised, been in Claire's thrall, most who knew her were. Perhaps that dependence was also about the familiar, the safe, an excuse, maybe, not to meet other people, do other things.

The sky darkened. She felt a splash of rain on her face. It was about to bucket down. They hurriedly joined the owners calling their dogs, a first flash of lightning followed by a roll of thunder, much closer than she'd realised.

She opened her umbrella. 'Let's make a run for my place.' Had she gone entirely mad?

They took off, laughing, dogs leading the way.

You could tell a lot about a person by the way they ran: hesitant, dull, competitive, self-conscious. Anthony was, she decided, athletic.

The rain came down, steady and soaking.

Lizzie's hips ached and her lungs protested but she was running, and it felt like she might live forever.

The rain intensified, downpipes gurgling, gutters floating with stupidity, roads puddling. They slowed, both puffing, dogs snorting and blinking. Thunder crashed, the air was electric. Setting off again, they walked at a pace, neither with the breath to speak. They pressed on, wind roaring, umbrellas limp and misshapen.

They arrived at Lizzie's, wet and cold, rushing to the protection of the verandah. They looked at each other, hair plastered to faces, shoes squelching, and burst into laughter. Lizzie headed off in search of towels, thinking *what now*?

Once they'd dried off, Lizzie asked Anthony inside. She had Margot to thank for the makeover. The expression on her daughter's face when she'd visited . . . A chaotic house, just another reason to stay away. She'd decided that if Margot were to drop by again, she would find her old home cosy and welcoming. It had not looked so nice for years.

She had started in Tom's room, working through one section of the cupboard at a time. The toys were the first to be sorted into a pile—what she would give away, what would be thrown out. It took her a very long time.

A year or two after his death, she had been going through his things, making decisions about what might be useful to another little boy, when she sank to the floor. She could not part with any of it: not his bright red raincoat, not his beanie with the pom-pom or the jeans just like Daddy's, or his little rubber boots. She had put all of his belongings into suitcases and thought she could never look at them again.

All these years later, Lizzie unpacked those same suitcases. Each item of clothing she held to her face, imagining his lovely Tom smell. She wept many times, but she had also smiled, recalling long-forgotten moments.

She ran up some sheers for the windows on her forgotten sewing-machine and painted the room. She dragged a comfy old chair up the stairs, and gave in to the trend for indoor plants, a pot plant filling one corner. A reading room, perhaps even a room to rent out. Decisions for later. Tom was beside her when she unpeeled the letters of his name from the door.

More thunder, lightning putting on a laser show. Fred trembled in a corner; Poppy was unimpressed. The old roof shuddered as wind gusts grew more extreme, Lizzie anxious it might leak, or worse, take flight.

Anthony's eyes flitted around the room. 'Lovely old place.'

Lizzie smiled. It was her home—she loved it, too.

She was about to make coffee when there was a tremendous crack. She leapt, sure the house had been torn in half, Anthony putting an arm around her.

Lizzie gasped. 'Did lightning just hit the house?'

Anthony shook his head. 'Something out the back, I think.'

Lizzie raced to the kitchen and jerked the curtains open. She cried out, arms falling limp beside her.

'Lizzie . . . ?'

The jacaranda was still standing, but at its centre burned a fierce orange glow. Two of its largest limbs, flung to the ground, pointed to the sky accusingly.

'Beautiful tree, such a shame.'

Lizzie closed her eyes. The jacaranda was Tom's tree.

The dogs came to investigate, milling around their legs.

She stared disbelievingly at the tree, its great network of roots loosened from the earth, spread wide as if searching for home. 'Maybe it can be saved.'

Anthony shook his head. 'Its roots, the way it's leaning . . .'

She opened the back door, wind wailing, rain coming down in sheets, lightning dancing across a midnight sky.

He pulled the door closed. 'You can't go out in that. The rain will see to the fire.'

The acrid smell of smoke seeped under the door driving them from the room, dogs following.

'That tree means a lot to you?' asked Anthony.

She took the photo of Tom playing under the jacaranda from the mantelpiece and passed it to him.

'Your boy?'

'Tom.'

'Happy memories.' He smiled.

She nodded.

'Perhaps Tom can help you plant another tree.'

'Tom died not long after the photo was taken.'

'Oh dear, I didn't realise . . . you didn't mention . . . I'm so sorry. To lose a child . . . Is there anything I can do?'

Lizzie rarely mentioned Tom to people who hadn't met him. It caught them off guard, they seemed to have no idea what to say, and would often hurry away as quickly as politeness allowed.

'Excuse me for a minute,' she said. Poor man, Lizzie thought. He must be wondering what he's got himself into.

In the bathroom, Lizzie splashed cold water on her face and pushed her hair into some sort of order.

He was exploring the bookshelves when she returned. 'Maybe I'm wrong about the tree. Maybe it can be saved.'

She shook her head. 'It will have to come down.'

Standing next to her in his sensible brown jumper, shirt collar turned up, she was grateful for his solid calm presence.

'I'm sorry,' said Lizzie. 'I've had quite the few weeks.'

'I know those weeks.'

'I lost my closest friend not long ago ... and, well, it's complicated.'

He nodded, his eyes gentle. 'I saw the story in the paper.'

'Rumours and gossip,' she said, grateful he didn't probe further. 'Now, about that coffee.'

Anthony touched her elbow. 'Give me your number and we'll make another time.'

They fed each other's numbers into their phones.

'Let me at least drive you home,' Lizzie said, enjoying the warmth of him beside her.

He shook his head. 'The rain's almost stopped.' He called Poppy and retrieved his umbrella, coaxing it back into a shape that would provide some protection. 'We're fine to walk.'

Lizzie stood close to the tree, soft rain falling, listening to the sputter and hiss of its dying breath. She leaned her head to the trunk, tears mingling with the sap oozing from its wounds, its life force ebbing away. The insects that nested deep within, the birds that sought safety within its branches, the invisible life it supported, fleeing or dead.

Her fingers braved the heat, found the notches she'd made to chart Tom's growth. She would ask whoever came to fell the tree to rescue that little fragment of history. The mulch she would spread on the garden; within that mulch were tiny particles of Tom.

Trees had memory, she was sure of it, feelings too, giving birth, nurturing and protecting, living and dying. It had watched over them, this tree, sheltered her when she sat bent in grief beneath its canopy, shaded Tom and Margot as they played. It had borne witness.

Tom came to her, tugging at her jeans. 'Do trees go to heaven?'

'Tree heaven,' she said picking him up and burying her face in the loveliness of him.

Together they said goodbye.

An arborist came to look at the tree, a last silly hope it could be saved, dashed. He walked around what was left of the trunk shaking his head. Squatting, he examined the roots, more shaking of the head. Men were such silent creatures.

'It has to go—much too big for a suburban backyard, anyway.'

'What if you were to cut below the burn,' she said, 'could it regrow?'

He pointed to the roots. 'Nah,' he said.

And so, they came. The men with their machines. She left the house with Fred, Tom's tree disappearing in seconds.

She heard the stutter of a chainsaw. And kept walking.

Opening the front door, Lizzie was unprepared for the light streaming up the hallway. For years, she had imagined a skylight. There'd be no need now. Fred darted ahead sensing something was different. She paused to gaze at the light filling forgotten corners and warming the floorboards. She took a deep breath and faced her loss.

They had been thorough, grubbing the roots and grinding the stump, the snake of tendons at the tree's base, roads and highways for Tom's trucks and tractors, had disappeared. A pile of mulch, a gaping hole.

The crows that kept watch from the chimney, the magpies that strutted the fence, the blackbirds always poking about for worms, had disappeared, too, their birdsong silenced as if struck mute by what they'd seen.

Fred stopped and stared, sniffed and circled.

Kneeling, Lizzie picked up handfuls of sun-warmed mulch, drifting it back to earth through her fingers.

She heard Tom calling, *Mummy, Mummy*. She looked up. And there he was, tiny beneath the jacaranda, blossom whirling and tumbling and catching in his hair, lilac blooms thick about his feet.

Yes, thought Lizzie, I am ready, I am ready to let him go.

CHAPTER 35

THE CARAVANNERS—THE NAME HER neighbours gave themselves—adored Alice. Someone who was once famous, living among them. Who'd have thought? She was the talk of the park. She hadn't had such interest and attention in years.

And she'd been asked to be the face of one of the summer fashion shows at the local shopping centre. What did it matter if it wasn't David Jones or Myer who'd extended the invite, local was the way to go, and *The Ageless Woman* had such a ring to it.

It was only now, from a distance, that Alice could see the patterns of her life, as silly in love as she'd been at fifteen. *Not again, not again*, the words on churn in her head. But there'd always been an again, always another time in another way that another relationship ended. Lizzie was right: she hadn't grown up, she did live in a fantasy world, a world she could manage, a world that helped her make it through each day.

Since fleeing Emilio's apartment, Alice started each day with a mantra: you are lovable, you are talented, you are a good person. And yes, you are amazing.

With much less rent to find each month, she no longer had to host cheese and dip soirées in far-flung locales, and she was getting more work as a life model. She'd surprisingly had a call-back from an audition earlier in the week. Apparently, the advertising agency were mad for her look. She would give their promotion edge, they said, she would give it cool. She'd never heard of *gated communities* until then.

She looked again at the company's website, links taking her to images of beaming elderly folk striding purposefully through an alien landscape of concrete and signage, men attired in spotless iron-pressed whites hitting it out on squash courts, and women, floaties encircling their floaty arms, performing water ballet in the pool.

It wasn't her idea of community, but it would be a few days' well-paid work.

Alice had joined The Caravanners after an unexpected wave of early summer heat had forced almost everyone from their cabins and caravans. They dragged whatever seating they could find, tattered deck chairs and falling-apart banana lounges, arranging them on the stony soil, half-dead trees leaning over them like old men. They sat together drinking beer and sharing potato chips. Alice was not to know the spontaneous gathering was to change, perhaps even save, her life.

One by one they introduced themselves, some giving their first name, others revealing a lot more. People from every background: single mothers, pensioners, Indigenous Australians, refugees, people with disability, others who, like Alice, you wouldn't expect to find in such reduced circumstances, including a doctor and a company director. They talked about the weather, whinged about politicians and cracked jokes about how they came to be living in a caravan park.

Whether it was the heat or the beer or the feeling of being among people who understood, light-hearted anecdotes soon became more serious. Late into the night they talked of lost childhoods, of homelessness, of addiction and poverty and racism, of illness and depression and prison, stories rarely heard unless they had a happy ending. Raw and real, the manner of their telling affecting, Alice knew immediately these were stories that must be told. But who would tell them?

The answer, when it came, was obvious: the stories were theirs—only they could tell them.

All they needed was a stage and a guiding hand.

Alice phoned Ursula.

Alice loved visiting Ursula in her tiny little terrace. Filled with books and plants and paintings, many of Ursula's own sketches and watercolours, it brimmed with life and joy.

Ursula hadn't blinked an eye when Alice told her she lived in a caravan park, twenty minutes from Ursula's house, as it turned out. She had lived a creative life and creative people made do, often with not very much.

'So, what do you think?' asked Alice, after pitching The Caravanners and their stories.

'I think it's a wonderful idea, thank you for asking me.'

'So, you're interested?' said a pleased Alice.

'Yes, but with one caveat.'

'Okay?'

'I'd like you to be part of it, to work with me.'

'Me? Really?'

'You were a journalist so you can write, you understand performance and audience. You know these people, they trust you.'

Alice didn't think twice. 'Won't we have to find somewhere first?'

'It just so happens . . .'

Run-down and wreathed in cobwebs, the Town Hall was past her best. Home to knitting clubs and the odd council function, her days of grandeur were long behind her. Neglected and unappreciated, there were holes in the plaster, paintwork was discoloured and patchy, great scabs of render swept into corners. But there was a stage and plenty of seating—even if of questionable comfort—and the structure was solid. She had lost her trappings but not her soul.

Refurbished in the art nouveau style, Alice imagined the heavy dark woods gleaming beneath grand chandeliers, glitter now concealed under thick layers of grime. Everywhere were magnificent columns and faded murals and stained glass of subdued blues and reds that, with a little elbow grease, would flame again.

'Cannot believe,' said Ursula, excitedly pointing out the crimson curtain that framed the stage. It was frayed and worn, but it still rose and fell. Rather majestically, thought Alice. Albeit in a cloud of dust.

Ursula had been granted permission by the local council, with some conditions, to use the hall. But it needed work.

Among the park's residents was a seamstress, a plasterer and a painter, who, the agreement allowed, could undertake minor patching. But for the most part, they cleaned. Ladders were begged, borrowed and perhaps stolen, cobwebs were sent swirling, floorboards scrubbed and buffed, walls washed, windows cleaned, glass and doorknobs and brass all polished. Nothing escaped Ursula's eye. Though still in need of major restoration, the hall soon recovered something of her past exuberance.

They had been overwhelmed with interest, a large number of The Caravanners wanting to be part of the production.

When all the cleaning and repairs had been done, Alice and Ursula sat in the front row drinking coffee, Alice imagining the stage coming to life.

'I've been thinking,' said Ursula, 'would you consider opening the evening with your story, your life story?'

Alice was flattered. 'My story?'

'I think you might have quite a story to tell.'

Alice took a mouthful of coffee. 'I suppose I have but . . .'

'You'd be wonderful, you would do it so well.'

'I'll have to think about it.'

Alice did think about it. She would once have jumped at the chance: centre stage, an audience, her life story. Yes, she had suffered as women of her age and class suffered: she had grown up without a father; she had survived sexual abuse and life-threatening illness; she had had the highs and lows of a creative life; and she knew what it was to be poor, to be excluded.

But she saw now that she had also had great fortune: she had never gone hungry; she had always had a home to go to; and people in her life who cared about her.

Her story paled next to those whose stories she had been writing these last weeks: stories of war and violence and death, of great tragedy and unthinkable loss, but also of courage and humour, of resilience and overcoming.

She wanted to work behind the scenes, support others to find their voice, encourage the telling of their stories. She had had her moment.

This time, the stage belonged to them.

Alice couldn't believe how Ursula carried the whole performance in her head. There was no set designer, no musical director or lighting person, no one taking care of audio or wardrobe. With Alice as her stagehand, Ursula was artistic director, stage and production manager, designer and producer.

Concerned she wouldn't have enough extras, Ursula had asked Alice to do a call-out in the community newsletter. She was deluged by locals, all certain the following year would see them on their way to LA.

Each day, Ursula set aside time to speak to whoever had a story they wanted to share. Alice was a journalist again, listening, asking questions, interviewing, taking notes, transcribing. Alice helped write and rewrite scripts. Looked for that moment which would make the invisible visible, the unheard heard.

They started the day with breathing exercises, movement, voice. Dance to find rhythm and energy and connection, Alice joining in. They improvised, they workshopped. It was transformative.

Planning stages were intense: how would the stories be told, which of the many stories would they feature on opening night? Ursula was disappointed at first that Alice had decided not to participate, but when Alice explained, she said she admired Alice all the more.

'We absolutely must have an opening night,' said Ursula. 'Invite the local community, celebrate their music, their food . . .'

Many of The Caravanners had never seen a play, the cost of a ticket enough to feed and house them for a week. Hardly believing they would be telling their own stories, they were full of anticipation and nerves.

They had almost all missed out on an education. Ashamed of the way they spoke, or anxious they did not speak English well enough, they were fearful people might laugh at them.

'Be yourselves,' Alice told them. 'Being yourself is the most powerful thing you can be.'

They had gathered for the last of the workshops before serious rehearsal began. There were issues to sort out with lighting, wardrobe and music, but it was at last coming together.

A vote had been taken on which two stories, each less than thirty minutes long, they would perform on opening night. Alice would then be in conversation with the two performers, all three later taking questions from the audience.

That afternoon, they were workshopping scenes from one of the two plays.

Tashid, who had come to Australia as a refugee, was to deliver a monologue about his time in detention. He was imprisoned for many years in a hotel in a suburb where lawyers and professors and surgeons lived. He was eventually freed. His home for the last six months had been the caravan park. Many of his friends were still in the hotel.

A hush as they took their seats, the first rehearsal.

Tashid remembers a song his father, who did not make it to safety, played on the oud.

The oud, melancholic and timeless, plays.

*

In the closing scene, Tashid addresses the audience:
I am twenty-four. I have been waiting in the hotel for seven years.
Who will speak for me?
The oud plays.

Alice and Ursula looked at each other, both moved.

The Caravanners might seem an unlikely ensemble, thought Alice, but on stage, their performances were raw and courageous, full of the drama and poetry of life.

CHAPTER 36

MARGOT WATCHED HER FATHER HOLDING a press conference, journalists surging forward, eyes feverish, necks craned. White-faced and grim-lipped, he denied everything. Beside him, Charlotte, standing close, eyes defiant as she stared into the camera. Margot was the only person, other than Ed, who knew she was pregnant.

Rumour mills, enemies within and without, undermining, lies and more lies. He was innocent. However, for the good of his party, he would resign. Forthwith. History would vindicate him.

Margot imagined how it might feel if Julian had an affair. One, she might understand. But one after another. Year after year. *A sex addict*, a colleague had been quoted as saying. What her mother must have put up with.

He had had the money and the opportunity to meet all his needs. But he wanted more than sex. She'd met men like him plenty of times. He wanted the thrill, the danger. He wanted to be adored, to be in love. *A distraction*, he'd said, a distraction from grief, a distraction from his mortality, too.

Her father had never acknowledged that Margot had been a sex worker. She blamed herself, for what father wanted to think about his daughter prostituting herself? She had only just grasped that it wasn't that he wanted to protect her, or even that he was ashamed, he was much more afraid of the media finding out, the headlines that would surely follow. Not a good look for someone whose politics was framed by family values. *Fuck his hypocrisy. Fuck him*. And Claire, Claire who had listened and tried to help in so many ways, had not once during those years looked her in the eye.

She played his latest message, his voice worn and scratchy. He didn't care about his career, he said, it didn't matter what people said about him . . . he was sorry, he loved her. There were things that would come out, things he was ashamed of, but they were in the past. Could they meet? Somewhere private. He could explain. This time she didn't stab delete.

Margot opened the door to her father, turning when he leaned to kiss her, stepping away from his arms when he tried to hug her. Rejecting him, hurt.

'I have to pick Jack up from kindy in two hours, so we don't have long.'

'Margot, I can't tell you . . . it's so good to see you.'

She walked him to a room adjacent to the kitchen, a place where the family gathered to watch television or play board games. She made coffee.

He hovered around the bench. 'There are so many things I want to say.'

A one-way conversation, thought Margot, where he justified, excused and generally bullshitted his way out of blame and responsibility.

'There are things I want to say, too,' she said, turning on the coffee machine.

'I . . . you must know how sorry I am.'

'No, Dad, I don't.'

He shrugged helplessly.

'You really think a sorry will make it all go away?'

'What would you have me do?' he asked, a flicker of annoyance quickly controlled.

She took mugs from the cupboard. 'A sign that you've reflected, that you realise the enormous hurt you've caused, that you take responsibility.'

'Isn't that what I'm doing now?'

'Didn't you want to wrap your arms around us after Tom died? Didn't you want to look after your family?'

'I wasn't thinking. I didn't know what I was doing.'

She pushed his coffee across the bench. They moved into the family room, sitting at a distance from each other.

'Not one night, Dad, but weeks, months . . .'

He grimaced, closed his eyes, opened them again. 'Tom was gone, your mother was away for weeks on end, I was lonely—'

She spoke in an enraged whisper. '*You* lost Tom, *you* were lonely, *your* wife was away . . . *you*, Dad, it's always about *you*.'

He rubbed his hand over the arm of the chair. 'Not just me, Margot.'

'Claire is dead.'

'And what about your mother?'

'Mum's fault, Claire's fault, not yours, never yours.'

It was raining outside, an unexpected downpour, ending almost as quickly as it began.

'Claire was Mum's best friend, someone I loved.'

He shifted uncomfortably in his chair. 'I did a stupid thing, we all do stupid things, things we regret, but it's a long time ago . . . life goes on.'

How easily he forgave himself.

'Is there anything else you need to say?'

She could see it wasn't going as he'd planned, that he'd expected to kiss her goodbye, pleased that he, in his magnanimous way, had apologised, that everything would then go back to the way it was, his conscience clear. In a week or two, he'd buy her something beautiful, jewellery perhaps, an expensive trinket that spoke of the love between father and daughter. He would be forgiven.

'I need to talk to you about Jane.'

'She seems like a very together young woman.'

'She's your daughter.'

'We've spoken, she bears no grudge, we're friendly.'

Jane had been right to keep her expectations low.

'That's it?' asked Margot.

He frowned. 'Margot, you expect too much. We're practically strangers.'

'You don't want to get to know her?'

'Let's not rush things.'

Even his closest relationships were transactional, thought Margot. He saw life in terms of getting away with whatever he could, of never admitting fault. She wondered when it would all come crashing down.

She took a mouthful of cold coffee. 'I'm going back to uni, and I've got some photography work, just a few hours a week.'

He showed no interest in what she might be studying.

'Work?' He looked around the room. 'You don't need to work.'

He wanted her home, like he had wanted her mother home. And now Charlotte.

'I'm going to need your help with Molly and Jack, ferrying them around, a few hours babysitting.'

'Is this penance?'

'Is spending time with your grandchildren penance?'

He shook his head. 'You know I'd love to but the next few months are going to be very busy, a baby on the way, and, cone-of-silence, I've had a job offer. It will involve a lot of overseas travel, so I'll be away from home more than I'd like. I discussed it with Charlotte, of course, but she couldn't have been more encouraging.'

How smug he looked.

'What sort of work?'

'Oil and gas. I was Minister of Resources for a long time, so my expertise . . .'

'Congratulations.'

He reached for his bag. 'Something else for the media to bleat about.'

She was thinking of Charlotte, home with three babies, her father away . . . history repeating.

'If you ever hurt Charlotte . . .'

He smiled reassuringly, his old self again. 'Darling,' he stood to go, 'you must see I'm not that man anymore.'

Margot woke suddenly, Julian murmuring in his sleep, hand reaching out. She sat on the side of the bed, sipped from the glass of water she kept on the bedside table. The dream began as it always did, Tom crying somewhere in the house, her panic as she ran from room to room trying to find him. It ended as it always did with Margot bursting into the lounge room, then running and running, her father calling after her. But this time she saw what she had been running from: her father and Claire on the sofa, together, the expression on their faces when they saw her, Claire crying out, her father chasing after her, lifting her in his arms, Margot hitting his hands away before sobbing into his shoulder.

This time she heard the voice, the words whispered in her ear: 'Just a bad dream, darling. We mustn't tell Mummy, we don't want to make her cry.'

CHAPTER 37

SITTING ON THE VERANDAH, GARDENING books piled on the table beside her, Lizzie allowed herself to imagine a new planting. In just a few days, roses that had sulked in the shade of the jacaranda were growing soft red shoots, and plants that hadn't flowered for years were coming into bloom.

Her phone flashed: Anthony. He was close by with coffee and the best macaroons . . .

She had been sure, after days without a call, that her past had hurried him away. At his age, why would you want to attach yourself to someone with so much emotional baggage? Then again, no one got to their age without emotional baggage.

Since mentioning him to Alice, she'd been having cold feet. Lizzie had been single a long time and, for the most part, hadn't regretted it. If sometimes she missed the intimacy and companionship of a relationship, she valued her independence more.

She'd had flirtations, and there'd been one-night stands. After Ed, Tim was her one close call. She'd met him through a mutual friend. A senior bureaucrat, they shared an interest in politics. Never married, erudite and handsome, she was instantly attracted.

It was months before she introduced him to Margot. The introduction, when it happened, went badly; Margot sullen, her contempt undisguised. And, as she was to discover, unrelenting.

Later came talk of moving in together, banter about where they might live, and what pieces of furniture would come with them, Lizzie questioning why she was contemplating anything long term.

One evening after dinner—Margot's grunts her only contribution to conversation—Tim took Lizzie aside, telling her a firm male hand was overdue. He listed punishments he would put in place should Margot continue to disrespect him and asked that Lizzie show her loyalty by giving him her full support. Lizzie listened attentively then ushered him out the door. She asked him to return the next day to collect his belongings and told him not to contact her again.

Now she had different concerns. Both she and Anthony were at a stage of life when ill health could strike at any moment. What were those statistics she'd read the other day? She couldn't remember exactly, but once over seventy, the likelihood of this befalling you or that accosting you increased alarmingly. Over eighty, it didn't bear thinking about. Her head filled with worst-case scenarios—she had a talent for worst-case scenarios. He looked fit enough, but who knew what was lurking. She thought of Claire and the sacrifices she'd made.

Overnight, her plans could all be upended. Instead of being his lover—lover, did she really think they might become lovers?—she would become his carer, the trip to South America she'd been saving for, becoming even more of a pipe dream, her freedom curtailed, her days filled with soiled linen and medical appointments. She reread the message. Did she even want to see him again? The passive way out—the most appealing—would be to ignore him, or she could respond with an abrupt *no thanks* so he didn't bother her again. Or she could put off a decision altogether and not get back to him for a day or two. By which time, the coffee would be cold.

She messaged back: *Coffee just what I need.*

Picking up the book resting in her lap, Lizzie's eyes fell upon the chapter heading: *Renewal.*

Anthony stood, hands in pockets, surveying the damage.

'Once the hole's filled in it won't look nearly so bad. It's not that you won't miss the tree, but you'll get used to it not being there.'

Lizzie moved the book from the seat beside her so he had somewhere to sit. Like most people, he thought he understood. He didn't. It didn't matter that Tom would now be a grown man, that decades had passed. She had lost her child and her child had lost everything he might have been.

'I'm sorry.' He turned to face her. 'I didn't mean to sound . . . I know it was much more than a tree.'

She rescued him. 'On the plus side, the house is filled with light and the garden has come to life.'

'You're all right, then?'

'Yes, I am.' She thought that she really was.

'Will you plant another tree?'

She shook her head. 'I'm thinking about natives, to bring the birds.'

He nodded approvingly.

'Can I get you another coffee?'

'I'm a one-a-day man but I wouldn't say no to a cuppa.'

One-a-day rang alarm bells. Was he one of those boring people—laundry on Wednesday, shopping on Thursday—not even a nuclear blast could change his routine?

He was leafing through her books when she returned. She felt momentarily assured: he liked gardens, he had an adopted greyhound, he seemed kind. As Alice would say: what's not to like?

'I've got nothing on this afternoon—let me at least make a start?'

'It's not a big job. I can do it myself.'

'We could do it together.'

Why was she hesitating? What was she afraid of?

'I think I've got a pair of gloves that will fit you,' she said. 'And we'll need sunscreen.'

They worked all morning, shovelling and wheelbarrowing, an old hat she'd found in the shed on his head, his sleeves rolled up. His arms were muscled, his tummy flat. He caught her looking and raised an eyebrow. She adjusted her eye to the middle-distance.

She remembered those times she and Claire had laboured together, digging and planting and planning.

'Penny for your thoughts,' he said.

'I was thinking about my friend, the friend who died. We often gardened together.'

They were by the veggie garden, gauzy plumes of fennel against a sunstruck sky, chorusing currawongs overhead.

He leaned on the shovel in the most attractive way, sweat and soil mingling. 'Your son, your friend . . . this could be a memorial, a place you come to remember them.'

This was Tom's place, a sacred place, not Claire's.

'I'm not sure,' she said, and went looking for the rake.

It was mid-afternoon before they'd finished. Anthony tidied things away while Lizzie went inside to make sandwiches. They sat together, eating a late lunch, blackbirds foraging in the newly laid mulch, honeyeaters flitting in and out of the abutilon, the first butterflies of summer.

'A good day's work,' he said.

She agreed.

Lizzie snuck sideways glances. He was slender to a fault, but his frame was strong. He wore his hair a little longer than most men his age, long enough to sweep his collar. Lightly tanned, his face was smeared with dirt and sweat, and mulch clung to his clothes.

'Do you think much about dying?' she asked.

He laughed. 'I think about it more than when I was forty.'

'Do you fear it?'

'I'm getting used to the idea.'

'Have you made plans? For dying, I mean?'

'You mean if I get some awful illness or the mind goes?'

Lizzie brushed crumbs from the table. 'Some sort of contingency?'

'I've told my family there's not to be any heroics, and the local doctor gave me a form to fill in, outlining my wishes. Beyond that . . .'

'You don't mind me asking?'

He shook his head. 'I guess with your friend dying, it's uppermost.'

'I guess.'

'Such a magnificent drama, if only we weren't the star.'

They grinned at each other.

'What will you do when you go home?'

'Think after today's effort I might be putting my feet up.'

'You better shower first.'

He surveyed her. 'You and me both.'

She rubbed a hand self-consciously over her face.

'The layer of dirt is very becoming.'

Was he flirting?

He smiled. 'If that's not being too forward.'

She glanced at her watch. It was time for him to go.

He stood. 'How about dinner? My place. I'll cook.'

She liked him. Intelligent but not pretentious, confident but not arrogant. But a relationship? Dinner? 'You can cook?'

'Very well, I'm told.'

Who had told him? she wondered. 'In that case . . .'

'I'll give you a call, arrange a time.'

After he'd left, Lizzie sat in the garden, Tom's name and height carved into all that remained of the jacaranda resting in her lap.

CHAPTER 38

ALICE KNEW HOW IT MUST look to Lizzie: the rotting fence, the shabby vans, the taint of poverty.

'I've been thinking . . .'

Aha. Alice knew there would be a reason for her visit.

'You are to move into my place tomorrow, take the upstairs, pay a small amount of rent so your working-class sensibilities aren't offended and pop downstairs for aperitifs at five each evening.'

Alice shook her head and laughed. 'We've already discussed this.' She would not be moving in with Lizzie. They were each of them difficult women, and difficult women needed not just their own room but their own space.

A man waved from a distance. 'G'day, Alice.'

'Lovely day,' Alice called back.

'We've missed you,' he yelled.

'When did you become so suburban?'

'It's called community,' said Alice.

'I know all about community, but best friends in five minutes?' Alice shrugged.

'You didn't tell me you'd been away?'

'Just a day or two—minor medical procedure.'

Lizzie's eyes scanned her face then fell to her chest. Medical procedures, where Alice was concerned, meant one of two things: work done or new implants.

'Oh my God,' said Lizzie, looking at her flat-chested friend. 'Your breasts?'

'I know.'

'Well, I think you look amazing,' said Lizzie.

'I think I do, too,' said Alice. She was already growing to love her more boyish incarnation. Androgyny was so *now*. The scars from the initial surgery had long ago faded to silver and she was planning an extravagant tattoo as soon as her latest wounds healed. No longer did her stomach sink at every mention of cancer and survival rates and metastases.

Lizzie hurried after Alice, cigarette smoke wheezing from one caravan, cooking smells, thick with heat and spice, wafting from another. Still trying to keep up, she darted in and around washing, precarious on flimsy lines, talkback opining some-where. Veering left at the shower block, Lizzie shuddering, they made it safely to the café.

Alice held the door open. She saw the disdain in Lizzie's eyes, the snootiness of the inner-city postcode. 'The coffee's as good as you get in Melbourne, only cheaper.'

The woman behind the counter looked up. 'G'day, Alice. Sit wherever.'

Other than a woman in a brightly coloured kaftan and a man in shorts and singlet, the café was empty.

Alice glanced at Lizzie's harem pants. 'At least there isn't a dress code.'

'Janice, I'd like you to meet Lizzie.'

'Any friends of Alice . . .'

They sat by the window with a view of the carpark, shiny four-wheel drives, fuel tanks no doubt brimming, noses pointed towards exits, ready and waiting to transport grey-haired explorers onward.

Lizzie wanted to know more about Alice's surgery—why on earth hadn't she told her—nodding sympathetically when she confided that up until the last minute, she thought she might not go through with it. She didn't want Lizzie to know how vain and cowardly she was.

She'd been living with Christopher when she'd been diagnosed. Her cancer had totally freaked him out, even before the surgery. He didn't visit her in hospital, not once, and on the day she was to be discharged, left a message with the nurses that he wouldn't be able to make it in to take her home.

She instead caught a taxi to the home they rented together. When she opened the door, the house was half-empty. He'd gone and taken almost everything with him. He left a note, the thought of her not having breasts . . . he was sorry, et cetera. Her shock was quickly replaced with relief. He was out of her life. But the feeling that she was nothing without breasts had persisted. Until now.

'I know how courageous you are,' said Lizzie.

'On the house,' said Janice, popping a bowl of Smarties on the table. She exchanged a conspiratorial smile with Alice who'd asked her not to mention anything about the rehearsals or the Town Hall.

She longed to share her new venture with Lizzie, but was fearful that if it fell through, that if something went wrong . . . *Wait a week or two*, she told herself, and for once, listened.

Alice was vaguely amused to see Lizzie so out of place. The café, more a takeaway, smelled of fried food and meat pies; chair legs scraped, tables wobbled, Neil Sedaka sang. Lizzie, bracelets jangling, gazed at the menu as if it were written in a foreign language before politely pushing it to one side.

If Alice were truthful, she'd hated the café, too, its yellowed pine tables, pathogens stewing in the bain-marie, the shitty soundtrack. But more and more, she appreciated its lack of pretension—no baristas, no name-dropping, no competing, no outfits that cost the price of a pandemic. No bullshit.

Their coffee arrived.

'So,' said Alice, 'news?'

'Well . . .' said Lizzie. She blew on her coffee.

'Waiting.'

'I suppose I might as well tell you . . .'

Alice tapped orange fingernails against her cup. 'Tell me what?'

'I've met someone. Or, at least, I think I have.'

'Someone? I'm supposing that someone is a man.'

'I've only ever been boringly heterosexual.'

'You've been on Tinder?'

'Goodness, no. I met him walking Fred. He has a grey-hound, too.'

Alice sighed dramatically. 'I thought you were going to tell me something interesting.'

'He invited me out for coffee . . .'

'Talk about swept off your feet.'

Lizzie glared. 'Don't make fun.'

'Does this someone have a name?' asked Alice, succumbing to temptation and selecting a brown Smartie.

'His name is Anthony,' said Lizzie. 'He's around my age, perhaps a little younger. His wife died a few years ago and he lives in my neighbourhood. We're friends, nothing else.'

'Friends?' Alice laughed. 'Don't you sometimes yearn in that big bed of yours?'

'Only for a good night's sleep.'

'Are there children?'

'Two daughters, both married.'

'Is he good-looking?'

'I'm not sure how good-looking he is. Quite a nice man, is how I'd describe him.'

'If there's a quite nice man on the scene, grab hold of him,' said Alice.

CHAPTER 39

'MUM.' LIZZIE KISSED HER MOTHER, who was almost swallowed by the chair. She lifted her mother's legs and arranged a pillow lengthways on the footstool, tucking it beneath her knees so her legs were properly supported. 'You look a bit peaky. Not coming down with something, are you?'

'Old age is what I'm coming down with.'

Lizzie laughed. She placed the beaker of thickened milk in front of her mother. She was vanishing before her eyes, bones visible beneath the translucent skin. 'Mum, you have to drink.'

She had raised her mother's weight loss with the doctor the week before. He'd shrugged and mumbled something about age and poor appetite and moved to the next bed. She had taken it upon herself to ask staff to keep a chart documenting what her mother ate and drank but rarely was there more than a scribbled entry or two.

'I won't be drinking no more of it.'

The nurse, when Lizzie got hold of her, was more sympathetic. 'We'll do our best, but with more than a hundred clients, and nowhere near enough staff . . .'

Lizzie understood too well the focus on the task, the bottom to be washed, the bed to be changed, human attentions lost to overwork and time management.

What must it be like to work in such a place? thought Lizzie. Not one of her patients was ever going home, no one would recover or resume their lives. And when they went, another with the same fate would replace them.

She fetched a serviette from the linen trolley. It wasn't just weight her mother was losing: the energy was disappearing from her voice and her eyes weren't sparking as they usually did when she visited. 'You haven't had so much as a sip.'

Her mother flapped her arm dismissively. 'The smell's enough to make you ill.'

'What are we going to do with you?' Lizzie said, taking the lid off the beaker. She spooned the gelatinous liquid into her mother's mouth. 'It's chocolate—your favourite.'

She had read somewhere that refusing to eat was a first sign of letting go of life. Well, she was certainly not going to let her mother starve to death. 'No pain? You don't feel unwell?'

'Perfectly comfy.'

If she could just get her to eat, she could have months, maybe a year . . . even two. Lizzie had been coming in every day for the last few weeks to make sure she ate at least one meal. She couldn't bear to lose her. Not yet.

'A shower, then I'll get you into bed.'

She shook her head. 'I'm that tired . . .'

Her mother never refused a shower.

'I've been thinking I'd like to have a word with the priest—his blessing before I pass.'

Lizzie tutted. 'That's a way off yet.'

Her mother smiled. 'Ah, my daughter.'

Beyond the door, the clatter of plates, the clang of a trolley, a smell of boiled vegetables. Another day.

It always felt strange that life outside went on, thought Lizzie, after saying goodbye to her mother. There was so much sorrow within those four walls she wondered how it could possibly be contained, that it must surely seep out under doors, escape through an open window, any chink or gap, the sadness affecting passers-by, causing them to stop for a moment and think of those hidden from view.

Two messages on her phone: the first, a request to speak at an International Women's Day event, and later, that same day, to chair a panel on the gender pay gap.

Who would have believed that decades on, women still didn't have equal pay and were still trying to sort out childcare. She remembered rushing out the door a few years earlier, to an International Women's Day celebration. The festivities were to begin with a lavish brunch in a gloriously renovated old ballroom and end with drinks at sunset on the rooftop of one of the city's most beautiful buildings.

Other than for a busy hive of people with vacuum cleaners strapped to their backs, Lizzie's street was deserted. Up and down the street they laboured, scurrying to and from vans with detergents and mops. Every one of them was a woman. Not one of them was white.

Lizzie went back inside, took off the t-shirt hash-tagged with a meaningless slogan and took Fred for a walk. They could keep their cupcakes and pink balloons.

She again declined their invitation.

The other message was from Margot. Was Lizzie free the following day? She'd bring lunch.

No matter how much you ran from it, thought Lizzie, there was, in later years, a balance sheet, a reckoning.

Lizzie and Margot were in the garden, Margot having just shed a tear for the jacaranda. 'Tom's tree,' she said.

They sat at the outside table, drinking tea and making small talk. Margot thought the house looked awesome, Tom's old room, especially. They were friendly, there were smiles and laughter. It felt good, like friends who haven't seen each other for a while, so much to talk about, so much catching up to do. Lizzie waited for a break in the conversation.

'Margot,' she took her daughter's hands in hers, 'I'm sorry, so terribly sorry.'

'Oh Mum, I'm sorry, too.'

'It's what I should have said last time you visited; what I should have said a long time ago.'

Margot shook her head. 'I should have been more under-standing, more forgiving, I should have loved you better.'

They talked then of hard painful things, hurts they'd kept from each other, from themselves. They cried and hugged and remembered and forgave. Margot told her mother how impos-sible and infuriating she was, how funny and kind and good. Lizzie told Margot how stubborn and maddening she was, how courageous and talented and full of grace.

They talked about Tom.

They promised that when they disagreed, given that they disagreed on almost everything, that they would talk it through, not ruminate for years on end. No more injured silences, no more excuses or justifications. No more would they withhold their love.

They came to the startling conclusion, that they were, in different ways, very like each other.

Mother and daughter after all.

Margot gazed out the window, thinking again about the conversation with her mother. They would learn, they would find their way, wounds would heal. She thought of her father, and Claire, who had fallen madly, stupidly in love.

He had abandoned her mother, abandoned her, too, unjustly blaming her mother for Tom's death. Only now did she realise that she had blamed her, too.

Charlotte, when Margot spoke to her, was surprisingly sanguine. She said anyone who made it in politics had things to be ashamed of. The difference between her father and the rest, was that her father had been caught out. They didn't mention the affair.

Margot had forgiven Claire. She owed her everything. You can't judge a life by one mistake, as foolish and as reckless as that mistake may have been.

The murmur of distant voices: Julian, Molly, Jack. Her family. A breeze fluttered through the open windows, the day soft and warm. Summer had arrived.

CHAPTER 40

LIZZIE WAS ON ANTHONY'S DOORSTEP with Fred, who had also received an invite. A lovely old verandah protected the house from the worst of the afternoon sun. In its deepest corner, a couple of chairs, pastel-coloured cushions, an unexpected feminine touch.

Lizzie rang the doorbell, the door opening quickly.

'Lizzie.' He sounded surprised.

'Didn't you think I'd come?'

He smiled. 'It may have crossed my mind.'

Poppy raced up the hallway.

Lizzie unclipped Fred's lead, both dogs sauntering off.

'Come on through.'

'You've done some travelling,' she said, noticing the photos on the walls.

'Miriam liked to travel.'

She followed him into the lounge room. Two spacious chairs and a sofa, newspapers scattered on the coffee table, shelves crammed with books, lamps, CDs.

'Nice,' she said.

He offered her a glass of wine. He was really quite handsome she thought, though the checked shirt was a bit daggy. Daggy was under-rated. Daggy was good.

She sticky-beaked while he poured the drinks.

'Well, cheers,' he said.

They raised glasses.

'Strange to think we've lived so close all these years.'

Even more strange that she'd accepted his invitation to dinner.

'To think we've been catching the same trains, walking our dogs in the same places, shopping in the same supermarket, paths crossing all those times without speaking a word. And here you are.'

Yes, she thought. Here I am. 'So, what have you been doing these last thirty years?'

'You think thirty years is a long time, that a lot should have happened, but when I look back on it, not much happened at all. You wonder where all those days went.'

Lizzie glanced at the photos on the mantelpiece, among them a young man who looked very much like Anthony with a pretty young woman nursing a baby, a toddler playing at their feet. 'Your family?'

He nodded. 'Miriam and our daughters.'

'Are there grandchildren?'

He pointed to photos on one of the bookshelves. 'Five of them tearing around different parts of Australia.'

'Not all living in Melbourne, then?'

'One of my daughters moved to Perth last week.'

'It's sad when they move away, you don't expect it.'

'You never know what they're going to do next. Our parents probably said the same about us. Still, there's Skype. Skype's a wonder, isn't it.'

She laughed. 'It is.'

'Tell me about your daughter?'

Lizzie was about to trot out her usual script but stopped herself. She liked this man. She didn't want any more secrets. 'The truth is we haven't been all that close. But I think—I hope—that's changing.'

'Relationships have their ups and downs.'

'It goes back to losing her brother. I wasn't there for her when she needed me.'

'Grief plays out in unexpected ways.'

She added to his qualities: good listener, compassionate.

He offered more wine, she accepted.

'You're a very attractive woman, Lizzie.'

Goodness. No one had said that for a while.

'You're quite an attractive man,' she said. Enough wine for you, she thought.

'Well, now that we've got our good looks out of the way, I'll get dinner going.'

She followed him into the kitchen.

'You said you liked curry?'

'I do.'

He donned an apron, gathered a chopping board, a sharp knife. Garlic, spring onions, lemongrass, chilli and ginger into the blender.

'Impressive,' she said, over the whirr of the blade.

He scraped the curry paste into hot oil and held out a wooden spoon. 'Could you stir?'

'Only under supervision.'

They stood side by side, shoulders and hips almost touching. Lizzie stirred as he added spices, the room filling with the fragrance of cumin and turmeric and coriander. Next was coconut milk, stock and vegetables. 'Rice and we're done,' he said.

Half an hour later, she was squeezing lime over her curry. 'This really is delicious.'

'Failsafe,' he said.

Lizzie approved of his table manners. Often people who lived alone ate like no one was watching. But not Anthony: small portions on his fork, no talking with his mouth full, mindful of the purpose of serviettes. Poor man, she thought, he has no idea he's passed the first test.

He volunteered that he'd been a journalist, retrenched years before he was ready to retire. Up until then, they hadn't talked about careers. At a certain age all the status that went with how you made your living no longer mattered.

She told him about her job in politics.

'The dark side.' He grinned. 'I don't want to have to send you home early, so I won't ask which party.'

'It hardly matters any more, you can't slip an envelope between them.'

'Are you still involved in politics?'

'Not politics exactly, some advocacy work, non-violent protest . . . that sort of thing.'

'Good on you.'

She asked if any of his writing was available online. He named one or two articles. She put down her glass. 'Don't tell me you're that Anthony Jeffries?'

'Yes, indeed, that's me.'

'My goodness,' she said. She had liked his pieces. 'The paper wasn't the same after you left.'

'Looking back, I'm glad I went when I did. The stuff that counts for journalism today . . .'

Lizzie raised an eyebrow.

'I forget you've had first-hand experience,' Anthony said.

'That's a story for another day.'

'Bread and circuses.'

'Something like that.' She smiled. 'Do you still write?'

'Every now and then. Sometimes they publish but most times I'm told I need to be less serious, more accessible, finish on an optimistic note.'

'*Relatable*,' said Lizzie.

'An editor once asked if I could find a more youthful photo so as not to put off younger readers.'

'I hope you told her—'

'I found a more youthful photo.'

They laughed.

She scanned the room. 'Is your house just as Miriam left it?'

He shook his head. 'Most of her things are gone, though it took a long time for me to get round to it. My daughters said it wasn't healthy clinging on. But when it's all you have . . .'

Lizzie nodded, hardly believing it had taken her more than thirty years before she could let go of anything that belonged to Tom. In the days after his death, she had tied his footy jumper around her waist, relinquishing it at the last minute so he could wear it one last time.

'I rearranged the furniture,' he said. 'Bought a few new pieces, cleared shelves of knick-knacks, removed a couple of rugs. That sort of thing.'

'You've never thought about an apartment?'

'I looked at one once—"up-market", they said.' He shuddered.

He cleared their plates, insisting Lizzie not do anything.

'You had a good marriage, I can tell.'

'We had our moments, she more than me, I think. But overall, we were happy. I was angry she died so young, if sixty is young. It's a funny thing that sort of anger because you don't know where to direct it or who to be angry with.'

'It can go in all sorts of directions.'

He gazed at her for a long knowing moment.

'You never met anyone else?' he asked.

'I haven't made it a priority.'

'I looked at those dating apps but they're not for me.'

Lizzie nodded. 'Like going for a job interview.'

'You don't get lonely?'

She did occasionally. 'I've been on my own a long time . . . If I need company, I've got friends I can call on.'

'I've always envied women their friendships.'

'You don't have friends?'

'I meet up with a couple of old journos for a drink every now and then, go bushwalking with my brother-in-law, and a bunch of us go to the footy. But you know us blokes, we don't talk about much other than work and sport. And now that we don't work . . .'

He made tea, teabags the only downside of the evening.

He looked at her, eyes crinkling with amusement. 'Confession time.'

'Already?'

'When I didn't see you after that first time we met at the park, I thought I'd scared you off.'

'Time gets away.'

'I like you, Lizzie; I think you might quite like me.'

Oh God, she hoped he wasn't going to kiss her or something.

'I'd like to be more than just friends.'

'I'm not sure what you mean.' She knew exactly what he meant.

'Not marriage or living together, but companions.'

Lizzie thought it might be time to go.

'I'm told I'm quite good company.'

She laughed. 'Indeed, you are.'

'And I can cook.'

'You certainly can.'

'I have a fine appreciation of greyhounds and gardens.'

Why had she come?

'We could go to the cinema, Sunday drives.'

Next he'd be talking about picnics. 'I didn't think anyone went on Sunday drives anymore.'

'The occasional night in front of the television, concerts, plays, picnics . . .'

'That sounds like quite a commitment.'

'Not all on the same day . . .'

'Companionable? Like brother and sister?'

Their eyes met.

'That would be up to you.'

'I'm complicated,' she said.

'I've noticed.'

'I'll think about it.'

'Don't think too long,' he said. 'It's not as if we've got time to waste.'

Lizzie pulled into her driveway, the night dark and still, Alice's words on repeat in her head: *if there's a quite nice man on the scene, grab hold of him.* And Anthony was a nice man, the nicest man. And she did want to grab hold of him. But always the what-ifs. They'd met, how many times? A few. If he were to stay overnight in her house, how would that feel? Or his house—both homes had their ghosts? Was she behaving like a lovestruck Alice, a silly schoolgirl? Losing her head because it had been so long since anyone noticed her, forever since she felt desirable.

But a picnic, now that she thought about it, sounded irresistible. She reached for her phone.

'Are you in bed?' she asked.

'No,' he said. 'I'm looking at the sky and thinking of you.'

'Are there stars?'

'More than I can count.'

'I thought I might come over.'

'I hoped you would.'

Here she was. Here they both were, reaching out to each other across lifetimes. They held each other. And for a little while, nothing else mattered.

CHAPTER 41

LIZZIE'S MOTHER'S FACE WAS GAUNT, eyes sunken, cheeks bony crests, lips ashen, the skull already revealing itself.

The call from the nursing home in the early hours of the morning to tell Lizzie her mother had suddenly deteriorated came as a shock. She had been doing so well, enjoying Lizzie's daily visits, even putting on a little weight. She should have been expecting it, but who is ever prepared for the death of their mother.

She bent to kiss her cheek. 'Mammy.' How cold she felt.

Her mother opened her eyes, stared, Lizzie terrified she wouldn't recognise her.

'My Lizzie,' she said.

Lizzie plumped up her pillow and smoothed the sheet. 'What you get up to when I'm not here.'

Her mother tried to smile.

'Any pain?'

She shook her head.

Lizzie dotted lanolin on the cracks opening up in her mother's lips.

'I'm soon to go to my Maker.'

Lizzie held tight to her hand. 'I'm here with you.'

'I'd have done it all different if I'd known.'

'Oh, Mammy. Who of us would not.'

'Darling girl,' she said, before drifting into sleep.

Lizzie could have insisted her mother be admitted to hospital, that she be started on oxygen, a drip inserted into her vein, sustenance delivered via a tube into her stomach. Her mother could be kept alive, for days, weeks, perhaps longer. Time together, time to make up for time lost. Delay the final goodbye. But to take her from her familiar surrounds, from the faces and voices she knew, the routines she understood. No, she would not do that to her mother. She asked that they keep her comfortable, that all active treatment cease.

Lizzie spoke to the nurse in charge insisting that it would be she who bathed her mother and changed her gown and saw to her hair. In her final hours, she wanted her mother to feel only the gentle touch of loving hands.

Margot arrived with Julian and the children, their great-grandmother somehow summoning up the wherewithal to make a fuss of Molly and Jack before they said goodbye, Margot soothing Molly before Julian shepherded both children out the door.

For one last time, the three generations of women were together, each knowing so much yet so little about each other. For how can you know someone's life?

When Margot left the room so Lizzie might have time alone, she lay on the bed beside her mother, arms around her. She talked of sunny days and soft rain, of cricket in the back yard, their trips to the beach, how she loved it when her mother laughed. She remembered her father, described the photo of them on their wedding day. When they were happy, how happy they had been.

The funeral was everything Lizzie's mother had wanted.

She was farewelled in the old church close to the home her mother had lived in for most of her life. With soaring ceilings and stained-glass windows, it was heady with perfume and occasion.

Going to church had once been an important social event, people gathering under century-old palm trees, showing off their Sunday finery and chatting long after the final blessing. The church was a place to come together, share news and predict the fortunes of the local footy team.

There wasn't a huge turnout. Most of her mother's friends had passed away or were too ill to make the journey and sit through a long Mass. Margot and Julian arrived with Molly and Jack, their great-grandmother's passing their first experience of death. The inevitability of loss, life's saddest lesson.

'I'll sit next to you, Grandma,' said Molly, 'and say one of Great-granny's prayers.'

Lizzie caught Margot's eye. They smiled. She was Margot's mother, Margot was her daughter, nothing could change that. They were taking it slowly, neither rushing the other. There had been an outpouring, Margot stumbling over words and feelings, sorrow and confusion and pain. Lizzie listened, walls all coming down, her heart open. She had lost one child, for too long forsaken another. She loved them more than life itself. You can't undo the past, thought Lizzie. But there was love, and where there was love, there was healing and hope and second chances.

Jane and Sam joined them, Sam one of the musicians fare-welling Lizzie's mum.

Lizzie had seen Jane talking with Ed and Charlotte, Charlotte now obviously pregnant, Ed attentive and friendly, all for public consumption, of course. Lizzie had seen Charlotte on television standing by a humiliated Ed, a Hillary Clinton, she thought, another woman who stood by her disgraced man. Lizzie, though she had been spared the public airing, realised she had done much the same thing. Perhaps it wasn't their partner, women stood by, but their family.

Margot and Ed were in touch again. Lizzie was glad of it. They were father and daughter, she didn't want them to be enemies. But their relationship had cooled, Margot had his measure. Her daughter had, in typical organised fashion, drawn up a roster, enlisting Lizzie's help, and for the moment, her father's, to look after Molly and Jack when she was working and, when later that year, she returned to study a master's in photography. It was as if, thought Lizzie, she had been given a second chance, to be the parent she could have been, should have been.

'Lizzie,' Charlotte leaned to kiss her cheek, 'I'm so sorry about your mother.'

Lizzie thanked her. 'We'll have to stop running into each other at funerals.'

They laughed self-consciously.

'Congratulations on the baby,' said Lizzie.

'Yes, quite a surprise.'

'You're well?'

'Yes, considering.'

Lizzie wasn't sure what to say. 'It can't be easy.'

'I'm seeing another side of Ed, a side I think you know quite well.'

Startled, Lizzie looked around to make sure no one could overhear them. 'If Ed hasn't already changed, I'm sure he will after this.'

Charlotte also looked around. 'He has a job which requires him to travel regularly, there's a baby to think of. I'm young, he's not. I will bide my time.'

'Charlotte, I had no idea.'

She smiled. 'I wanted you to know the truth, you deserve to know the truth. But you must promise you won't say anything to Margot. It could make things very strange between us.'

'You can trust me.'

'I know I can.'

And with that, she walked away.

Mourners were avoiding Ed, keeping their distance.

Ed had been cancelled.

The extent of Ed's misconduct should not have surprised Lizzie. He was not the first, he would not be the last. *Same old same old*, Alice would say. To get to the top you have to do the business. Hadn't Alice once said, give Ed enough rope and he'll hang himself. And so he had. He would not go to prison but his political career was finished. He would, as Lizzie had predicted, never be prime minister.

Still, Ed was nothing if not a survivor. Even if his new job didn't work out, he'd eventually be invited onto boards, he'd write his memoir, be in demand on the speaker circuit.

Right on cue, Ed wandered over and passed on his condolences. Lizzie politely inquired after him.

'A few years ago, no one would have cared. These days, a whiff of scandal, any misdemeanour no matter how small or how long ago, and a man's done for.'

As insightless as ever, thought Lizzie, hurriedly bringing the conversation to a close.

Claire's affair with Ed, Lizzie would never quite understand. She knew, though, that Claire had lived in penance for her one lapse. She had also loved and nurtured the daughter who she, for years, had abandoned. Not once had she censured Lizzie—Lizzie was her dearest friend; she loved her, she loved Margot. It was the least she could do.

Alice was there, too, deep in conversation with Molly, Molly giggling, Alice basking. Molly was right; Alice was fun. Alice, forever young.

The casket, solid oak with gold handles and a lining of white satin, was engulfed in flowers. Her mother was dressed in her blue frock. She wore stockings and heels and her favourite lipstick, her hair in soft waves, in her hands, a posy of roses Lizzie had picked from her garden. Numerous passages were read from the bible, hymns sung, prayers said, speeches given. Lizzie remembered her funny, brave, tenacious mother, who did, as we all do, her very best. 'Ave Maria' and 'Danny Boy' rang through the church. Mourners wept.

Yes, she could hear her mother say, it was a fine funeral, *a very fine funeral indeed.*

CHAPTER 42

LIZZIE LOOKED AGAIN AT THE ticket to one—no, two plays—that Alice's friend, Ursula, who she was yet to meet, was directing. Opening night—what would she wear? Alice had not mentioned a word of these plays, so the invitation had come as quite a surprise.

She pulled her red dress from the plastic bag, glad now it hadn't made its way to the op shop. She liked it. Anthony would like it, too. He was still to be introduced to her friends, but not tonight. Tonight was Alice's night.

Lizzie smoothed her hair and polished her glasses. She stood back from the mirror. Yes, she looked very *opening night*. She smiled: Alice a budding playwright. How was she feeling? Lizzie wondered. Nervous, excited? All of the above? She did so love a late bloomer.

She pulled the door behind her. Such an ordinary life, she thought, but extraordinary in the way all lives are extraordinary.

*

Backstage, Alice could hear the hum of the gathering crowd, people enjoying a drink and finger food, not your usual hors d'oeuvres, but fragrant, lovingly made offerings from all over the world.

She peeked through the curtain—its dull dusty red transformed into an almost sumptuous crimson, if you didn't look too closely. What a buzz there was. Friends and family and community, chandeliers dazzling, late sun setting the stained glass ablaze, every seat sold.

A journalist from the local newspaper had arrived, Margot was snapping photos of the crowd, and Jane was chatting with whoever would chat with her, a vox pop for the radio show she produced. Sam was playing.

They would all be missing Claire tonight, Lizzie especially. She would be circulating, putting everyone at their ease, talking to anyone looking left out and making whoever she spoke to feel they were the most interesting and important person in the room.

Lizzie and Margot found their seats.

Lizzie checked their tickets.

Alice had reserved the seat between them for Claire.

The lights dimmed, the curtain rose.

Lizzie's hand reached out in the darkness just as Claire's hand had reached out to her all those years ago. 'Claire,' she whispered, 'I'm here.'

ACKNOWLEDGEMENTS

THIS BOOK BEGAN IN 2017 with a question: why do so few books feature women in their sixties and seventies and beyond? If you eavesdrop for even a moment, you'll discover that it is older women who are having the most interesting conversations. And the most fun. Anecdotally, older women make up the greater number of visitors to art galleries, they also fill seats at writers' festivals, theatres and cinemas. They mother and grandmother and volunteer. They are, in other words, the beating social and cultural heart of our communities. They are not zany or sweet or quaint—or only occasionally! They are who they have always been, only older, brimming with energy and optimism, laughing and raging, loving and overcoming. They have lived long lives, they have seen much. And they have stories to tell.

How this book made its way from the Allen & Unwin slush pile to the legendary and beloved Jane Palfreyman is still a mystery to me. Never did I imagine that Jane would read my words, that she would publish me is the stuff of fairytales. Endless heartfelt thank yous, Jane, for seeing the story I wanted to tell and supporting me to tell it. I am so thrilled to be an Allen & Unwin author.

A huge thank you to the wonderfully intuitive Genevieve Buzo for your many brilliant editorial insights and for pushing me to delve deeper. To Jessica Friedmann, much gratitude for your meticulous copyedit and acute observations. Thank you, too, to the eagle-eyed Christa Munns who makes everything happen, and proofreader extraordinaire, Pamela Dunne. I'm also indebted to all the behind-the-scenes folk at Allen & Unwin; I'm sure I'm not the first to label them The Dream Team, for pulling everything together so seamlessly. And a big thank you to artist Melanie Vugich, for the gorgeous artwork on the cover of my book.

In 2021, I was very fortunate to be awarded a place in the Australian Society of Authors' mentorship program. Being mentored by the exceptional Nadine Davidoff was an absolute turning point for me. Huge thanks Nadine, for believing in the story and showing me what was important in the novel.

Thank you to Antoni Jach's wonderful Novel Writing Workshop Masterclass XXV, whose feedback helped me work through some of the problems I was encountering at the time. Antoni's Masterclass is where I met all-round lovely person Liz Walton. I can't thank you enough, Liz, for all your support.

I am indebted to Melanie Ostell, who was the first person I talked to about this novel, and who later gave wise and insightful feedback on my two shitty first drafts.

Deepest thanks to talented writer and editor, Clare Carlin, who long ago saw some potential in my writing. I am forever grateful for your support, generosity and kind heart.

To Caroline Miley, thank you for your friendship and for cheering me on. Thank you, too, for your art-world knowledge and expertise, much of which made it into this book. Mistakes, my own.

Big thanks to Maryrose Cuskelly, Catherine Johnstone, Chris Ringrose and Marilyn Miller, who gave wise and considered feedback on early drafts of this book. Thanks also to Maryrose for so generously answering my many questions about the publishing process.

To dear friends, Mira Robertson and Ana Kokkinos, thank you for your many kindnesses and our wonderful writerly conversations.

Thank you, Kathleen Maltzahn and Koula Neophytou for many years of friendship. Your loyalty and encouragement have meant so much.

And thank you to long-ago writing group who I first met at RMIT PWE—Lucy Treloar, Kate Richards, Jenny Green, Dana Miltins, Clare Strahan, Julie Twohig—many fond memories.

I have learned from many wonderful teachers on the way to publication, including the amazing Lee Kofman and brilliant RMIT PWE teachers, including Toni Jordan and Penny Johnson.

To my children Stephen and Ben Bolton, I love you. And, yes, it's finished! And thank you Stephen and April for my grandson, Theodore, an unexpected and precious gift, who I love more than life itself.

To my very dear sisters, Cathy Meades and Josephine Pitsiava, what would I do without you? You are kind and funny and I adore you. Thank you for always being there.

Big thanks to Lisa Kenway and super talented Debut Crew 2024 for being great fun and great company, and generally being brilliant and awesome.

To my wonderful neighbourhood and community, thank you for the many delicious offerings that made their way to my front door.

To my English teacher, Michael Walsh, who in Year 9, told me that one day I would be a writer, thank you.

To my partner, Frank Coenders, you are everything and more. This book is for you.